Will Text For Love
Ashley Gill

Ashley Gill

Names: Gill, Ashley, author.

Title: Will Text For Love / Ashley Gill

Description: First Edition. | Oregon: Ashley Gill, 2026.

Identifiers: ISBN 979-8-9942506-0-0 (trade paperback)

Subject: Love story

First Edition: January 2026

Printed in the United States of America

Book cover design by Jordan Riley

To my fairy godmother,
I couldn't have gotten through my emotional twenties without you.

Contents

Chapter 1

Present Day

January

I can't stop rubbing my knuckles over my heart. That gut punch from last Friday still left a mark. My mind starts to drift off, playing every hurtful detail on a loop.

"So, umm... listen, I've had a good time getting to know you these past eight months, but I really don't want you to keep holding out for me," Dean had said over the phone, and I could hear the tension in his vocal cords.

"Oh," I'd paused, "Ok." I was shocked he had said it in such a blunt way. I'd needed to let him know how I was feeling too, so I said, "Umm, I've been trying to call you and talk to you lately. I know you said you didn't want to start anything right now, but I really do like you and I don't want to see this end." By this point I had started pacing the length of my room.

"All relationships end, though," he'd said, and his words had felt like a tornado of rejection in my stomach.

"Ouch—" I'd stopped making the indent in the carpet. "That's not what I expected to hear," I had replied, completely honest. "Can we talk again in the future? Like the good ol' days? I miss our hours of talking and texting." I had tried another angle, who cared if I sounded desperate.

"No. I don't think that's a good idea. We aren't going to be together in the future," he had replied with another gut punching phrase. This one knocked the wind out of me. I had dropped to my knees on the carpet, feeling utterly defeated.

Squeezing my eyes shut, I try to erase the memory. In my twenty years of life, I've never been so heartbroken. I lift my hand to wipe away the tear that's falling toward my ear, partially from the pain of the memory and partially from the length of time I've kept my eyes open without blinking.

It's so early in the morning, the sun hasn't come up yet. I'm trying to get myself out of bed, but my limbs won't move and I've found myself stuck in the concrete that is made up of sheets and blankets.

Rhythmic noises are coming from across the room, as if a bear was sawing logs right next to me. My Southern Californian roommate, Juniper, is sleeping in her bed on the other side of the room. Snoring is her only negative trait. She doesn't have to wake up for her shift for another hour—lucky her.

I, on the other hand, have my alarm set for 5am so I can get ready and be at work in time for my 6am shift. I'm going to need the strength of all the stars in the galaxy to muster the energy to peel myself off the bed. It's going to be more like a fruit-roll-up getting peeled off the plastic wrapping it lays on. Sticky, jerking, struggling, ultimately not wishing to be parted from my dear friend, the bed.

I lift my head, do a slight side crunch—as if I'm copying a Richard Simmons workout video—then I relax and plop myself back on the bed. I'm going to have to stay here forever it seems. I wiggle my legs back and forth, and find that they feel like a pot of spaghetti noodles that were cooked for too long. I'm scared to try standing in case they collapse right under me.

It's been fifteen minutes now, since my gentle lullaby of an alarm has gone off. That's the kind of alarm I prefer. Not the ones that are like two pans being banged together to wake you up. Nobody needs that kind of negative energy to start their day. I prefer to be slowly annoyed by the gentle sounds of flutes.

A heavy sigh escapes me. I knew I wasn't worth dating. I'm too clingy, too emotional, too desperate.

If that phone call we had a week ago wasn't enough to explain it to me, it's becoming especially clear now, because it's been three days since I texted him, **"Hey man, how's your day?"** and he still hasn't responded. For the past eight months we've been talking regularly. Okay, so it was getting less and less frequent toward the end, but I had such high hopes that things would turn around again.

My chest feels like someone set ten newborn puppies on it, as a movie slideshow of our conversations continues its never-ending swirl of memories in my head. When he told me, "We can't be together now, but maybe someday," or "I think you're my dream girl," I believed him.

My eyes keep watering, and I start rubbing my temples to stop my brain from pulsing. I feel like I've been wounded. My blood is metaphorically pouring onto the ground, but I have no medics around to cover my gaping wounds. I want to give into the never-wanting-to-get-out-of-bed feeling that is swimming laps in my subconscious, because I now realize that all the dreams I'd been holding tight to with my toddler-strength grip, aren't actually going to come true.

I forcefully kick the blankets off my legs, as I realize I now have to grieve the future I hoped to have with him. The daydreams had gotten so strong. I now see I've lived a life all in my head with someone, but it was never actually real. I realized too late that I liked him and hoped he would be my first boyfriend.

The last corner of the blanket is still stuck to me, and I kick it so hard I bang the wall.

Oh crap, I hope I didn't wake up Juniper.

I lay silent for a minute and realize the bear saw is still going. My mind is reeling, I have to let go of the dates I thought we'd have, the vacations I thought we'd go on, and the dream house I thought we'd buy together. No use moving on since the best part of my life is over, I'd rather have the bed eat me whole than function like a normal adult today.

I've wasted enough of my 'get ready' time now. If I don't peel the fruit-roll-up off the bed, I might have to call in sick and I don't want to do that. Luckily, I love my job too much to miss even a day of it. I finally complete the side crunch that would make Richard Simmons proud and throw my noodles to the ground. After staring at the floor for five seconds, I hoist myself up as if by some magical strings. With my baggy shirt and comfy plaid pajama bottoms on, I drag my feet to the bathroom leaving scuffed up carpet rugs in my wake.

There is no pep in my step as I walk to the Jack and Jill bathroom that is shared with the bedroom on the other side. One of my housemates, Kim, lives in that room and she doesn't have to get up for work yet, so I have the sink all to myself. Kim is the kind of nature-loving, outdoorsy person you'd expect to see coming from Montana. Everyone who meets her loves talking to her because she's so nice.

I splash a giant amount of cold water on my face to bring back some life to my sagging features. I'm looking at the sad face of someone who's heartbroken because she didn't realize that daydreaming gets you more attached to the idea of someone rather than the reality, and now she's not in a relationship. This wasn't even a relationship. I don't know why I'm calling it that. We were nothing more than two people, whose souls were drawn to each other, and then after a series of events, we lost that bond because emotions got too scary and real.

As I wipe the water off my face with a towel, I see a couple wrinkles that had recently shown up. Like I had aged five years overnight. Fresh heartbreak robs you of any ounce of happiness you might've found in the world the day before. The blonde strands of hair around my hairline are all wet now and I try to dry those off. Trying to give my face a little help, I start applying mascara to my eyelashes. I get a little too close to the inner eyelid and blink fast. Dammit. *That tracks.*

As I'm cleaning off the smudge that could be my new aesthetic, all these thoughts start swirling in my head. Was I too clingy? Was I too honest? Maybe it was because I shared my heart too late with him? All I have are questions at the end of these eight life altering months and only one answer. I'm not the one for him. I won't be the one for him. This door is closed and will never open again. Make that one answer broken up into three different ways.

My zombie feet re-straighten the carpet rugs on my way back to the bedroom and I find my clothes with the light of my phone. I try not to wake Juniper up while I get dressed in a pair of jeans and a t-shirt. Grabbing my bag, then my book, I head off to work.

I'm the shift opener at The Grand Coffee. I get to make lattes for a living. It's actually super fun. This little mom and pop coffee shop is so chill and the customers are so nice that it's turning into my dream job. Flipping on the lights when I get to the shop, I take in my surroundings. This long narrow shop with its brown and burnt rust colors is going to be my haven for the next eight hours.

Once I put my stuff down behind the employee counter I walk over to look in the coffee bean cabinet for the brown paper bag that is our house coffee and start working on grinding the beans for our brewed pots. The smell of freshly made coffee escapes into the air. I take a deep breath and hold it in. A flat smile comes to my face. I'm filled with the most ethereal endorphin rush. Coffee smells have a way of lifting the spirits even when life is trying to give you the sad puppy-eyed blues. I flip on the open sign and get back to my mindless tasks.

Unfortunately, mindless tasks can only do so much to keep my brain from reeling. Maybe every time I meet a guy I should come right out at the beginning and say "Hi, my name is Elise and I'm a chronic emotional spiral-er. I spiral when a food I want at the store is unavailable. I spiral when a friend cancels on me. And mostly, I spiral when a boy I like doesn't respond to my text messages or phone calls. So buckle up, buddy." Maybe that'll weed out the ones who don't have enough emotional intelligence to handle a hard conversation, instead of ignoring the girl you were falling for just a few months prior. Completely ghosting someone is one of the most effed up things you can do to a person.

"Hello," a voice came out of nowhere. I snap my head behind me to see a customer standing at the register. "Oh, hi. How can I help you?" I wipe my hands on my apron and walk over to the register.

"Can I get a medium hot vanilla latte, no foam, please?" She stares down at her wallet as she places her order.

With wide eyes full of embarrassment I punch her order into the computer. I didn't even hear the bell on the door go off. I must have wandered deeper into the abyss of my own thoughts than I had realized. Being a barista is the only part of my life right now that I can be fully distracted in, and maybe a little too much.

I grab a cup and it slips out of my hand. I fumble for it in the air to see if I can grab it before it touches the dirty floor, but my fingers are too slippery, alas it falls to the ground.

Now that one's trash. Get it together, Elise.

Grabbing another cup, I pour the milk into a steamer pitcher and start heating it up. The white noise sound of the milk heating up keeps me grounded. Not to mention having to remember if the customer said decaf or not. It's just second nature to go for the regular espresso beans instead of the decaf espresso beans. *She doesn't want decaf, I'm sure of it.* First world barista problems.

Once I hand the customer her to-go drink, I finish my last morning prep task then head to a chair on the wall for employees and sit down with my book. I open up *Thomas Taylor and The Treasure Within* and start reading. I'm putting all my trust into this book to keep my thoughts on one topic. Magic.

At home I feel all of the emotions of the 'break-up'. Gosh, I can't believe I'm still calling it that. 'Break-up' feels too advanced for what we were. If there was a word for two people who were obsessed with each other and then the other person just slowed down their momentum because of those pesky emotions, *that's* what we were.

My brother-in-law, Fred, suggested I read the *Thomas Taylor* books because he figured they could help me stay sane during these depressing heartbreak months. Fred married my sister, Emily, eight months ago. Their wedding is where this all started.

I've never read any of the *Thomas Taylor* books before and I find myself swept up into the pages of this magical land. Turns out Fred was right, this book is truly wiping my brain clear of any intrusive, emotional thoughts about my current lonely situation. Those thoughts can go burn in a dumpster fire behind a Waffle House.

I know I need to feel the emotions and move on, but I've felt them pretty deeply lately and now I could use a break. I'll process them later today, but first, a school full of kids learning magic!

I work alone at The Grand Coffee for most hours of the day. It's a small, cute, little place that just opened up a year ago and they're still building up their customer base so I have a lot quiet time. It's not too bad when I'm here alone. I get to listen to music, podcasts or read a book.

The owners are pretty chill, they know what it's like to be on shift here. They're not your typical micromanagers that need to have a shackle around your neck and control every part of you while you work. As long as we get our prep work done and all the dishes clean then we are free to spend our time between customers within the pages of a book.

I made it through four chapters of *The Treasure Within* before my next customer beeps in through the headset. We have an outside speaker that customers can order from and then drive up to our window. "Good morning." I greet them with my best customer service voice. "Hello. Can I get a small Iced Mocha, please?" they ask. "Of course. Anything else?" I ask hoping their answer is no so I can selfishly get back to reading where these intrusive thoughts leave me alone. "No, that's it," they reply. "Perfect. Drive up to the window and I'll get it ready for you."

Iced drinks are the best kind of drinks to make during early shifts, when the morning rush can get overwhelming, I don't have to do much else but throw the shot in with the mocha syrup and stir. *Cold milk, ice and then I'm done*, the cup slips to the ground as the milk carton knocks into it. I drop my chin to my chest. *Gah, this is not my day.* I quickly make another one, this time making sure I have a good grasp on the cup and container.

I hand the customer their drink and sit down to read about what feels like my escape from reality.

I manage to devour a few more chapters of the book before the front doorbell rings as someone opens it. This time I hear it and I lift my head.

"Oh, hi, good morning," I say as I look at the clock on the back wall.

"I didn't realize it was 7am already. Wow. This morning flew by like a bride that doesn't want to get married."

Juniper, my roommate and my eclectic best friend, walks into the employee-only section in her colorful flowing outfit that displays both her tattoo sleeves and goes to clock-in. "I'd love to be at that wedding. The drama. The thrill of what's going to happen next. Count me in, baby," she says as she enters her password.

"You're not wrong," I say chuckling, and turn back to my book. Still no morning rush.

Juniper and I usually do the morning shift together. One person handles the drive-thru orders over the headset and takes payment at the window, while the other person listens to the orders over the second headset and starts preparing the customer's drinks and food.

When I first started here, I didn't know the difference between a cappuccino and a latte. I was a real coffee virgin, the last one of my kind. Now, I can tell you what a tidal wave is—a shot of espresso with a shot of heavy cream on top (not mixed!), then you throw it back into your mouth and the hot and cold swirl together like a tidal wave before you swallow. It's a sensational oral experience I highly recommend.

I've been in Georgia and doing this job for four months now. I'm basically a seasoned barista at this point. Throwing drinks around like a talented juggler. Getting orders out fast. I like to think I'm a contributing member of society.

Once I hit the tenth chapter I hear Juniper taking an order from the drive-thru headset for a 16oz, hot, cinnamon latte, with low-fat milk and a sausage breakfast croissant. I set my book down on the chair and start making the drink. We fall into the rhythm of the morning. We're like two people in a dance, working around each other and anticipating what each other's next step will be. Even when the orders start to pile up, neither of us gets stressed out. Two people taking on seven customers is no problem. We focus on our task at hand like a couple of Santa's elves that know what's at stake if we don't finish our work on time.

"It's been a nice, steady morning today," I say as I'm wiping espresso beans off the countertop.

"I agree," she replies as she hands me her signature drink of the day.

A hot coconut mocha. One sip and I'm on the beaches of Maui, looking out over the ocean as the sun rises. Then, with lightning speed, I'm brought back to the coffee shop and say, "I couldn't ask for a better way to distract myself." I don't make eye contact with her because an uncontrolled knot comes to my throat as tears well up in my eyes. I swirl my coffee around in the cup while my lower lip begins to quiver.

"Ah hun, I'm so sorry." Juniper comes over to put her hand on my back. She knows everything that's going on, so I don't have to explain myself more than that.

I turn my head, and this time, make eye contact with her. A small smile barely reaches my lips when the bell above the door goes off. More customers start to show up, and we have to get to work again.

I get lost in the sea of lattes before me. I pump syrup in each cup I have in front of me and I eyeball the amount of milk I need in the pitcher. As the milk is steaming, I grind my coffee grounds. After filling three portafilters I tamp them each down and manage to pull a few perfect twenty-five second shots. I learned in orientation, that if the pull is too fast the shot will be sour, too long and the shot will be bitter. I feel a small amount of bliss as I pour and stir everything together. I feel confident when I'm working. An unfamiliar feeling at this point.

I bring my drinks to the pickup window. "16 oz Raspberry Latte," I say loud enough for everyone to hear. "16 oz Caramel Latte", "16oz Peppermint Mocha". The three customers each saunter up and grab their respective drinks as they give me a smile before they turn and head out the door. Wow. That confidence was fleeting. I want another rush of people to come in so I can do it again.

"I love those morning rushes." I brush off my forehead with my left forearm as I wipe down all of the equipment so it stays clean for the day.

"I agree. The morning has flown by nicely with these macro rushes." Juniper looks at the clock on the back wall. It's almost time for her to leave.

She cleans up the back kitchen area from all the food, and I finish wiping the front down. When we finish our cleaning, we settle into the two chairs along the back wall and pull out our books. Gorgeous and funny beyond her years, Juniper is a huge book reader. She reads about two books a week, devouring them whole and spitting out the bindings.

I don't know how she can read so fast. It takes me a good month to read a book. However, this *Thomas Taylor* book might be finished in a week.

I'm twenty and single. I feel like a spinster even though it's normal to get married later and later these days. Being single at my age is like being in a pool with jeans and a heavy jacket on. It's a struggle. Luckily, *The Treasure Within* is engaging enough to put that thought out of my mind...for another few minutes at least.

I take a deep breath and melt into my chair. The rest of the morning rush is just two customers. I don't bring up our interrupted conversation, because I don't want to feel that knot forming in my throat and the burning feeling in my eyes again. The sad puppies that have made their permanent residence on my chest need to be ignored right now.

An hour later Juniper clocks out and I'm left by myself to finish the morning shift alone. Magic, wands and best friends swim through my mind as I finish the rest of my shift. Once the afternoon girl gets here to relieve me, I head home.

I live in a charming two-story house in this small town of Tyrone, Georgia, with eight other people. Most of us know each other and are connected in some way. Emily and Fred live here, as well as Fred's parents, Mitchell and Sarah, and Fred's sister, Juniper. Then there's me and my brother, Forrest, along with Kim (one of Emily's prior bridesmaids) and Josh (one of Fred's prior groomsmen).

We're all, basically, family except for Kim and Josh. I decided to be a part of this metaphorical commune because I've never felt so known by a group of people before, in my life. I met everyone at Fred and Emily's wedding and haven't wanted to be separated ever since. Plus, it made financial sense in this economy.

Kim has gone to her shift at the aquarium for the day, so I have the bathroom to myself again, to take a shower. Kim actually has a pretty cushy job. She works part-time at the Atlanta Aquarium and feeds the dolphins and big fish. She went to college to become a marine biologist. Lucky for her, she got a job inside her field of expertise that relates to her degree. Not very many people get to say they are doing their dream job, except for Kim. She is one of the lucky few.

I start putting my stuff away from work as my feet begin to feel sluggish and fill up with concrete. I struggle moving around my room as my body has lost all the pep it mustered up for my shift today. I sit down on my soft bed to try and think of what I'll do to fill my time, and my mind, this afternoon. Too bad you can't escape your emotions forever; they're always lurking there like a troll in a dark cave. Ready to jump at you.

I pull my phone out of my pocket and open up my text thread with Dean. I want to see how he is doing but he's probably done hearing from me after that haunting phone call we had last week. I can't help it, though, so I start typing.

"Hello there, what's up?" I pause and stare at the words I just typed out on my phone. Do I actually want to send it? My eyes move up my screen to my last text to him, "Hey man, how's your day?" The timestamp is from three days ago.

I hit the delete button. I don't want to be the desperate girl who keeps texting the guy that isn't responding to her. I keep staring at my phone, but maybe he got busy, read my text and forgot about it?

I convince myself *this* is the truth, so I type out another text. One that seems more carefree this time, less boring. "Hiya toots, how's it hangin'?" I look at it and decide this is the one. He'll remember that I'm charming and will want to respond. I hover my finger over the SEND button and wait for a minute. I slowly lower my thumb to the screen and send it off through the airwaves to reach Dean on the other end. My body feels a rush of cold running over it, quickly followed by a wave of sweat that covers every inch of me. I turn my phone off and hope I don't obsess about this text all day. He'll respond back. *Yeah. He'll respond back.*

Juniper walks into our room and says, "Hey Esel, I thought you might like another distraction today. Wanna get some Thai food?" Esel is the nickname she gave me soon after we first met. I like to think that I'm a Bavarian beer girl, who eats only cheese, when she calls me that.

Juniper's been helping me process everything with Dean. *Oh Dean, we could have had such a fun life together. Our humor fits so perfectly that it would have just been laughter upon laughter for yeeeeears.* I involuntarily wipe the sad sweats off my hands onto my shirt. I want to stay away from these raw feelings just a little longer.

"Yeah. That sounds great! When do you want to leave?" I don't hide the eagerness in my voice as I look at her with unblinking eyes. She knows me so well. She can easily see behind the facade that I'm trying to show the world. Our friendship means everything to me.

"Great, love. I'm thinking in 15-minutes?"

"Perfect. Let me get ready really fast." Now I have to get out of my coffee shop clothes and decide what I'm going to wear on this winter day in Georgia. Shouldn't be too hard, it's only sixty degrees outside.

Chapter 2

Past

May

It's a nice spring morning in May. I'm sitting on a soft, cream-colored couch on the edge of a large living room. My bare feet are propped up on the coffee table in front of me and I lean on a pillow that's tucked under my armpit. I take a deep breath and let it out as I look at the cuticles of my dominant hand. It's been an hour now, of me waiting to be told what is happening next. Behind me is my mom, Katherine, who is talking to Sarah, Emily's soon-to-be mother-in-law, about the upcoming week and the order of events in which our two families will soon be joined.

The topic of rain is on everyone's mind since rain is the only thing that is forecast for the BIG DAY. No matter how many times we send good vibes into the universe to change the weather, it's holding on tight to its Saturday spot. Redding, California, doesn't typically have rain. It's known for being blisteringly hot, but not this year. Since the weather is determined to rain, Emily wants to have a Plan B for her Plan A.

My ears turn into the bell end of a stethoscope when my mom starts talking, "Emily has it all figured out. We'll set up the chairs outside when we get there tomorrow. Then the next day, if the rain hits an hour before the ceremony, we'll ask everyone available to pull the chairs inside and arrange them in a circle around the room."

"Perfect. We'll be ready for it. I don't want this special day to be less than perfect for our kids. I want everything to be as magical as Emily imagined it," Sarah says with a dreamy look in her eyes.

I've known Sarah for a total of two hours now. She is the most bubbly and confident mother of an adult I have ever met. Usually, life beats people down after fifty years of life, but Sarah doesn't seem to let it. She has so much optimism she could outshine the top five, best kindergarten teachers in the country. She seems to want everyone around her to thrive and that quality showed up within the first two minutes of meeting her.

"Yes...it will be great," my mom says slowly. She's very practical and straightforward, it doesn't seem like she knows what to do with someone so bubbly.

I'm not convinced there'll be enough people to help make this last minute change happen so I twist my body around on the couch to face them in the kitchen and ask, "How many people will be there an hour before the wedding to help move chairs and decorations if it rains?" I try to hide any tone in my voice. I've been sitting here for so long, waiting to hear the plan for the day. And I forgot to bring a book for the week so I'm extra impatient.

"Probably about twenty between the ushers, groomsmen and both extended families helping," my mom says.

"Cool, cool," I say while nodding. "That sounds like it'll be enough people. I know the bridesmaids won't be there because we are getting ready over at Cindy's house, and I don't see us all being ready and at the venue a whole hour before it's supposed to start." Cindy is the maid of honor, Emily's right-hand lady. "Yeah. That's perfectly fine. We'll have it taken care of, no problem," my mom encourages with her confidence in putting out any wedding-day venue fires.

I turn back around on the couch and when I look down at my cuticles the mothers continue, "This afternoon will be mani's and pedi's."

"Oooh," Sarah says, clapping her hands together. "I love that!"

"Mmhmm," my mom says flatly and I can feel her blank stare at Sarah even without looking. "And then this evening the bachelor and bachelorette parties are happening." I feel a scratch on my head that can only be my moms. I pat my mom's hand to acknowledge her gesture but stay facing toward the living room at my very captivating fingernails.

"Then, tomorrow will be the wedding venue setup, rehearsal and rehearsal dinner afterward," my mom finishes.

"I can't wait to see them practice! Two perfect kids getting ready for their perfect wedding. It's going to be so perfect," Sarah says with glee. Emily is one lucky lady. To get such an optimistic mother-in-law would be such a delight.

"Yep. They deserve it," mom chimes in a response.

I start to tune them out as I focus on these hang nails that really need some tending to. As I'm picking at a particularly stubborn piece of skin that won't come off, I start to wonder what kind of groomsmen will be at the wedding. A hopeful smile crosses my face at the prospect. This might be the most exciting thing about being single and in a wedding, all the—potentially single—groomsmen I'll meet soon. One of them could be my next crush.

I don't know what kind of friends Fred keeps around, but I sure hope he has some good ones. I know him about as well as anyone does when their sibling falls in love in a different town, then brings home a guy that tries to impress the family, but you stay skeptical for a while until you realize he's the real deal, and when, eventually, they announce they're engaged, you're happy for them. It might have taken me a minute to decide my feelings on him as a good guy for my sister, but that's only because I love her and want her to be with someone who deserves her love. After getting to know him over time, I can confidently say he is a good one, and I'm so happy for Emily for finding her life partner and bringing a loving brother figure into the family for me and my other siblings.

My family decided to share a giant house with Fred's family this week. I like to think of it as a family commune. One of Emily's friends is lending it to us for the duration of the wedding festivities. It's large enough for our decent sized party of ten. When we all arrived at the house last night, we said some quick "hello's" to each other then found our rooms and went to sleep. It was really late and nobody had the energy to talk more than that.

Along with Sarah is her husband, Mitchell, and their daughter, Juniper. Mitchell is a quiet man. I've probably heard a total of two words out of him since being here this morning, but you can tell he's kind. Juniper is my age and I can see us being friends if we were ever living in the same town.

Juniper dresses like an eclectic hippy and dyes her hair dark red. Her expressive sense of style has me very aware of the boring jeans-and-t-shirt look I'm often sporting. I don't like to wear things that draw attention to myself. I prefer to be a wallflower. My blonde hair and blue eyes often get me noticed, and I don't mind as long as strangers don't talk to me.

After the giant breakfast everyone helped out with (everyone except the lazy people who set out plates and silverware-i.e., all the men in the families...and me), I sat on this couch, and I've been here ever since. Juniper steps into my view and asks, "Hey, do you want a Henna tattoo?"

Her hippie side showing. However, I'm a big fan of henna tattoos, so I guess that makes me a hippie at heart.

"Absolutely." I smile and get up to follow her to the kitchen table. She positions a chair in front of her and points her hand at it as she takes out the supplies to be able to draw a brown temporary tattoo on me for the wedding.

I sit down in the chair. "I love these things," I say feeling elated to get a fun design on my foot to show off. "I actually lived in Hawaii for a few months at the end of last year." She looks up at me with surprise in her eyes. "It was for humanitarian work," I add. "Not too glamorous, but my friends and I'd go get Henna every other week."

"That sounds like it would be fun, actually. Anything that brings you to Hawaii can't be too much of a drag," Juniper says while she mixes the paste together. "What island were you on?"

"You're right. I have no complaints that it took me to Hawaii." I sheepishly smile. "I was on Maui," I say looking down at the ground. Whenever I tell people it was Maui they start to get excited and my stomach flips uncomfortably.

"Oh. Pretty," Juniper replies as she pulls out a couple pages of designs she can do with the henna. "What design do you want? I have these ones here that I can draw. Take a look."

I look back up at her and my body relaxes. If I was an onion that takes ages to reveal each new layer, then this moment feels like the first layer got pulled back. She hasn't acted like all the other people I've mentioned living in Maui to. Feeling comfortable again, I grab the pages from her and flip between the designs. "Hmm. Let's see." There are so many options I don't know what to choose from. "Ooooh, I like the flower one. Makes me think of the ones I had on the island. Can you put it on my foot?"

"Sure can, girly," she says, grabbing the tube she put the paste in and squishing it to the tip of the bag.

This is the first time Juniper and I have really interacted with each other, and I love how quickly I feel comfortable. That's rare for me. When Juniper makes a practice swipe on a napkin I ask her, "So do you have a job?"

"Yeah, I work at this place called Teavana. It's this tea shop chain down in Southern California. We sell loose leaf tea and tea lattes," she pauses, looking like a surgeon preparing for an operation as she makes her first swipe of the flower petal on my foot, then continues, "I love tea. I'm making the tea for the rehearsal and the wedding. I could tell you all sorts of things about it. If you tell me a few things about yourself, I could tell you which kinds you would like."

"Oh, fun!" I say, and then I give her some descriptive words about myself to test out her skills, "I like traveling, spontaneity and funny people."

Juniper bites her cheek to concentrate as she continues to make the petals of the henna flower, then she says, "Hmm. I bet you would like a black tea with floral notes. Black tea is the most common kind of tea all over the world so if you like traveling then you couldn't go wrong with that. Then the floral notes because you would appreciate the humor in drinking flowers."

As I'm watching her do the swooping lines of another petal I say, "You might be right! I didn't know I could be whittled down into a tea flavor."

"It's a gift."

"Ha!" I squawk, "The best gifts are always the rarest."

"Don't tell too many people. They might want to turn me into a circus act and I'll have to roam the country with a gaggle of carnies." I knew I'd like her. Sense of humor was on point.

"That would be terrible! Because then you would lose out on practicing your second gift. Henna drawings. This flower looks amazing!" I lean forward and admire the art she is creating on my foot.

"Thanks. If I can avoid being stolen away to be a part of a tea-specifying-circus-act then maybe I'll open up a shop to do henna tattoos." We both laugh and look down at my foot to watch her work as she adds the final touches.

"There you go. Now let it sit for 30 minutes before washing it off. The gel will become dry and start to flake off," Juniper directs me.

"Will do," I promise, then stand up and start to waddle like a duck, back to my seat. Lifting my foot off the ground a little bit just in case contact with the ground will disturb my temporary flower tattoo. I've always wanted a tattoo but henna is the closest I've ever gotten.

I can't wait to get our nails done soon. It will really make this henna tattoo pop.

Across the room my dad and my brother, Forrest, start a heated game of Slapjack. With all their loud slapping and pushing, they nearly topple each other onto the ground. During all the ruckus they're causing, my other sister, Esther, and her husband, Michael, come through the front door. They live in town, so they don't have to stay in this family commune for the week.

"Hey Es," I say to Esther, and then give a nod to Michael. I relax a little bit more now that she's here. Esther is my sister bestie. We've always done everything together ever since we were kids. She gives me encouragement when I need it. It's hard now that we're older and don't live as close to each other anymore.

"Hey Els," she replies, as she gives the rowdy guys a wide berth to come sit down next to me.

"Whatcha got going on here?" she asks with a curious smile over at Dad and Forrest before she quickly has to cover her face as a few cards fly through the air.

"Oh, they're just being crazy boys," I say chuckling, and pick up a card that flew to the couch next to us, flying it through the air back to them. "Are you guys having fun over there?" I ask.

"Yes," Dad and Forrest say in unison, as they change their roughhousing to an arm-wrestling competition. I laugh at them and turn back to Esther.

"Besides the boys being wild, I just got a henna tattoo on my foot," I pause to point at the coffee table to direct her eye, "and we all just got done eating breakfast. What about you?" I ask.

"We ate breakfast and came here. I didn't want to miss out on any family fun." She nods to the lively arm-wrestling match happening.

"Fair enough. This is Fred's sister, Juniper," I say gesturing behind me at the kitchen table, and Juniper pops her head up to smile when she hears her name. "She is doing henna tattoos if you want one," I offer on Juniper's behalf.

"Oh! I'd love one," Esther looks over to Juniper to see if she acknowledges her enthusiasm.

"Pop on over to my seat of torture," Juniper says as she adjusts the chair in front of her. While Esther sits down to get her own henna tattoo, I tilt my head back and rest it on the couch, wishing for a book to read.

After thirty minutes I go to the bathroom to wash off my dried tattoo paste under the running water in the bathtub. A quick rub of the hand over the area and the stuff falls off easily, leaving behind an adorable brown flower. It's perfect. I wonder if one of the groomsmen will notice.

I walk back to Juniper and Esther to see that Esther chose a string of vines wrapping around her ankle. Juniper is just finishing up when I say, "Look at my flower, you guys. It came out so good!" I prop up my foot on an empty chair next to them.

"Nice work," Esther says, leaning in for a look.

"You like it?" Juniper asks without making eye contact.

"Yes! It'll look great with the pedicure I'm going to get later today," I say enthusiastically.

Chapter 3
Past
May

I t's party time! After the mani-pedi's were done we all went back to our respective lodging to get ready for the bachelorette party and eat a quick dinner. It's evening now, and all the girls start showing up at Cindy's house. She has a pretty big house, the only part of it I get to see, though, is the spacious living room. It has a ton of seating for this large group of twenty. All eight bridesmaids plus eleven of Emily's closest friends. I feel an uncomfortable ball start to form in my stomach as I enter this giant social gathering. I don't stand for longer than it takes to get a mocktail, having seen an empty spot on the couch that I want to claim.

As I walk further into the living room and look around, I think to myself, *Cindy must be a very put together person, because her living room is very clean.* I feel like my slobbiness is stinking up the place as I sit down on my target couch. Almost all of her furnishings are white; it's like we're inside a cloud.

There's a piano that has a lot of little gift bags on it in the corner for prizes, and a fireplace roaring on the far south wall. I secretly hope I win a prize during one of the bachelorette games tonight. I don't know which games they will do but there's always quiz type games at these shindigs. As everyone has arrived, we all snuggle into the couches, our drinks in hand.

Our MC for the night, the lovely Cindy with her red straight hair pulled half up, stands in front of us all, "Alright everyone, welcome to Emily's bachelorette night!" She sings as a couple of "whoop, whoops," leave the women's lips. I wish I could come across so poised in front of a large group.

With a smile in Emily's direction Cindy presses on, "I have a few clean bachelorette party games for us tonight. For the first one, I'm going to ask you a bunch of questions and you'll answer them on the cards I've made." I sit up a little straighter in my seat as she passes the pile of little papers to her right. I love guessing games. We all grab one and give it to the person next to us so it can go around the circle quickly.

Sounds like the first game is going to be a rip-roaring good time. With a name like, "How Well Do You Know The Bride?" how could it not be? I can feel my competitive side start to bubble up. I always try to win at least one game at these events.

Luckily, tonight they aren't playing the WORST GAME EVER IN-VENTED, a secret undercover game that some bachelorette parties, or baby showers, have where you can't say the secret word "bride" or "baby" or else you'd lose the clothes line clip you were given when you first arrived, that you'd attached to the bottom of your shirt.

My skin always feels like it's crawling with anxiety the whole night when this game is played. I feel like a failure when I say *the* forbidden word. And everyone yells and points at you if you say it, like they found you with your pants down. Some women will just out themselves at the beginning of the event and yell "BRIDE" or "BABY" and then hand their clip to the person next to them, so they don't have to worry about that stupid game the whole time. Those are the stressful party games that some hosts like to torture us with. Thankfully, poised Cindy has our backs tonight.

I'm feeling cocky with this first game. I wiggle in my chair as I hold my pen ready. This should be easy since I've known Emily my whole life. Cindy starts her questions as soon as the last person gets their pen. "What is Emily's favorite color?" I smile, easy, blue.

Then the next question, "What year did she graduate High School?" I cover my paper with my drink hand and write 2018.

Boy, we're getting quite a few soft balls lobbed at us with these questions. Too easy. Give me something to think about.

"When was her and Fred's first kiss?" Shoot. I scrunch my lips together and tap the pen on my forehead. Umm, two months into dating? I write that down.

"What was Emily's first car?" Oh crap, I look up at the ceiling. I know it was white, my eyes dash down to the carpet. Maybe a Honda Civic, or Honda Accord? I write down the latter.

Cindy continues on with a total of twenty questions for the group. There's laughter and giggles as we all answer each question while trying to keep our drinks from spilling and our answers hidden from the women sitting next to us.

When the game is done, Cindy reads off the answers and we tally our scores for the winner. I definitely lost with my high score of *twelve* out of twenty questions answered correctly. I guess knowing her my whole life wasn't really a leg up. The winner was Esther with a grand total of *nineteen* out of twenty questions right. The only one she got wrong was Fred and Emily's first kiss.

We all clap for Esther as she throws her long blonde hair over her shoulder and walks to the piano with prizes. I look over at Juniper, squished between a couple petite black haired twins, and catch her eye as I give a clap to hide my jealousy. "Happy for her," I mouth to Juniper with a look that says I-wish-I-was-the-one-that-won. Juniper slowly claps with me and mouths with a nod, "Next time." I laugh, feeling known already in our one day of friendship. A true kindred spirit.

As we're waiting for the next game to start, one of Emily's old roommates, Harper, who is sitting next to me wearing the prettiest floral dress that goes really well with her ankle boots and messy bun, leans in and says, "I didn't do good at all. I got eight out of twenty right." She laughs as she puts one hand over her eyes, "We were roommates for three years in college. Doesn't look like I have much to show for it."

"Tell me about it," I say, laughing along with her, finding common ground, "I've known her for twenty years and I only got twelve right!"

The uncomfortable ball in my stomach from these social settings is beginning to shrink. I'm not generally the type of person to lean over and talk to others that I don't know, but the atmosphere in here is very homey so I'm starting to feel like I know these ladies. I watch the women all around the room lean over to one another and start gabbing about how many they got right. No one got close to Esther. Rightfully so.

The next game we are given is called 'Him or Her.' This one is another list of twenty questions that is testing us on how well we know the groom or the bride. To my surprise Harper ended up winning. I'm happy for my new acquaintance to get one of those much coveted piano gift bag prizes. She deserves it.

"Ok everyone. Our next game requires us to get into teams of three," Cindy says.

We stand up and everyone starts looking around the room at each other to see if anyone knows what's going on. I stare at Cindy, I could burn holes into her forehead trying to see if she's giving away what kind of game is next. Confused but compliant, I look at everyone starting to group together into respective teams and join my own group of three. We wait for Cindy's next instruction when she says, "And make sure at least one person in each group has a car here." We ask around, do some more shuffling to accommodate this next request and finally have our teams established. In my group I have Esther and Juniper, and so, my discomfort is now nonexistent.

"Now, this one is called Bachelorette Scavenger Hunt!" she says and I hear everyone say, "Ooooh," like it was rehearsed. We are given our scavenger hunt paper with all the questions on it. "Take a minute to read over the questions, and then when I say, GO, you can all run to your car and start! The first group back to the house gets to pick a prize off the piano," continues Cindy with her instructions.

Esther, Juniper, and I look down at our list and see the various tasks we need to collect, photograph, and touch. Once we feel like we have a handle on our tasks we look up and wait. When all the groups are looking at Cindy she says, "Ok. On your mark, get set, GO!" My legs feel like they could fly and my gut feels like it's twisting as we run out of the house like a crowd leaving a fire and into our group's car.

"Ok! Ok! Let's go to the theater first and take a picture with the movies that are playing tonight!" Esther says. Juniper skids out of her parking space as we all squeal like a couple of twelve-year-old girls, heading to the theater. We see cars driving in all different directions trying to create the perfect route around town that will hopefully lead back to Cindy's house the fastest.

"I want to win, you guys!" I playfully slap the paper against the back of the headrest.

"I will move this car as fast as I need to in order for you to get a win, girl!" Juniper replies with matched enthusiasm.

Esther claps her hands together and says, "Yes! Let's do it! I know this town like the back of my hand, we can get in and out of everything as fast as humanly possible with me here."

"I always get so competitive in these party games." I put one hand over my face, "It's embarrassing."

"At least you have passion," Juniper replies.

Esther and I make eye contact and laugh. "I love that you call it passion and not my ugly competitive side," I say to Juniper.

"I'm a girl's girl. Every trait you have will always sound positive coming from me. So, let's go get you a gift bag!"

"I need that," I reply, feeling my heart swell. I can feel another onion layer pull away.

After we take a picture of the movies playing at the theater, we move onto the task that says, "Take a picture with 3 strangers." We are in the perfect spot for that because the theater is brimming with strangers, so we wait like an awkward glob of three for the ideal unassuming group to pass by.

You don't attack an unknowing creature quickly, lest you startle them, so we slowly walk up to a group that seems like they'd be up for our shenanigans and start with, "Hey...We're doing a scavenger hunt. Will you guys take a photo with us so we can win? We need a picture with 3 strangers." They were perfect sports and said YES! We get our photo and thank them profusely.

I take a couple slow breaths as the adrenaline rush from asking complete strangers for help starts to settle down. Juniper, Esther, and I stand in a circle around the scavenger hunt list and see that we have to go to any grocery store and buy three candy bars, a box of popcorn and a movie. The two girls run to the car and I'm left thinking, *this is oddly suspicious. I wonder if we'll be using these items later tonight? Wait, why am I wasting time standing here, who cares,* and I run to follow them to our car.

We drive to the closest grocery store, WINCO. As we run from our parked car to the entrance, we see another group of girls running as well. When I look at them more closely, I realize it's Emily's group, also making their way to the sliding glass doors. My feet pick up the pace. One of the girls makes a loud squealing sound and we keep running to be the first group there. Once inside I frantically look right and left for the proper aisles.

I'm almost to the box of popcorn when I get distracted. I hear a group of guys laughing and talking together. Some of them look strangely familiar so I slow down. I see my brother, and the man in the middle, I know exactly what group this is. It's Fred with his groomsmen. He has short shorts on, with a crop top t-shirt that shows off his belly, which is allllll hanging out, and it has the word GROOM written across it. I start to feel secondhand embarrassment for him, but I have to admit, it's nice seeing him goofing off so freely. I'm happy my sister found a man that can have fun without taking himself too seriously.

Esther noticed them too and asked, "Hey guys! Umm...whatcha up to?"

One of the groomsmen that I've never met before chimes in and says, "It's Fred's bachelor party. We're giving him his most embarrassing last day as an unmarried man. He gets to be paraded around town like a crazy dude in a crop top and booty shorts. He has to buy some beer and then yell, 'I'M GETTING MARRIED!' when the cashier takes his money."

"Woooow. Suuubtle," I say with a chuckle to myself.

"Then what?" Juniper asks curiously.

"Then we'll go to the movies with him like this," the groomsman replies. "Any public place we can take him to utterly embarrass the man."

Just then the other group of girls, that has Emily in it, finds us in the aisle and Emily starts laughing at Fred. The bride and groom share sweet eye contact and laugh. As they're talking, I look behind Fred at some of the groomsmen. Each of the ones I tried to make eye contact with had this demeanor about them that told the world 'I'm married or unavailable.'

Just as I'm about to look at the ground to play with a piece of dirt I see there, I catch the eye of one of the groomsmen on the right side of the group. He's looking right at me. My eyes blink a few times too many and I cross my arms in front of me. I smile at him to acknowledge that I see his eyes and he smiles back. Sprinkles of goosebumps cover my arms and my stomach hurts all of a sudden.

Who is this guy, eye flirting with me? I wonder to myself. I look down at his left ring finger that is hanging down at his side just to be sure. No ring. I look back up at him to take in his face. He's insanely tall, definitely a few inches over six feet. He's got dark brown hair that is covered with a baseball hat, and blue piercing eyes that could match mine. He's also got a sharp jaw and braces-level-straight teeth. Tall, dark, and handsome hasn't ever been my type, they all seem like players to me and that's never been the kind of person I'm into.

Confusingly enough, there's a powerful confidence coming from his posture that is drawing me in. I squint my eyes. I refuse to be sucked into a player's charms.

His smile gets bigger and it makes me realize I've been staring at him for a long time. I flush, pull my arms even tighter to my body and look down at the piece of dirt I gave the middle finger to a minute ago. Too bad there's about fifteen people here, and too bad I'm too much of a wallflower to say anything out loud.

When I look back up, he is still looking at me, making me feel another pull at my stomach. He mouths the word, 'Hello' at me and I quickly say back, 'Hi' without actually making any sound.

He darts his eyes from me, to Fred, back to me, then to Emily. Like he's making sure I see them and their silliness over Fred's attire. I laugh a little out loud, nod my head and scruff my shoe on the ground. I look back up at him, and he rolls his eyes all the way around, dramatically. I smile and shrug my shoulders.

"Emily clearly loves him," this groomsman mouths at me. I smile and look over at Emily and Fred. They can't take their eyes off each other even though this is definitely not the most normal situation. I look back at the groomsman and nod while mouthing back, "most definitely." I feel like we're creating an inside joke with charades, and I'm here for it.

Breaking eye contact with him, my eyes follow someone walking down the aisle. I suddenly remember why we're here. I wish I had more time to continue miming with him, but my competitive soul tugs and reminds me that I've got a game to win. If we stay here any longer the other groups might get back to Cindy's house before us. I whisper to Juniper and Esther that we should duck out.

Twisting my lips sideways I quickly wave a hand at the groomsman and turn my back to the popcorn aisle. The others wave goodbye and follow me. We book it as fast as we can to get a head start from Emily's group. After a few seconds I see movement out of the corner of my eye when her group realizes what's happening. We rush to the other aisles for our candy bars and pick out a good movie.

After purchasing our scavenger hunt items at the register, we run back to the car. We rapidly make our way to a few more places, getting pictures of us touching a statue in town, and the three of us with our hands in a 'body of water.' Once we get all the items on the scavenger hunt done, we drive as fast as we, safely, can back to Cindy's house.

We pull into the driveway, and a rising surge of adrenaline hits my blood. I'm still not sure if we are the first ones to arrive. There is one car sitting in front of the house, but I don't know if that is an extra car of someone who is in another group or if it's a car from someone who arrived just before us with their group.

I can't open the car door fast enough and we run up the stairs to the house to finish the game. My heart bursts with curiosity as we open the front door and see it's only Cindy standing in the family room yelling, "You're first!" She opens her arms wide, then flutters her hands toward herself and says, "Now show me all your items and photos to see if you completed all the scavenger hunt tasks."

We pull out all of our stuff and show them to her. "Yep. Yep. Everything's there. You guys WIN!" she says now clapping. "Go pick a prize for yourselves!" I feel a sense of satisfaction now that I've finally gotten my own gift bag of prizes.

When everyone else starts to arrive they see us and each group who enters gives an audible, "ahhh," followed by a "great job," to be good sports about it.

Cindy addresses the room once everyone has arrived back, "Now this scavenger hunt wasn't for nothing. You all went to get popcorn, candy, and a movie. Let's put the movies on the table and we can all vote on a movie to watch to finish off our evening." What a fun night. We all agree on *Legally Blonde* and enjoy our popcorn and candy bars for Emily's last day as a single woman. And I'm one day closer to the wedding. *I wonder who that groomsman was.*

Chapter 4

Past

May

Half of us from our family-commune-house arrive at the venue, Elks Country Club, for rehearsal. I drove with Juniper and her parents, and when we walk onto the property, we realize we are the first ones here, so we settle into a shady spot under the trees. I sit down next to Sarah, Juniper and Fred's mom. Her lighthearted and fun personality is so captivating. I feel so drawn to lighthearted people, probably because sometimes I'm uncomfortable in my own skin that I want some of their light happiness to enter my world. To influence my personal atmosphere.

"Want some?" Sarah says as she offers me almonds and blueberries.

"Sure," I say as I reach for a few. I've never thought of eating almonds and blueberries. I'm more of a popcorn and candy bar kind of person.

"Looking forward to the wedding?" she asks me while grabbing a few berries herself.

"Yeah, I love weddings. Getting dressed up in a nice dress, making an effort to look pretty, the vows, the dancing. It all speaks to the romantic side of me," I reply as I reach for more 'snacks,' "I'm also extremely happy for Emily and Fred. I love seeing people in love. Plus, Fred is going to be a good humor addition to our family." I let out a happy sigh that brings a smile to my face before I put the food in my mouth. I love being around funny people. I hope to be funny someday.

"I agree. Fred is my favorite son and you guys will love him as a brother-in-law," Sarah laughs. "Speaking of perks at a wedding, I hear that there's some potentially single groomsmen here, " she says as a grin spreads across her face.

"Ha! I definitely want to hear more about that." I wink at her. "I'm keeping my eyes peeled." We both laugh lightheartedly. I feel so happy to think that maybe I could find someone at a wedding. Especially this wedding. The one that is coming at the perfect time in my life as I'm young and single.

"I heard the best man is single." She nudges me with her elbow.

"Thanks for the heads up," I say sarcastically and pull my legs up to wrap my arms around them.

"Mom, don't say that like you heard it from a little birdy," Juniper chimes into our conversation, "You've known him practically his whole life. You know he's been single for years."

"Yes!" She tilts her head back to laugh, "You got me. He's Fred's best friend actually. They've been besties since middle school. He's a very nice guy. His name is Dean," she says with a smile.

Juniper gives me the side eye as if she sniffed out a mole in our midst. I tuck my chin and chuckle into my chest.

I think to myself, *since he's the best man he's like wedding party royalty, I won't be interacting with him much.* So I push down any hope that tries to bubble up about this guy.

To be polite, though, I respond to Sarah, "Oh that's fun. You'll have to point him out to me when he gets here."

"He's already here." She looks behind me and nods her head.

My heart nearly leaps to the other side of my chest, and I feel sweat break out on my skin. Could this be the moment I see *the* guy that could be my next crush? "Oh really? Where?" I ask with so much chill I don't even recognize myself. Though, inside I've got a big adrenaline rush going.

She nods to the group of people that just arrived. "Right there."

I see a group of guys walking over to set up white folding chairs in front of the wedding archway, "The one with the blonde hair?" A smile creeps up to my lips. I undo my arms around my legs, crisscross them on the ground, and lean forward in this guy's direction.

"No, not that one. I don't know who that is. He might just work here at the venue. No, no, the one over there. At the end of the aisle with the two chairs in his hand. He has the baseball cap on, over his dark hair, and he's towering over the other groomsmen," she says, trying to redirect my gaze.

"Ohh. You mean that guy?" Now I'm zeroing in on who she is talking about. The one with the typically handsome looks and sharp jaw. My head does a double take. I recognize him. I squint my eyes. He's the one that mime flirted with me in the grocery store last night when we ran into Fred and his groomsmen.

"Yes!" she says to me. I genuinely appreciate her effort. Every unattached girl needs people like this on her side.

"Oohhh." I draw out the word. I hope I don't disappoint her with what I'm about to say, "He's kinda....not my type. I don't fall for the tall, dark, and handsome look. But thanks for keeping an eye out for me." I say even though a part of me knows that I feel this intangible pull toward him.

"No probs girl. But it's not just about looks, ya know. He has a great personality," she says, trying to convince me of this guy who is probably like another son to her. I look back over at him to see what she sees.

"You're probably right, but I'd rather be certain about the person I'm with." I look down at the grass feeling like I'm disappointing the coolest mom figure I've ever met.

"Fair enough." She rubs the top of my shoulders.

Just then, the pastor that is marrying the happy couple calls everyone over to the archway. As we all start to congregate around him and bunch up in a very second grade, unorganized circle, he starts to explain the order of events that Emily and Fred want. Once he's done explaining he gives the floor to Emily to pair us off.

Emily points to a guy named Haydon that I will be walking with, and we go to stand next to each other. My eyes instantly go to his ring finger. Taken. *Dammit... The search continues.*

As we start to line up to practice walking in a straight line down the aisle, to a song that has an eight count, I catch the eye of the best man and he smiles. My stomach decides to play jump rope, twisting in circles...I instantly look to my left and pretend to examine the leaves on the trees. That's weird. I look down at my stomach and talk to it with my mind. *What are you saying? We're supposed to be on the same page. I'm not into guys that ooze charm. Remember?*

The only thing I know about him is that he's single and has a lifelong friendship with my soon-to-be brother-in-law. My stomach has gone off the rails; it needs a new conductor leading it.

I'll give my stomach some grace though, this Dean guy is charming.

For the next twenty minutes that we are practicing this unpaid modeling gig we all signed up for, my mind goes on auto pilot, and I keep looking around for Dean. I can't control that pull I feel toward him. I want to make eye contact with him again. I succeeded a couple times and each time I remembered to smile instead of my normal resting chick face. I rub my hands on my pants to dry them off.

I feel like I'm going to end up talking to this guy more than I had initially thought. I look at my hands that keep perspiring and have a talk with them in my mind too. *What is happening? They're just glances. Nothing is going on. I don't want him.* The pastor and the wedding coordinator, Shannon, ask us to all start back at the beginning of the aisle again, so we congregate back there as we wait for the next command.

The smiles that Dean and I are exchanging make me feel alive again. That has to be why I'm feeling nervous and sweaty. There's no other reason I'd be looking forward to a smile from a guy I don't want to be interested in and haven't even exchanged a single word with. I look down at the ground to give my stomach a break.

"Hi, I'm Dean. What's your name?" I jump from the sound of the voice behind me.

"Oh hi! My god, you scared me." I put my hand to my chest and catch my breath. "I didn't see you coming. I'm Elise. Nice to meet you Dean." I hold my hand out to shake his. Something I learned from my dad.

"Nice to meet you too," he says, reaching out to accept my formal greeting.

Then he asks, "So what do you say we both stand and object at the wedding tomorrow?"

"Umm." My tongue feels too fat to make words.

"I don't think these two are gonna make it. They're too much in love. That kind of love just makes more love and more babies." He holds my eyes with his crystal blue ones.

"I uhh..." can't form words apparently.

"That's not what every red-blooded American wants. And in order to end this epidemic we have to take a stand. What do you say? You with me?" He holds a fist up into the air and gives me a side grin.

"No?" I finally get out one word, unsure of how to respond to his banter.

He laughs out loud. "I'm just kidding. I've never seen Fred happier. It's disgusting." He smirks.

I want to banter back but all of my insecurities have me standing stiff as a board, with a resting B face, wondering how I could contribute to this conversation.

"Yeah, disgusting. Who wants a happily ever after? Barf," I say as I twist my fingers into the corner of my jacket and see only blue. I wiggle my shoulders back a little to signal my muscles to relax.

"So you get it!" He laughs and winks. "I'm the guy who gets to hold the rings in this shindig. I don't think Fred remembers all the times I lost my pencil in school. I'm not very reliable with small objects. But hey, if he wants to place his whole future in my hands, then why would I deny him the chance?" he says playfully, then glances over at where Fred is standing.

"So, you're the ring bearer then?" I ask with a cheeky smile.

"I guess I am. I had to wrangle a couple of bears to get the gig but now I'm top dog, or uh, bear I guess, and nobody can take that title from me," he replies quicker than I expected. His smile looks so effortless.

"You should be proud. Not everyone can say that about themselves," I reply back even quicker.

"I'm gonna get a plaque made." He doesn't stop holding my gaze.

"That's smart. Commemorate it. Make it your headstone." I tilt my head up a little to take in his height.

"Yeah, it'll say 'here lies the ring bearer, top dog, or uh bear I guess'."
He shifts his feet but stays locked in.

"I'll be your witness. The title is yours." I look down at his feet.
They're pointing right at me. Did I see somewhere that says people point
their feet in the direction of their desire?

"Good. I'll need that." His smile has me captivated. "Ooop. I'm being
waved over. This best man business is hard work, it's driving my life," he
says as he walks away from me.

"Oh, ok. Bye," I stumble. Just when it was starting to get good and
confuse me even more.

Dean walks toward Fred to get some kind of instruction on where
to stand. I see Dean gesture in a way that I can only assume means he's
deciding which pocket to put the ring in for safekeeping and easy access
on the special day.

I see now what Sarah meant about Dean having a good personality.
How did I just get lost in his eyes for half that conversation? Damn, why
do all the ones I'm not interested in have to be so fun to talk to?

Chapter 5

Past

May

Setting up the venue and the ceremony rehearsal ended a little later than expected.

"Where's the rehearsal dinner at?" I ask Esther as she stands at the end of the chairs waiting for Michael to be done with his conversation so they can walk to their car.

"One of Emily's friend's houses I believe." She puts her jacket over her arm.

"Can I drive there with you and Michael?" I cross my arms in front of me as I look around for my backup plan if her answer is no.

"Sure. We have room," she says as Michael starts to walk over.

"Sweet. Thanks!" We start walking to the parking lot.

I hop into the back seat and get settled. Michael gets in the driver's seat and asks, "Can I pass this back to you to sit on the seat?" as he passes back his camera bag.

I grab the camera bag from him, "Yeah, that's fine."

As I buckle up, I hear the other backseat door open. When I lift my head, I expect to see Esther climbing in, but instead I'm greeted by Dean. I feel like a rolling pin just ran over me. My mouth drops open a little bit.

"Hi," he says.

"Hello," I manage to say back as a swell of excitement rushes in and I'm suddenly very aware of my hand placement.

What should I say? What will be witty enough to make him laugh? I can't believe how excited I am because I've already written him off as a hard no. There's just no stopping my heart from feeling what it wants to. So, *what do I saaaaay? Something funny...something funny...something...funny...*

"Is this seat taken?" he asks with a smile.

I laugh. *He's funny. I feel awkward.* I want to be funny so bad but I don't know what to say. I also don't want to make things weird by being silent for too long. "Umm, noooo..." I say hesitantly, trailing off trying to come up with a witty comeback. Nothing is coming to me. I scratch my arm. Stupid nerves.

He sits down in the empty seat next to me.

I see him look down at the camera bag and then he lifts his eyes back up to meet mine, "I feel like there's something between us."

I look down at the camera bag, and his joke hits me all at once.

"I've noticed," I say with a breathy sound to my voice, a lift to the corner of my mouth and a tilt of my head.

"So you see it too?" He stares at me as if he's reading me like a book.

I laugh out loud. "Indeed, I do. At least it's not a pile of baggage, holding us back from talking to each other." My heart starts racing. Too much? Too deep? Dammit.

Moving past the awkward silence the entire car is certainly feeling, I try to tease him and say, "So you couldn't find another person to ride with? You picked us as a last resort?" He is wedding party royalty after all. This doesn't seem like the car for him.

"I thought about hitchhiking to the rehearsal dinner, but this was faster. I'm putting my precious life in Michael's very capable hands," he says as he pats the back of Michael's shoulders in front of him. I breathe out the air I was accidentally holding in. He's playing along with my banter! *Maybe I can be funny?*

"Plus, we got to talking, and it turns out Dean skateboards too, so we decided to stop at a skate park before the rehearsal dinner. We have thirty minutes to kill," Michael chimes in.

"Oohh, how fun! I love watching people skateboard. I used to have a guy friend in high school that skated. I watched him a couple times, so I'm down," I looks sideways as I think about John who stopped talking to me after I turned down his feelings for me. I remember thinking he wasn't tall enough.

"Cool. I love it too," Esther inputs from the front seat.

"I was hoping you'd say that. There's nothing worse than dragging someone to a skatepark, making them watch me skateboard and them wanting to vomit the whole time." Dean takes his hand off Michael's shoulder and crystal blue meets crystal blue again.

"It'll be quite entertaining to see if you fail at it too," I say with a smirk combined with a ball of anxiety where my diaphragm should be. I'm trying so damn hard to find the right amount of teasing to give him.

"Now that you're watching, I'm gonna be extra careful." He winks.

We spent the short five-minute ride talking about skateboarding. The tricks he knows and the tricks I can pronounce. I've never skateboarded myself, but I've definitely watched it in my teen years and learned the lingo. I'm trying to impress him.

I'm scared to admit that I love this attention from him. All the pep talks to my body aren't doing any good. I can't put words to what's happening, but I'm starting to give into it.

Once we get to the skate park Michael and Dean head toward the, larger than expected, concrete park. There's quite a lot of people here and I lose track of Dean for a minute but then find the guy with the captivating demeanor across the way, like an invisible magnet drew me to him.

He's really good.

As I'm standing next to Esther, I start to daydream about this being our future. What if I end up with Dean and this is a normal weekend for the four of us? What if Michael could have a brother-in-law that he had something in common with. Esther is my closest sister. Since we're just two years apart from each other we grew up basically at the same time. It would be awesome if I married a guy that could be friends with Michael. I'd love to spend more time with Esther and daydreaming right now has me excited to see the four of us make that happen.

Now that Esther is married and not living at home anymore, I'm constantly wishing we can spend more time together. The thought of this being a normal outing for us makes me so happy. I can see a future that brings me so many fulfilling moments.

Dean heads in my direction and stops to do an ollie right in front of me. He lands it and makes eye contact. When he smiles I can practically see the dental sparkle on his teeth. Show off. I secretly like it.

"So, what do you think of Dean?" Esther asks, breaking me away from my silent interaction with him.

"Umm there's nothing there," I lied. I don't actually know what is going on inside of me to be honest with myself, so I can't even be honest with her.

"Oh really? He seems so cool. And I thought I was picking up a vibe between you two." She looks over at me to try and coax me out of my not-sharing-any-information shell.

"I think he's funny. But he looks like a player. Which is fun to flirt with, but I don't think it can go the distance. It's too bad. Otherwise, he would be my perfect guy." I look down at the ground and kick a rock that was just sitting there minding its own business.

"What if you're wrong about him and he is actually a decent guy? I didn't notice Michael at first. But he kept pursuing me and I noticed him more and more. His personality surprised me. Now I think there's no one I'd rather be around, than him." She squints her eyes against the bright sun, folds her arms in front of her, and smiles over at her beloved.

"Umm, you could be right," I say, not taking my eyes off Dean as I'm talking to her.

"You could just see where it goes without telling him that you don't know if he's a player or not? Who cares if it takes a few interactions. You can just wait and see. Then if it doesn't happen and you don't start to see his true colors, you can just stay friends," she says with convincing confidence.

"Hmm. I see what you're saying. I'll keep that in the back of my mind," I reply, breaking my eyes away from following Dean down the skate bowl and finally looking her in the face.

"Good," she says. "Have you noticed that he keeps looking over here, at you?" She pushes her shoulder into mine.

My stomach leaps, my head snapping in his direction to see if I can catch his eyes, but he's riding off in the opposite direction.

Esther smiles to herself. "Not interested huh?"

"Shut up," I say as I try to hide a smile. We both laugh. She knows me so well.

We continue watching the guys skateboard and once the time we're trying to kill is up, we all load back into the car and head for the house where they're hosting the rehearsal dinner.

As we're driving, comfortably with the camera bag still placed between us, Dean starts asking me questions about myself.

"So, what kind of hobbies do you have?" he asks as he rolls his window down.

"Umm I like reading books and knitting right now. My hobbies change every year," I reply, as the wind starts pushing my baby hairs all over my face, I look over at him.

"Hold on. I didn't hear that. The wind is too loud." He rolls his window back up. "Say that again."

After I repeat myself, he says, "That's honest. If my hobbies changed every year, I'd have a hard time recognizing them."

I laugh but try not to show my growing interest. "Honesty is the only way I know how to talk," I reply.

"That's refreshing. I like a person who can tell the truth about their grandma tendencies. Grandma's the new thirty, ya know? You're two-thirds the way there," he jokes.

"Hahaha. What's the other one-third?" I ask

"Waking up early because you went to bed early. Be honest. I won't make fun of you if that's you too." He points a finger in my direction.

I laugh out loud and grab it out of the air. "No. That one I don't do. But I nap. Nothing better than a good two-hour nap in the middle of the day. Don't touch my naps." I release his finger and threaten with my own finger pointed at his face. "You can't take them away from me."

Now, he's the one grabbing my finger out of the air. "I wouldn't dare."

All the heat goes to my pointer finger as I'm now very aware of its existence. "Thanks," I say. "So, what about you? What are your hobbies?"

"Well, my main hobby is camera bag stabilizer," he gestures, releasing my finger and grabbing for the camera bag between us.

"Wow. Eventful. And might I say, that sounds very life fulfilling," I reply, placing my new favorite phalange on my lap.

"Oh, you have no idea. There's always a camera bag lying around that needs holding. I can't tell you all the places I've traveled to for this hobby. Okay, I'll tell you. Four. But they've all been the state of California. I'm always around very artistic people. Anyway, no other hobbies. That's it," he says with a shrug.

"Ha! So skateboarding earlier today was beginner's luck? First time ever doing it?" I ask jokingly.

"You caught me. Looks like I have two hobbies." His smile sucks the air out of the car.

"Nothing gets past me," I wink, grateful for the words I was able to put together this time, even with a tongue that didn't seem to want to operate.

"I believe it," he says. "So where do you live?"

"In Washington right now. What about you?" I say as I settle into my seat. Quickly feeling increasingly comfortable with someone I only recently met.

"Southern California," he replies. "What town do you live in?"

"It's a little town called Yelm. About forty-five minutes east of Olympia."

"Ye-uh-el-mmm. Hmm can't say I've ever heard of that town."

I laugh. "You're saying it weird. It's Ya-el-mm. Yelm."

"It's a weird word. Hard not to say it out loud to see what it feels like falling off my tongue." He stares at me, sticks out his tongue, and scrapes it against his teeth.

My heart skips awake. Now all I can think about is what his tongue would feel like on mine. I shake my head.

Wait, he's not my type. Is he? Stop it, Elise.

"Fair point. A lot of people say that about the town's name," I reply as I break our goosebump inducing eye contact. I turn to look out the window and try to stop the thoughts running rampant in my head about his tongue.

"So do you like it there?" he asks.

I turn back to face him and say, "Actually, it's too small for me and too familiar. I want to live in a bigger town. I'm somewhat of a nomad and like to travel around a lot to experience new and different places." I'll admit, I'm trying to impress him with my cultured experiences.

"Ooh, the nomad life. That's the dream," he says, opening his eyes wide and drifting them over to watch the road. "Someday I'd like to skip off to another country with no more then a days notice."

"You should! That sounds like so much fun," I say as I pull my arms tight around me.

"I could embrace the nomad life. Go anywhere, do anything, be anyone, meet everyone," he finds my eyes again. "So, where to next, Miss Nomad?" he asks as he's fiddling with the zipper on the camera bag.

"Georgia. I've applied for a school over there and just recently got accepted. I'll be preparing to leave this summer," I say just as Michael turns a corner and I start to lean into Dean a little bit. The turn is so sharp I can't fight gravity fast enough to pull myself off him. When I look up to see what he's thinking, I notice he's staring down at me with no protest. We stare at each other in silence and wait for gravity to ease up. Feels like gravity is casually trying to be a wingman.

"Sorry about that," I say as I'm finally able to lift myself up.

"No worries. We can't all win the fight against gravity like Superman." He then reaches over and straightens my shirt sleeve for me. It had somehow been pulled down during the "corner smooshing car game."

"Thank you," I say as I look down at his hand touching the skin of my shoulder.

"You're welcome." He seems more nervous than I've noticed all day. "So, umm," he stumbles over his words, "Your next life is gonna be as a...southern bell."

I smile. "When you say it that way it sounds so charming." I bat my eyes like a debutant.

The car slows down. "I think this is the right place," Michael says quizzically as he's looking for the house number.

Breaking away from my conversation with Dean I say, "Oh cool. This place looks like a log cabin." We pull up the long driveway and find a spot behind twenty other cars parked at the house.

"Yeah. Emily said it's her mentor's house," Michael replies.

"That's so nice of them to let her use their house!" My mouth drops as I stare at the many walls and roof peaks that make up the side of the building I'm looking at.

After Michael has parked the car, we all get out and walk around the house to the front door. Dean skips up beside me and continues our conversation. "So, if I needed a sweater would you be able to knit me one?"

I jump. "Oh! Umm. I'm not that good. I could basically knit you a square or a rectangle," I confess.

"So a blanket then?" he asks.

"Well, I've never knitted a blanket before. Just scarfs. I could knit you a scarf all day e'ry day. But I could probably try my hand at a blanket," I offer.

"I'll take one of your scarves if you have the time." He winks at me.

"Okay. I'll knit you one." I look up at him and wonder when the next time we'll see each other after the wedding will be. But I still agree.

I walk into the house and leave Dean behind as I notice that the inside matches the feeling the outside gave me. I'm greeted by a magnificent, vaulted ceiling that spans the entire entryway and living room. As I get past the foyer my eyes go up and to the right, seeing a balcony with a railing that I can only assume is where the upstairs bedrooms are. As you walk into the living room there is a sliding glass door that goes to a beautiful wooden/stone deck outside.

This rehearsal dinner doesn't look like it's just for the people in the wedding party, but rather, for the bride and groom's entire community. I feel my body shrink into a tiny version of myself. I just want to find a corner to sit in and observe everyone here.

Once I walk out onto the deck, I see all the food. I smell barbecue in the air and my stomach grumbles. Seeing Juniper out on the deck I walk over to her.

"Hey there. Nice to see a familiar face," I say, a little relieved that I can just hide out during this party next to someone I feel comfortable with.

"Hi. There's so many people here, I'm glad you walked over. I didn't know who to talk to." She confirms my exact feelings.

"Me either. Sometimes I get so overwhelmed at gatherings I just like to find people I know so it looks like I'm mingling, but really, I just stand around one or two people the whole time." I look over at her and admit my giant gathering secret.

"I do too!" she says. So we stand on the deck in comfortable, age-old-friendship silence and start watching everyone else mingle and chat.

They all seem like they know each other and there's a lot of "Hiiiiii!" and "How are you?" and "Whatcha been up to?" comments with hand gestures and waves. I feel myself shrinking less now that I have a friend to wallflower with.

I break our silence, "I love weddings, but I don't look forward to the big parties that require me to mingle with strangers. Oh! Or the cleanup part. It's always the family that gets stuck with cleanup." I pretend to stomp my foot.

"Hmm. Never thought about that. Yeah, that is a drag! We should tell Fred and Emily that for this wedding we're changing the rules. It's their party, but they get to clean it up. We can't lose!" she says, elbows bent and palms pointing to the sky.

I laugh so hard that tears start to come out of my eyes. "YES! I am so on board with this! I don't see how it could go wrong!" I exclaim, wiping the laughter tears from my eyes. I've never made a friend that I click with so quickly or get along with so well.

Just then, Emily comes out to the deck and tells everyone to gather around. Once everyone came close enough, she started to talk.

"Thank you everyone, for being here and wanting to celebrate with us. As a physical thank you we wanted to feed everyone a nice meal. Since the way to everyone's heart is through their stomach, we figured this would be the perfect appreciation gift. We love you all, and feel very loved that you all chose to come here and be with us. Sooo...dig in!" Emily turns around to walk away and then snaps back, "Oh! And, umm, immediate family and wedding party goes through the line first." Emily nods as she finishes her speech.

I'm glad she said that the wedding party can go through the line first because I am starving, with an exclamation mark behind it. These moments are always awkward to see who gets to go through the line first. You don't want to seem too eager and run up there, but if you wait too long to go up to the line you might miss out on some of the good stuff that runs out fast. Social settings are complicated.

Once Juniper and I get our food we go and sit down inside the house, on a bench they put in the grand foyer room. Dean comes up to us and sits down next to me with his plate of food in his hands. "Hey ladies, mind if I join?" he asks.

"Sure," Juniper and I say in unison.

As he sits down the sides of our legs touch each other. Neither one of us makes a move to pull away. I feel a rush of electricity fire through my nerves ending in a lightning show in my stomach. I look down to remind it of the pep talk we've had already. *Don't you remember what we've talked about?*

"So, since these two love birds are basically celebrities, we need to find a celebrity mashup name for them that we can use for the rest of their lives. What do you two think of Fremily?" Dean proudly states.

"That sounds like a great name. I guess the conversation ends here for the best celebrity name. We can't top that," I say looking over at Juniper to see what she thinks.

"That's pretty spot on where celebrity mashup names are concerned," Juniper nods in agreement.

"How long did it take you to think that up?" I ask as I put some potato salad in my mouth.

"I've given a total 3 minutes of thought to this." Dean smiles and takes a bite of his hamburger.

"Geez. They should hire you at the celebrity rag headquarters. They're missing out on your magic skills," I say while trying to cover my mouth that is now full of food. Not wanting Dean to have the image of food falling out of my mouth stuck in his head. Not exactly the 'charming' vibe I was going for...

"I've applied. Waiting for a call back as we speak," he says with a nod of his head as he chews another bite.

"Is this another one of your obscene hobbies?" I nudged him with my knee.

"You got me. Celebrity name enthusiast right here," he says with a mouth full of food and points his thumb at his face. Okay, so maybe I didn't have to worry so much about my image around him after all.

I laugh, look down at my plate of food, and see that our legs are still touching.

Chapter 6

Past

May

It's the big day! All the bridesmaids are at Cindy's house now, getting ready. I look over at Emily who's sitting on a kitchen chair while Cindy does her wedding day hair. They talked about the style last night at the rehearsal dinner. Emily told Cindy she wanted a cascade of curls that were pinned up on the back of her head.

Emily stayed at our family commune house last night. Her final night as a single woman was spent with her family. It might seem strange to other people, but for us it's not so strange because we're the 'weird' family that likes spending time together.

As Emily is getting all kinds of curls and bobby pins put in her hair, I'm waiting to get my hair done by Esther. I have such thick hair that it takes a good hour to do anything with it, which will give me time to think about what interactions I'll have with Dean today.

Maybe I should look him up on Facebook and scroll through his profile to see if I can see him as less of a player by the photos he choose to post. I'm sure there's one that doesn't make him look so tall, dark, and handsome...I grab my phone to open up the Facebook app.

I see a notification pending and click on it. The back of my neck goes cold as a rush of shock washes over me. It's Dean, asking me to be Friends on Facebook. Shocked, I look up from my phone as if to share this moment with someone around me, but with no one there I look back down.

Oh. My. Gosh. I didn't even have to do that creepy Facebook stalking thing everyone does. I accepted his request and went to his profile.

There's a lot of photos of him at work, some skateboarding photos, and more photos with friends. I notice the baseball hat that he was wearing when we first met in quite a few pictures. If he stopped wearing that baseball hat, I think he'd look less like a player. I find one photo that I pause and look at. This one is kind of sweet. His styled hair is pushed back on his head, almost like swooped hair that stays still. My back softens a little, I can see him as a "sweet guy" in this one. He's standing next to some people in an office. I only assume these are coworkers. He looks comfortable and confident. Like someone you'd want to get to know.

I give a heavy eye roll to nobody. I feel confused. I put the phone down on the coffee table beside me and started paying attention to Esther walking over to me.

"Do you want some curls in your hair?" Esther pulls the straightener out.

"Yeah. That would be lovely. Are you going to use the that or a curling iron?" I'm unable to keep the shock out of my face.

"This. I just have to twist it and it adds curls to the hair. Easy peasy." She smiles at me like she just shared a secret.

"Oh. Awesome. Well after you curl them can you try to pin them in a way that doesn't make my hair look too big, I already have enough volume as it is," I say with a laugh.

If I could give my hair density to people as a gift I absolutely would. I have too much oomph for one person to handle. It's not fair to the rest of the world. My hair has volume that only goddesses could comprehend...or someone from the 80s. If I was a teenager in the 80s, I'm sure I'd be popular at my high school. I wouldn't even need to tease it or hairspray it. They would chant my name down the halls and push each other out of the way to sit next to me in the cafeteria.

"I can do that. No Problem," she says. "So whatcha thinking about?" she gets to work on the first strand.

Which topic do I admit I was just thinking about? I'll go with the easier one. "I'm thinking about how voluminous my hair is and that I'd love to share it with people," I reply with no lie. It's not a lie if you tell just one and not two of the topics on your mind.

"Oh. Interesting. You wouldn't by any chance also be thinking about a certain tall, dark-haired gentleman that will be in the wedding today as the best man, would you?" she asks.

Wow. Is it written on my forehead? Did I write "DEAN" across my face last night?

I don't like to lie so I finally admit to her, "Mayyyybbeeee." I feel like I just got a tooth extraction.

"Elise! He would be so good for you! He's funny, charming, playful, interesting. I think you should consider giving into the feelings you're clearly trying to stop yourself from having," she winks, "And he seems very interested in you. He tried so many times to stand next to you at the rehearsal and the rehearsal dinner yesterday. You have to have noticed." She pauses to let it sink in.

"This guy is into you and if you just give it a chance you could be into him too," she talks through the bobby pins in her mouth as she tries to hold up a curl on my head.

"I know. I like his banter sooooo much. But what if that's all he's good for? Some laughs. What if he doesn't know how to go deep and have normal conversations?" I ask her rhetorically, looking down at the locked screen of my phone that sits on the coffee table.

"You'll never know if you just give him this one weekend to show you. It takes longer than that to get to know someone," she says, shoving a bobby pin into my mane.

"God, you're right." I let out the air in my lungs, not realizing I was even holding my breath.

"Just saying," she shrugs.

"I did notice that he's drawn to me..." I trail off before admitting that I'm also drawn to him. I'm not ready to say that out loud yet. Even if she sees it already.

I reach for my phone and unlock it. "He just asked me to be friends on Facebook."

"Wait, what!" she exclaims, enthusiasm written all over her face. If she didn't have those bobby pins to keep in her mouth her jaw would have dropped.

I open up my Facebook app to show her, "Yeah, I think I could get past the baseball cap phase...eventually. Here, look at this photo." I swipe through a couple to get to the one I want to show her. "He's kind of sweet looking in it, right? What do you think?" Her hands are busy, so I hold up my phone closer to her face so she doesn't have to lean down.

"I'm sorry, I'm still stuck on him asking you to be friends on Facebook!" she squeals. "I love this for you! I can't stop smiling. He could be the one!" she vomits out before she even sees what I'm trying to show her.

"Don't get ahead of yourself. Facebook friends is nothing serious. I just want you to tell me what you think of this photo for now," I wiggle my phone in front of her eyes, "Am I right? No baseball cap makes him look kind right?" I ask, feeling my arms get tired in this statue of liberty position.

"Let me see then. I'll get a good look at him." She looks down at my phone for a second then twists a strand of hair around her finger and pins it.

"Yep. I can see it." She nods. "No doubt, cute as a button."

"Give me more than that, please. I'm not asking about cute, I'm asking about kind. I've got the weight of this decision on my shoulders," I say dramatically and aching.

"Ok. Let me finish this final pin, and...there, ok. Let me have the phone."

I hand her my phone and rub my shoulders.

She does some zooming in and out on the photos. Some trombone moves of the arms, giving this moment a little flare of the dramatic to really make sure she's seeing him correctly. I smile and appreciate her antics.

"Yes! He looks very kind without a baseball cap. Maybe you are putting too much pressure on the baseball cap and you should just get to know him to find out if he's kind and not a player like you think?" she says as she hands the phone back to me.

"Yea, you're probably right," I let out a heavy sigh, "I feel so vain even caring about this. I wish I didn't, but it seems to be holding me up. I just think it gives him the image/vibe that he is a player, which is a pretty big turn-off for me." I give the photo one last glance as I place my phone back down on the coffee table and hit the lock button.

"Well, time will tell. We'll have to see how the cookie crumbles," she says reassuringly.

I look back at the mirror we propped on the couch and continue watching her do my hair. I start to daydream about the 'what ifs.' It's possible that the reason I am drawn to Dean is because we are meant to be and I just need to get over these high expectations I'm having for him.

Ugh. I let out a heavy sigh. Is this a lesson? Am I learning a valuable life lesson? The kind that sticks with you until you're in your sixties and you're telling all your young coworkers about? *It's okay to be with a guy that you don't instantly see as the one. You can really build a bond with someone through friendship and then it grows into something more. Trust me,* I'd say to the youth.

When Esther finishes my hair and we get dressed, we head to the venue with the few of us that are ready.

I honestly didn't think any of the bridesmaids would be at the venue early, but as it turns out, I was wrong. Plus, the rain decided to come in full force today. On the drive over I got a text from my mom saying, **"The wedding coordinator needs some help transferring the wedding chairs and decorations from outside on the grass to the main ballroom inside. If any of you girls get done early, I wanted to let you know what you're coming to."** My mother ladies and gentlemen, always being kind and considerate.

Once we get to the venue we walk to the back part of the building and head down the massive green hill to the grassy part where a group of people are starting to carry white chairs up the hill. I spot him in his black suit with his dark brown hair. No baseball cap.

He starts walking up the hill with two white chairs in each hand. We pass by each other halfway down the path and he catches my eye. "Hey there stranger. Fancy meeting you here. You come here often?" The eye contact is making my heartbeat faster than a racehorse.

"Almost every day this week. It's my new stomping grounds." I show all my teeth in a cheesy grin

He throws his head back and laughs, then says, "I hope to see that smile more often."

"You like it?" I blush.

"I like a lot of things about you, Elise." He stops walking, still holding the folding chairs and stands in front of me...towering.

I can feel the pink in my cheeks get warmer as we stand there in complete silence. "I...uh...thank you." I say the only thing that comes to mind.

"You're welcome," he sets a chair down to free one hand. He reaches for my empty right hand and lifts it up to his mouth to kiss the back of it.

My whole body gets weak as I stare at his lips touching my hand. My breathing gets heavier as I notice his dark hair being kissed by the sun. We make eye contact and it feels like the minutes stop.

Hearing some talking crest the hill, we both look over to see who it is and without thinking I do a slight tug on my hand and he lets go. Reaching down to grab the chair he says, "See you up there?"

"Yeah. Yes. Yep," I stumble. I watch him walk up the hill and then turn to grab my own handful of chairs. *I shouldn't have quickly pulled my hand away. I hope that wasn't embarrassing for him.*

As I'm about to walk back up the hill I see him at the top of it, starting to come back down with hands empty in a slight jog.

He makes his way straight to me and says, "Here Miss, let me get those for you. There should be more gentlemen around here helping out. It's a shame that I'm the last one on Earth." He pivots and walks back up the hill with a charming smile, and my chairs in his hands. Looks like my hand tug didn't phase him. I feel like a giddy schoolgirl hoping to catch the eye of a boy I like in the school hallways.

I can feel the happy bubbles come up to my chest, and a smile that can't be wiped off stay permanently on my face. He makes me feel like I'm the only person he sees here. Like somehow the celebrity of the wedding party notices *me*.

I don't want to tell him that, even after his gallant gesture. I still have to grab some more chairs and head back up the hill. That would ruin the moment. He was acting like such a gentleman. I laugh to myself. *The last one on Earth.*

The next handful of chairs and I make it up to the top of the hill, but right before I can make it to the building Dean comes running out and swoops the chairs out of my hands. "You can't be carrying these! They might ruin your pretty dress. For me, it won't be a big deal because I'm not the star of the show. Plus, this black suit could hide anything."

I let him take the chairs out of my hands. "You're right. My, also black, dress would show everything if I got it ruined." I wink, look down at my dress and then back up at him. He smiles and we both turn around to go back to our duties. I'm really enjoying that he'll say anything just to have a reason to interact with me.

I get to the top of the hill with the last of the chairs, walking as slow as possible and looking around for Dean to see if I could think of a way to interact with him again. When I spot him I see that he's now with the horde of groomsmen and the groom himself.

It looks like the photographer has collected them and they're walking around to find a spot to take the groomsmen's photos. The high I was just feeling makes my sinking heart feel more drastic as I watch him walk away.

They must be getting a jump on the photos and getting the grooms-men ones out of the way. I pick up the pace to finish my task.

Making my way into the building, I wait for my eyes to adjust from the bright light outside to the dim light inside. I set my chairs in the semi-circle being created, then look for the wedding coordinator. When I spot her I walk over. "Hey Shannon, need anymore help setting up in here?" I ask.

"That would be great. Thanks for offering," she replies. "I have mason jars in those boxes over there on the floor." She points to the wall closest to us. "They need to be moved around the corner to a drink table that will greet all the guests as they come in. Can you bring them around?"

"Absolutely. I'm on it," I say.

I walk to the wall that she was pointing at, pick up the first box and head around the corner. As I turn the corner to drop them off at the drink table, I see Juniper. She's standing there wiping off all the mason jars.

"Oh, hey there. I have a delivery for you," I say with happy surprise, "Didn't know you were inside. How's it going? Is this your station?" I know Emily put family and friends in charge of projects throughout the wedding day.

"Yep. I'm the tea wench," Juniper says as she opens her arms up diagonally.

"That's the best kind of wench," I chuckle. "Where would you like me to put this box of mason jars? I have a few more to bring over here after this one." I shift my feet from the weight I'm carrying.

"You can place them right there," she points to the floor at the end of the table, "I'm working my way through everything that Shannon gave me and grabbing all the wide mouth mason jars from all those boxes. If I don't have enough to fill the table then I'll move on to other boxes people have donated," she says.

"Perfect." I set it down where she tells me. "I'll be back with another," I say as I turn around to go back and get the rest of the stack Shannon pointed out to me.

When I set down the final box I start digging through it to help her find the wide mouth mason jars. I see some movement in the corner of my eye and look over to see who it is. I'm met with the sight of Dean and he's looking down at me as he's walking down the hallway.

"Bathroom break. Being a groomsman model is harder than you'd think. The trade isn't respected enough," Dean smiles as he slows down his walk to the bathrooms.

"I bet. Standing there in just one pose for twenty minutes must really wear you out," I cheese.

He laughs and says, "You're next," then continues walking past me toward his bathroom destination at the end of the hallway.

I don't stop smiling as I look down at the box I'm digging through and put the next mason jar on the table for Juniper. I sense Juniper standing still and when I look over at her I see that she's staring right at me. "What?" I ask.

"Umm...what was that? Did I detect some flirtation vibes between the two of you?" she asks as she slows down the strokes of wiping out one of the mason jars in her hand.

I blush. "Maaayyybbeeee," I say. This might be my new signature word now.

"Oh. My. God. This is like a movie! Who actually finds a groomsman at their sister's wedding and the guy happens to be your new brother-in-law's best friend?! This is too good. Too good," Juniper says as she shakes her head with a smile on her face.

I laugh and continue blushing. "I don't know if it's anything. It probably won't even work out because he lives in California and I live in Washington, soon to be Georgia."

"There's always long distance. And if you really hit it off you could just move to California and ditch Georgia." She flutters her hand in the air like it's no big deal to move your life for another person.

"I'm not sure I'm the type of girl to move to a different state for a guy," I place two jars on the table for her.

"Dean is a great guy. He's top-shelf quality. You won't find anyone more loyal. He's like a little puppy that wants to make people laugh." Juniper nods nonstop at me with wide eyes now.

I laugh out loud. "Those are some very convincing qualities."

"I wouldn't lie to you," she says with a straight face, but it doesn't last long because then she breaks out in a smile.

"Fair enough," I say, very aware of my smile not yet leaving my face. "I believe you. Everyone is trying to convince me that he is someone special. I should probably start listening to you guys."

I see Dean come back down the hallway. As he's walking toward me with unquestionable eye contact, I want to say something but nothing clever reaches my brain. We don't break away from looking at each other when he says, "You're doing a great job at placing those jars on the table. Seriously, no one else could nail it like you are. I wouldn't want to even attempt it myself because it's so intimidating."

"I wouldn't dare ask you to try either, just in case it's embarrassing for you to fail so hard at it," I say with a smile. Returning his banter is way easier for me then starting the banter myself.

"That's so thoughtful of you," he beams, then continues to walk down the hallway and out the doors to take more groomsmen photos.

I haven't had a guy make me smile like this before.

I keep pulling out wide mouth jars from the boxes for Juniper, and when I look up at her she's staring at me again. "Shut up!" I say, like a thirteen-year-old girl.

"I didn't say anything." She shakes her head. "Just absorbing what's happening," she quips as she takes the jars I'm handing her.

Chapter 7

Past

May

The last-minute wedding changes got finished before the guests started to arrive. The ceremony is colorful and vibrant, with giant pieces of fabric crisscrossing above everyone's head in all the colors of the rainbow, mason jars filled with flowers of the same colors are lining the floor following the pathway of the aisle. The wedding arch is in the middle of the room, and all the guests are seated in an almost full circle around it. It feels very fitting to have the guests completely surround the bride and groom as they get married. Kinda poetic, like you're supposed to have your community of people surround you through life.

The wedding party has been told to congregate in a back room while we wait to be cued by Shannon for our debut walk down the aisle. This room is so small it feels like we're the full contents of a bag of Doritos stuffed into a much smaller plastic baggy, bursting at the seam.

"Since I have you all here, I want to let you know that, after the reception is over, the photographer has asked for you guys to all group up outside on the grass, in front of the double glass doors. As long as it's not raining." Shannon points in the vague direction of outside with a smile. We all nod our heads for fear of using our voices and the oxygen gets sucked out of this tiny room.

Shannon leaves us to go get the music started. After what felt like the longest time with my fellow cheese flavored chips, I hear the piano player start to play music in the background. We start our aisle walk, meeting up at the front archway, and ending with the pastor asking, "Who gives away this bride to be married to this man?"

Emily stands there looking absolutely radiant in her wedding dress and her eyes locked in on Fred's when my dad replies, "Her mother and I do." I like that my dad includes my mom in this response. All mothers are giving their daughters away too.

Everyone watches as our loved one pledges their heart forever to the person standing across from them.

Emily is beaming up at Fred as she says her vows. When I look over at Fred I see a small glisten in his eyes. I love that Fred loves my sister so much. When Fred starts to proclaim that he'd lasso the moon for her I feel my heart grow three sizes and really appreciate that my sister has found someone that will protect her heart so gently. Hearing both of their vows makes me tear up and I feel beyond happy for these two people to be committing unconditional love to one another forever. I wish them nothing but happiness. I'm excited to have Fred be a part of our family now.

We laugh, we cry, and then, the ceremony is over before we know it. They kiss with an uproar of celebration and screams, then make their way back down the aisle as Mr. and Mrs. for the first time ever.

As the good little sheeps that we are, we make our way outside to the rendezvous spot that we were told the photographer wanted after the wedding. Invisible bugs start swimming around in my stomach as I start looking around for Dean and notice that we are close to each other.

I want to get his attention so I throw my head back and laugh at something that my walking partner, Haydon, said and maybe I laugh a little louder than I should have but I can't take it back now. It worked though, a few seconds later Dean walks over to our group and stands next to me, our arm hairs practically hugging.

"What did I miss?" He puts his hands in the pockets of his slacks and looks around the circle for the person who told the joke.

"Just telling a story about something my two-year-old did last night," Haydon says dryly.

"I can't compete with that. I don't have those kinds of stories," Dean shrugs.

"I'm sure you'll find something else to say that's equally funny. You always have a comment up your sleeve," I say to Dean. Everyone else in the circle fades away as I look at him.

"My jokes are so natural I don't even have a sleeve to hold them in. But...uhh...how much do you think I can bench press?" Dean asks, not skipping a beat from this challenge I gave him. He holds two thumbs out with palms pointed toward each other in a punch-line kind of gesture.

"Uhhhh," my mind goes blank as I try to figure out where this is going.

Haydon laughs, clearly in on the joke, then says, "Best in Show! I love that movie."

Dean smiles and continues, "250. I can bench an easy 250."

I'm standing there trying to get what's happening but it's totally going over my head. "Am I missing something?" I ask with an awkward grin on my face.

"Oh, sorry. It's a quote from a movie," he says and he pushes his arm into mine.

Now insanely aware of my arms hairs I try to reply back, "Ohh. I'm tracking now. Is it a new one?"

Haydon and Dean both look at each other, then Dean says, "No. It's probably twenty or thirty years old. Not very many people liked it in its heyday, so I'm not surprised you haven't heard of it."

"Gotcha," I say.

"So how did you like the wedding?" Dean asks.

Happy he asked me a question, wanting to keep this conversation going as long as humanly possible, I say, "It was so good. Sweet, and fun. What they said to each other during their vows was adorable."

"I helped Fred write those words," he deadpans.

"Oh really?!" I take a step back and look at him up and down.

"Umm. No. Sorry, that wasn't a very good joke. I shouldn't have taken credit for something so meaningful." He runs his hand through his dark brown hair, looking a little embarrassed.

"It's ok. You said it so confidently, I easily believed you." I slap his arm. He makes me feel like I'm in high school again.

He pretends to rub his arm. "I have a problem; I make everything a joke. It just flows out of me," he says.

I see movement around me, but I stay zoned in on him. "Yeah. I've noticed that all the things you say are basically jokes. Can you be serious at all?" I ask bluntly. It's something I've been wondering about lately.

"I can. I have a serious side too. I hope I can show it to you someday." He winks at me, a playful but genuine look on his face.

"I hope so too." I cross my arms and smile as more invisible bugs plague my stomach.

"Alright everyone," the photographer claps, "gather around, you beautiful people, and let's get you into some fun wedding party positions."

I break away from his gaze and remember where I am. I'm instantly self-conscious of anyone noticing that Dean and I have some kind of connection.

We start walking toward the photographer and I start to think, *this banter, this chemistry—it's like kryptonite to me. I'm usually a timid introvert, but I actually want him to notice me.*

The photographer places us close to each other in the first pose and electricity fires through my body and out my fingers when our arms touch. I can tell he's thinking the same thing because every time we accidentally touch he looks at me and smiles. I secretly hope the photographer keeps placing us next to each other. I welcome any opportunity to be close to him. Especially the opportunities that don't make it look like it's my idea.

For the next half hour of photographs we are weaved in and out of being close to each other. Each minute I feel like I'm being electrified, while the butterflies in my stomach are frantically raging around like there's too many motorcycles looping around The Globe of Death all at once. I'm a circus act all by myself. I haven't noticed how many times I've been told to smile because Dean's presence has been distracting me. I can tell the photographer is winding down and my mind starts to wonder. *I hope that we're placed next to each other inside at the dinner portion of the wedding.*

"Awesome. Thank you, guys! You all did great." The photographer clasps his hands together. "Now, let's have just the bridesmaids. Men stay close because I'll use you in a little bit too."

All the men move to stand a little bit away and we do our bridesmaid group photos with Emily. Every new pose we do I look for Dean and we make eye contact. He smiles at me and I feel happiness enter my bloodstream.

"Perfect! Ladies you are all done! Fred and Emily, you two stay with me. The rest of you are welcome to leave or linger. I've been told there is tea and snacks to keep you company while you wait for the photos to be finished," the photographer announces to the bridesmaids.

As we start to walk away I see Dean being pulled in to take some photos with Emily and the rest of the groomsmen, so I decide to go find someone that I don't have to stress out about talking to. I find Juniper inside at the tea table talking to Esther. *There we go.* I make a beeline for them and join the conversation.

"So, I think you would love an iced earl grey tea," I hear Juniper say as I come within earshot. Sounds like Juniper is using her circus skills to pinpoint a tea drink that Esther would like.

"You're gonna want to listen to her!" I say as I rest my hands on the tea table. They look at me and start to laugh.

"I'm gonna have to try that," Esther says, "Fill me up barkeep." She slaps the table playfully and all the mason jars clank together. Out of shock she grabs the jars closest to the edge and bursts out, "Oh! Sorry."

"No problem. Nothing broke." Juniper deadpans, "This time."

Esther gets wide eyes and looks at me. "She's joking," I say, smiling.

"Oh yeah, sorry. You're good. Let me get that one for you," Juniper says as she turns to the drink dispensers behind her to fill up a mason jar full of ice with earl grey tea.

"I'd believe anything she says. Yesterday I went to a tea shop in town and I tried a black tea with rose after Juniper had recommended it, and I really enjoyed it!" I say to Esther, giving Juniper my stamp of approval.

"Oooh, good credentials, that's all I need to hear," Esther says laughing as she grabs the drink that Juniper hands out to her.

Esther turns toward me, takes a sip of her drink, and says, "I saw you chatting with Dean out there. Any good conversation happen between you two?"

Juniper perks up at this question. Anticipating my answer she puts down the next mason jar she had in her hand and leans on the table toward me.

"Ha! There was a lot of back-and-forth banter. He joked about writing the vows and I commented about him not having a serious side," I say, recalling the short and sweet of our conversation to them.

"That's fun. I've seen his serious side. I know it's there, but he doesn't show it that often. At least when I'm around. Fred has said they have deep talks when it's necessary," Juniper assures me. Someone walks up and asks for a mason jar of strawberry mango tea.

I stay in silence until they leave, then I say, "I hope so. It would be nice to have some more serious talks with him."

"I think you will. Knowing Dean, he'll probably find some way to get your number and then he'll text you," Juniper says while organizing the rows of mason jars left on her display table.

"Oh, reeeeally? Well, that'll be interesting." My heart flutters at the prospect of texting Dean as another person walks up and asks for a mason jar of green tea.

As the three of us find another topic to talk about, we get interrupted by the photographer who came in to wrangle up the family for some photos with the bride and groom.

Since we're all siblings of the happy couple, Juniper, Esther, and I walk outside to join Emily and Fred in the obligatory photo op. I feel so cute and pretty, I hope Dean notices my confidence.

The photographer is directing us on where to stand, and that Emily's immediate family should group together, when I see Dean out of the corner of my eye. I can feel him staring at me and I try my hardest not to make eye contact. Is he trying to get my attention? I see a kid running in his direction and I pretend to follow them with my eyes just so I can catch a glimpse of Dean.

Ouch! My stomach is playing with a jump rope again. Twisting in circles. Yep, I was right. There he is staring at me and not breaking eye contact.

I'm not going to lie, I love the attention. I love being noticed as long as I'm not the center of attention. Cue my noticed-wallflower propensity.

"Awesome! Thank you everyone. Now it's time for the groom's family to step up with the groom," the photographer announces to us all.

My family breaks away and Fred's family goes in for their photo. Dean walks closer to me to watch this next round of photos.

As he stands next to me, he says, "You did great. I can only hope that my photos come out half as well as yours will."

Butterflies.

"One can dream," I respond with a smile. Our arms barely touch, yet tingles run all the way through my body. Dammit. This chemistry is insane.

We stand together in silence while we watch the photographer weave Fred's family in and out of poses. I lift my foot to pull up the strap of my yellow high heel wedge that keeps falling down today and say, "So umm..."

At the same time, Dean says, "I uhh..."

"No, you go first," he says quickly, while looking down at me.

"Oh." I put my foot back down and start to rub my arm. "No, you go. Mine wasn't important."

He chuckles, "Mine either, but I wanted to say, I uhh...noticed your little henna tattoo on your foot there," he points down, "It's cute."

"Oh!" I follow his gaze, "I just got it a couple days ago. Thank you for noticing." I smile to myself, realizing he has fulfilled a secret wish of mine: that a groomsman would notice.

"You're welcome. Where can I get one?" He smiles.

"I think that Juniper is selling them inside, if you want to grab a spot for one." I point behind me, to the glass windows, at the pretend location of my new friend.

"Awesome! I'll go run right now!" He makes a move as if to start a quick sprint right here, but lets up and chuckles, "Nah, just kidding."

I smile at the image he just created in my head.

"So now, what were you going to say?" he asks.

"Ah yes, umm...I was gonna say, I like your hair that way," I look up at the strands, whilst actively fighting the urge to run my fingers through it.

"Oh, this old thing?" he says while running his own fingers through it. "Thanks. I'm not normally a hairdo type of guy. I just throw a baseball cap on and call it a day most of the time."

"I've noticed." I touch his elbow with mine. "You have really good hair actually. You shouldn't hide it away."

"Gee Elise, you're making me blush," he says as he pretends to hide his face with one of his hands. "Speaking of hair, you have some great locks yourself," he adds, and then he reaches up to touch one of the strands dangling across my cheek, and I swear my face is going white.

"Th-thank you," I stutter and reach for the hair he just played with to tuck it behind my ear, quietly looking down at the ground.

"Don't hide it away in a messy bun all the time," he says and I look up at him to see his charming smile sending heart eyes down at me. I rub my stomach to remind the swarm of killer bees inside that they can calm down now.

Chapter 8

Present Day

January

I've noticed that it takes a while to get used to a new town especially if you don't have a car, like me. The group of us moved to this little town in Georgia just four months ago. Half of us for school and the other half because they wanted a change in life. Luckily, Juniper has a car and lets me borrow it whenever I need to get somewhere further away than 5 blocks. It's also fortunate that we live downtown and I can walk to the grocery store, the bank, and to my Grand Coffee job within minutes.

Juniper and I have spent the beginning part of this school year going around to different Thai restaurants in the area, finding which one serves the best Thai food. It's also helping us learn the roads and see what other things this town has to offer.

Tonight was one of those nights we were trying out a new restaurant, excited to see if this could be on the top of our list when it comes to Thai food restaurants. We were seated really quickly at a booth inside of this very empty, low light, Thai restaurant that is attached to one of the local grocery stores. "So whatcha gonna order?" Juniper asks me as she opens the menu that was just placed in front of her by the waitress.

I give a heavy sigh as if breathing out fire deep from within my lungs. Thankful for the distraction but still very much trying my hardest to push the thoughts of my text message to Dean from my mind. I'm controlling my hand from reaching into my bag and checking the locked screen for his name. I know I'm prone to getting stuck in a downward spiral about things outside of my control, and I also know I should probably work on that, but knowing and doing are two very different things, and when my heart is involved like it is with this whole 'Dean situation' it's easier said than done.

Talking finally pushes the painful thoughts from my mind, "I'm gonna order their Thai fried rice. I've decided that whenever we go to a new Thai place I'll just order the fried rice because that will tell me if it's the authentic food that I remember from when I was in Thailand." I open the menu to look for their fried rice even though I know it's always a Thai restaurant staple.

I was in Thailand for about three months to help out a humanitarian group and have developed a taste for authentic food from the Land of Smiles. Sadly, the first two months I was there, I got so homesick for American food I'd have eaten deep fried crickets for a whole day if it meant getting a taste for the food of my homeland. Instead, I just ate fried rice every day. So now it's my baseline, my standard for Thai restaurants in America to see if they are worth my time or not.

"Whatever floats your boat, babe," Juniper says as she's looking down, perusing the Pad Thai section of the menu.

"I know. I know. So boring. But once I know what their fried rice tastes like then I can move on to bigger and better menu items," I say not budging, then I shut my menu satisfied with my choice.

"Just teasing. You can order whatever tickles your fancy, love. You're the queen bee of your life and I wouldn't want you to choose anything other than what makes you happy," Juniper says, forever the word artist. She's always spitting out phrases that bring life to the air.

"Thank you." I fold my arms in front of me and beam. "What are you going to order?" I return the question.

"Pad Thai with chicken. I can't get enough of the sauce they make for it," she says as she flips the menu over to look at the drinks on the back.

"It's a winner," I say, flipping to see the back of the menu as well.

The waiter comes over and we order our food and drinks. I choose a one-spice for my fried rice and Juniper chooses a three-spice for her Pad Thai. We both get the Thai tea because, of course, that is something else I lived on in Thailand. What is truly unfortunate is that not every Thai place makes it the same. Most of them make it too sweet and then I need to thin it down with extra milk. In my opinion, true authentic Thai tea should closely resemble the flavor of dirt. It often sounds strange when I describe it that way to people, but it needs to be more dull than sweet.

"Sooooo, how's it going?" Juniper asks in that obvious way that I know means she's wanting to know how I'm coping with letting go of Dean.

I fiddle with my fingers and slowly start talking. "I'm sad. All the time. I'm definitely grieving him and what we could have been and I'm not sure when the sad feelings will go away. I didn't want to get out of bed this morning. I nearly morphed into a set of sheets and blankets." I pull at a hangnail and continue, "I feel like I'm constantly thinking about him which makes me want to text him. I know I have to let him go and the constant texting makes me seem clingy, especially after that last conversation I had with him." I vomit out all my feelings. I have to catch a quick breath to continue my monologue. "I feel like we could still text as friends. But I guess I only want that because I'm secretly hoping he'll find me charming again and will end up wanting to rekindle something. I did send him a text right before you walked into the room this afternoon...It's been three days since my last text to him, so I hope he doesn't think I'm being too much," a heavy sigh escapes my mouth, "I was doing so good by not texting him. I'm literally fighting the urge to text him every day. I think I might have to delete his number from my phone, though, if I can't stop." I take another deep breath and this one hurts my lungs. "I always catch myself thinking 'well now that it's been BLANK number of days it'll be alright to text him again. He won't think I'm being clingy or too needy because I've waited so long between texts.' And I convince myself to text him EVERY! TIME! Then I start back at the beginning of all of my mental anguish and go through the grieving process again. Because he, inevitably, doesn't respond to me and then I start to spiral. Again." Bleeeh. I can feel my internal organs collapse now that it's all out.

I look at Juniper, searching for some kind of pity in her eyes. She's surely thinking, "Poor girl, can't keep it together for longer than two days before bothering the guy again," or "Poor girl, needs to get a life and stop being so obsessed."

When she finally starts talking, after what felt like minutes but was really just five seconds, she says with compassion in her eyes, "It's normal to grieve it and be sad about it. Let yourself feel those emotions. You have permission to be sad about this loss." Forever my emotional coach.

All of the bones that were holding me upright now collapse and I slump my shoulders. While I exhale and my head falls down, my words come out muffled, "Are you my fairy godmother? You always know what to say to me." I lift my head and give a sad smile with tears forming in my eyes.

Telling Juniper all my thoughts, insecurities and feelings makes me feel like I'm unlocking the ability to fully process it. I can't move on if I'm still holding onto hope that he'll text me and say he's changed his mind. The truth I'm ignoring is I KNOW I need to move on. I've been trying to play it cool on the outside for everyone else but hiding the fact that I'm dying to hear from him on the inside. Juniper has always been able to see right through me, ever since we met.

"It would be my honor to be your fairy godmother," she says.

"Excellent. Can I request something? Turn my feelings for him off so I can move on?" I ask, clearly looking for a way out of this emotional journey I need to have.

"Sorry, love. Fairy godmother's code of conduct states we can't alter people's emotional state of being. These things must only be felt and walked through in real time," she replies with clear cheek to her words.

We both start laughing as the waiter brings us our food. I can smell the umami in her Pad Thai as it gets placed in front of her. Those noodles have always tasted dry to me but everyone else seems to love them. I look down at my fried rice and have high hopes for it as I take my first bite.

"Hmm. You know something I just thought of, maybe you could think of this like a break. Like someday it'll still happen and you'll get your happily ever after," she says.

When Juniper says this I start bawling right there in the restaurant over my fried rice. Those words evoke a sense of longing, waiting and desire that is never going to happen. It makes me lose all control of the heart broken emotions that I've been trying to hold so tightly inside. I get a rush of every emotion I've had since I realized I need to let him go. I keep thinking that maybe it's not the end, maybe we'll end up together someday, maybe he is the right person for me. But eventually I always end up thinking that I should forget about him, that maybe he just isn't the right person for me. All these thoughts hit me like multiple waves crashing on top of me as I lay sprawled on the cold sand, one blow right after the other. Every time I try to lift my head above the water I get hit with another wave of disappointment.

My hope and heart went from 'this could still happen' to 'there's no way this is going to happen' in a split second. I lose control of the parts of me that I was trying to hold together as the tears keep flowing.

Juniper doesn't act bothered by my tears. She just sits across from me with her arms gently placed on the table giving me space to feel. Her encouragement for me to feel my feelings has me realizing that tears are probably good and healthy to express. So when she just sits there with an empathic look in her eyes, while tears roll down my face, without either of us talking, I feel seen. If it wasn't for Juniper I don't think I'd be able to get over this guy in a healthy way.

When I'm done crying Juniper says, "Sorry I said that. I thought it would be more helpful than it was. I wanted to bring it up, but it wasn't the right thing to say in this situation. So sorry." I can see the genuine care in her eyes.

"No, it's alright. I didn't know I'd have such an explosion of emotions when you said that. I guess I just realized all the hope and devastation all at once. I really, really thought this would happen someday and I've been holding onto 'someday' for too long now."

Juniper reaches across the table and pats my hand. "You've got this girl. There is no shame in your process. Grieve. Be okay. Grieve. Be okay. Let the process take its course. There's not just one way to feel all your feels," she says.

"I appreciate that. It's so annoying to be emotionally involved with a guy that's not involved with you anymore. Makes you think you might not have had something special after all. I don't even know how I let my heart get here," I say, forgetting that I was eating fried rice a few minutes ago.

"Anything can happen if it's a slow fade. The good part is that you're recognizing it right now and able to see it for what it really is." Juniper twirls some Pad Thai noodles around on her fork and takes a bite.

I look back down at my hands because I've been thinking about something lately that I'm not quite sure how to talk about. After taking a few moments, I look back up and say, "I think all of my relationship heartbreak stems from when I was seventeen. My biggest high school crush literally crushed me. He was everything I wanted in a guy and then he pulled the rug out from under me."

Juniper holds eye contact with me and says, "Wow. What happened?"

"He told me that he wanted to go back to his old girlfriend and date her again. Like I didn't even matter to him," I say solemnly.

"What?! No way! How long had you guys known each other?" She asks with a little scream in her voice.

"Well...we had been talking every day at school and then on the phone every night for four months. So when he told me he was done out of the blue I was broken."

Jumper drops her eyes and shakes her head. "Oh man, of course you would be crushed. What a jerk! Were you guys ever official?"

"Not officially. Everyone in school thought we would be a perfect couple, but he never ended up asking me to be his girlfriend. I think I've been a little timid with the idea of love ever since then." I let out a deep sigh. "It's crazy because it's so psychological. I want to be loved but I'm scared of love at the same time. I don't even realize I'm pushing a guy away until it's too late."

"Maybe it's time to heal from all of that? Now that you're recognizing this very big moment in your past you could start moving forward and realize that you are worthy of love. Seventeen-year-old Elise deserves love," she says, before adding, "so does twenty-year-old Elise."

Tears well up in my eyes as I hear her say this. "I agree. She deserves love and doesn't need to be scared of it anymore." We sit there in silence as I let it all sink in. I don't have anything else to say. I feel like admitting all of my emotional feelings has drained me dry, like the last bit of coffee at the end of a straw.

We return to our food and chew in silence. Based on their fried rice I can confidently tell you that this restaurant is not one of my top restaurants of Thai food in the area. Probably won't be coming back here, but it was fun to get out and find some sort of routine back in my life rather than hole myself up in my bedroom and mope.

Chapter 9

Past

May

I walk inside to go to the restroom so I can splash some water on my neck to cool down. It was just a cheek graze, but it might as well have been more because I feel tingles all the way to my fingertips.

Before I head down the hall I stop in the reception area to look at the names on the placement cards, which are lined up behind the plates on the wedding party table. If anyone asks, I'm just looking at the menu, but if I'm being honest, it's because I'm curious if I'm being seated next to Dean.

I cross my arms in front of me and slowly walk down the wedding party table that is placed in the center of the room surrounded in every direction by all the chairs and tables for the guest. I want to check out every name, it's like the first day of school where you get to see your assigned seat and who you are being seated next to in hopes to flirt with them all semester. I stop in my tracks once I notice my name card, I'm placed on the far-right side of the table, very far away from him. I saw his placement card, he's right in the middle of the table on the opposite, 'groomsmen,' side. About five places down from me. Bummer.

I head to the ladies' room and turn on the faucet. I get some water on a paper towel and dab it on my neck. Until now, I really thought I wasn't attracted to him, as he's just not my type, but I'm starting to feel like I might have been mistaken. It's the way he so effortlessly finds ways to talk with me, and the way he always knows how to make me laugh. I'm always drawn to lighthearted people, and I love how their light shines through and reaches me deep inside. When it comes to social interactions with strangers, especially the flirty kind, I always have such a hard time knowing what to say. With Dean I'm starting to feel more and more at ease, and it's making me more confident in our conversations.

A smile crosses my face as I replay the way he smiles when he's told a joke that he knows is gonna hit just right. The way he makes everyone in the room feel seen. I saw him straighten Fred's suit before some of their pictures together and I started to think of him less as a player and more as an attentive person. I feel this pull in my chest, I want to know everything about this guy.

As I'm looking in the mirror I pat my hair to see if all my bobby pins are still in place holding my giant beehive up. Esther actually did a good job making my horse tail thick hair look like a normal amount of volume. I wasn't expecting Dean to notice or even touch my hair. Now that he has, I feel like I want him to notice more things about me. Screw my wallflower bent.

Oh, wait! I forgot, I have to fill out my food card. I pull myself away from my salon work to go find my menu card placed on my assigned plate. I remember seeing something about chicken, salmon or beef for dinner.

I make my way back to my seat and look up to see Dean sitting in the chair across the table from my spot...wait, what? I stop in my tracks and look from side to side, feeling a little confused...and...elated. His placement card was supposed to be in the middle of the table. How is he *here*?

As the realization hits me I start to feel my heartbeat quicken. *Oh my gosh!* A slow smile crosses my face. I'm so flattered. I wish I'd have been bold enough to do that. But I just can't ignore the fact that I don't like being too obvious about being drawn to someone.

I sit down in my seat. "Hello, fancy meeting you here," I say with a knowing smile on my face.

"Oh, hey. I didn't realize you were sitting here too. Small world..." he says, clearly lying, but opening his arms up gesturing at the seat across from him.

"Yes..." I tilt my head to the side and squint. "Very small, indeed." I fold my hands together before placing them on the table.

He looks down and clears his throat before speaking, "So, umm, do you know what entree you're picking?" he asks as he grabs his menu card to look at the options we get to choose from.

I smile at how awkward he is being, and play along. There's descriptions under each line item. Love that. I lean in to read.

"Hmm. I'm gonna order the chicken. I'm a sucker for a cream sauce." I say laying my card down on the table to mark it and then looking up at him with a teasing smile.

He gives me a wink and looks down at his food card to read the description then says, "Hmm. That one sounds good. I'm a sucker for omega-3's. I think I'm gonna order the salmon." He looks down to mark his choice on his menu. "If you're nice to me I'll let you try a bite." He folds his hands in front of him and leans on the table.

"Ha! I can't promise anything," I say, trying my best to tease him back as I clasp my hands together and lean on the table toward him. I can smell his cologne from here and it's intoxicating. I try my best not to close my eyes and take a deep breath in while he's looking right at me.

"I'll take it. At least there's potential for a shared meal," He lifts up his glass of water from the table and takes a drink without breaking his eye contact.

I feel my cheeks go warm. If there was a record for never taking your eyes off someone in a twenty-four-hour period, then he would win. Feeling prickles start to cluster in my chest, I say, "I bet you say that to all the girls."

"Nah. I only say that to girls that are mysteries to me." He puts his glass down.

"I'm a mystery to you?" I ask him and scoot my chair forward for a guest trying to get through the sea of chairs behind me.

"Yep. You walk around with this quietness about you and that is drawing me in. I find myself wanting to learn everything there is to know about you," he admits, mirroring my own thoughts toward him.

I don't think my cheeks could get any redder. I feel so exposed, like he can see right through me. I'm constantly wondering if I'm funny enough, pretty enough, interesting enough. I hope that he can't see my insecurities written on my face.

"I'm an open book. What do you want to know?" I ask, like I just started up a game of truth or dare and don't know what the outcome will be.

"Are you dating anyone?" He leans forward on the table, matching my posture.

A smile crosses my face. "No, I'm not seeing anyone."

"Good. Good. That's good." He looks down at his hands, I haven't seen this look on his face before, he looks unsure of what to ask next, but after a long pause he adds, "Sooo, what are some of your favorite hobbies?"

"You asked me that one yesterday," I say as I now look down at my hands feeling like I just pointed out an embarrassing piece of spinach in his teeth.

"Oh, right. Reading and knitting. I knew that," he laughs. "I was listening." My relationship status clearly has him discombobulated.

"But I do have another hobby to add," I say trying to save this moment. "I really like watching tv and playing volleyball." I scrunch my nose with a cheesy grin. He finally stops looking at his hands and looks me in the eye.

"TV is a great pastime. And volleyball! Elise, are you an athlete!? Color me impressed." He brightens up, looking deep into my soul with those crystal blue eyes.

His enthusiasm for me keeps my cheeks blushing. His sole attention is something I'm starting to crave.

"I like to think so." Now *I'm* fumbling in my brain trying to think of what else to say. Like trying to find something in a filing cabinet, I just put it there a minute ago and now I can't find it. "Umm, but not quite anymore..." *Wow, his eyes are so blue.* "Because I'm not actually playing volleyball like I wish I was." Man, I feel like my brain is short circuiting.

"That part doesn't matter. You actually want to be playing a sport. Not everyone is like that. I know I'm no athlete. Not unless you count skateboarding, but people who actually want to go play a sport and they're coordinated and stuff, that's rare." He sits up straighter, like encouraging me in my hopeless pastime is somehow bringing life to his bones.

I smile back. I'm falling for this guy and that's not at all what I expected to be feeling toward him. It's got to be the eye contact, or the genuine interest in who I am as a person. It seems that Sarah and Juniper are right, he does have a great personality. "Thank you. That's such a nice thing to hear." I smile at him and we sit there like two idiots smiling at each other in silence for a long time until he says, "You're welcome."

Now that he's done showering me with compliments I want to give him one too, "For the record, I think that skateboarding is a sport. It requires balance, core muscles, and coordination. All the things a regular school sport has going for it." I tilt my chin down without breaking eye contact, as if to say, be proud of yourself.

"Thank you for the validation." He slowly reaches across the table and puts a hand on top of my folded hands. "The magic of a compliment. You just made me feel like a million bucks, Elise."

I release one of my thumbs from their cage and wrap it on top of his hand and say, "You're welcome."

I start to breathe heavier. A small breach in physical contact between us and my nervous system is firing off like it's being shocked by an electric current. I smile. He smiles. Is anyone watching? I should look away. This is embarrassing. I reluctantly release the hand he's not touching to feel the warmth in my face.

I'm pulled back to reality when my shoulder gets hit by someone sitting down next to me, both our hands quickly moving back to our laps. "Hey guys! Ah, here's my seat. I finally found it. Ooph, my feet hurt so bad." One of the bridesmaids, Kim, joins us.

I look over at her and notice how her perfectly curled blonde hair falls across her face as she's rubbing one of her feet...Looking up at Dean through my eyelashes and then over at Kim I say, "Hi."

"Hi." Dean parrots and lifts his hands off his lap to put them behind his head.

"What are you guys talking about?" Kim asks, unaware of the tension she just broke up. You could cut our chemistry with a knife, and her unexpected arrival just took a machete to it.

"Oh, just our hobbies." I touch my neck to see if the heat reached down there and smirk on one side of my mouth while looking over at Dean.

He catches my eye and releases his hands from the back of his head to gesture with a thumb at me. "Yeah, Elise here is a full-on athlete and I'm sitting feeling like a lazy couch potato who likes video games and chips," Dean says, secretly flirting with me while Kim sits across the table from him.

I laugh at his compliment, "I like video games too...I guess that's another hobby I forgot to mention." I lean toward him across the table again because the magnetic pull between us is too strong to fight.

"Now you're just trying to make me feel better," Dean says, waving one hand in the air as if to playfully dismiss what I just said.

"I swear I'm not. I only tell the truth. Although, I do *only* like the 2D Nintendo Mario kind." I laugh at my very immature video gaming skills.

He leans toward me from his side of the table and says, "The 2D Mario was the best. You've got good taste."

I shake my head, smile and look up at the ceiling. This guy oozes sincere charm.

I hear Kim ask next to me, "What sport?" Changing the tone of our conversation away from flirtation, *like a sopping wet blanket*. I shake the thought away, Kim didn't know she just interrupted us, it's not her fault that she just wanted to sit down in her assigned seat.

"Volleyball," Dean and I say at the same time, not taking our eyes off each other.

"Oh, that's a fun one. I have some friends that play volleyball in the park every now and then. It's a good time," Kim says, contributing to the conversation.

"Elise!" Dean says with a slap on the table, a little too hard and makes all the glassware chime against each other. His eyes widen as he grabs his and my water glasses then he continues, "This is what you've been waiting for, no?"

"Dean!" I say to match his enthusiastic voice but I hold back on copying his gesture, "But I don't live in Redding. So, unfortunately, it doesn't benefit me."

"Ah well. Worth a try," Dean says and lets go of the water glasses he was holding.

The seats at our table start to fill with the rest of the wedding party. Guests are also finding their seats around us, as the reception part of the evening is soon to commence. I hear a couple talking behind me about how nice it is to go to a wedding after they just had their own wedding a month ago. Then in front of me a couple of guys give each other a high five and a hug, in the most bro-like gesture. Whenever there's a wedding you can always feel the love in the air and everyone catches the vibe, even the bros.

"Are there no groups you could join where you live?" Kim asks and I'm pulled back into my conversation with these two.

"None that I have found so far, unfortunately," I reply looking down at my hands, like I let her down with my sad volleyball journey.

"Oh, bummer. If you ever move here, I can include you into our volleyball park games," Kim says.

"I appreciate that. Thank you, but I'm moving to Georgia at the end of the summer to go to school and there's no chance of me coming to Redding anytime soon," I say, straightening my dress as a nervous tick. Making eye contact with either of them, while I admit this, feels awkward, like I don't want to see the disappointment on their faces or something. Each for a different reason.

"Oh, bummer," Kim sympathizes and starts to fiddle with the water glass in front of her. "Georgia seems nice though, I've been thinking about moving there myself!" She looks over at me and widens her eyes.

"Whoa, wild! Are you going to the same town as Fremily?" Dean asks looking at me, using the celebrity mashup name he just came up with yesterday.

"Oh my gosh, Kim! That is so cool!" I respond to Kim's new information, then I turn to Dean. "Yeah, Fremily, my brother Forrest and I are trying to find housing over there, but we'll probably just wing it when we arrive. We don't know the area at all, so we don't really know what kind of apartments or houses are close to the school." I sit back in my chair so my body language doesn't cut Kim off anymore.

"Fred told me that he and Emily are excited for Georgia. I hope it doesn't take him away from the West Coast for too long. I'll miss that guy if it does," Dean says and that reminds me how close they must be. I keep forgetting that he is my brother-in-law's best friend. Not just some rando groomsman.

"I bet. I hate moving away from friends-ooph," I involuntarily let out a noise as someone making their way behind me, trying to squeeze through, accidentally conks me in the shoulder. I turn around to make eye contact.

"So sorry," she says as she puts their hand on my shoulder. "Tight squeeze. I should have just said 'excuse me' instead of thinking I could fit." She let out an awkward chuckle.

"No worries," I say, scooting my chair closer to the table to make more room for her, undeterred by this possibly embarrassing moment.

"I feel like my friends are constantly moving away from Redding," Kim chimes in without skipping a beat, "This place is like a hub for people to come to for a short amount of time and then leave for their next adventure."

Dean and I give her a smile of acknowledgement. "Sorry, that's happening to you." I pat her on the shoulder. "I've heard that about Redding."

"Feels like a season of change. It would be funny if you were moving somewhere too, Dean," Kim jokes as she takes a drink of her water.

"I've actually been thinking about moving up to Bothell, Washington. I have a friend up there, and I've been telling him I'd live in the same town as him someday. I'm thinking it might be time now," he says while making eye contact with Kim but sending a quick side eye in my direction.

"Oh really? That's fun!" says Kim, enthusiastically.

I stare at him as I realize the weight of his confession. "Wow!" My eyes don't break contact. "How interesting that you would be moving to the state that I am moving away from. So crazy!" I look down at my hands as it sinks in. The fact that I'm moving away from Washington and him to Washington is kind of strange, like two ships passing each other in the night.

Another realization quickly bubbles up inside of me. This means every time I come home for a visit he'll be just an hour away from my hometown and we could see each other!

"I know. Life is funny like that," Dean says. "But it's been in the works for years and I'm finally at a place in my life where I can make that move. It's not definite yet, but I'm about 70% sure it's gonna happen."

"I hope that works out for you and you enjoy it up there." I flatten my lips into a smile. "It rains a lot, do you know what that is?" I wink. I can't hold the laugh in for too long.

"I've heard about the rain. It's water from the sky, right?" he deadpans.

"Yes. That's right! And it gets everything it touches wet," I return the joke with matched seriousness.

"Fascinating. I can't wait to learn more about it. We don't get very much of that 'rain' in sunny Southern California," he counters.

"There's not much to it. Just wait a couple days and the rain will start to fall." I laugh, he clearly doesn't know what he's getting into. A California boy in the Pacific Northwest. It's beautiful but that beauty comes at a price, the sun.

"What month do you think you'll move?" I ask as I reach down to straighten the strap of my high heeled wedge shoe. It keeps falling down and this might be the last time I straighten it. If it does it again I'm taking them off for the night—they're going to high heel prison.

"Sometime next year. Probably January or February," he says.

"That's exciting. But also, good luck with that. You won't have to wait longer than 30 seconds. In the winter it rains nonstop," I keep teasing him. Seeing how far I can push this bit.

"You guys are so funny!" Kim looks back and forth at our faces.

We break away from our banter and look at her. Then we all laugh. It seems like sometimes we get so caught up in our own conversation that we forget people are around us.

The atmosphere in the room starts to shift when we hear that the bride and groom are about to enter the room. The wedding coordinator directs all of our attention to the two glass exterior doors where Fred and Emily will be entering for the first time as man and wife. Like two show ponies being paraded around the room. We don't have to wait long before those doors burst open. The photographer's camera clicks rapidly and the whole room erupts with 'whoop's' and 'yeah's' as we all clap and cheer for the happy couple.

The last couple of the bridesmaids and groomsmen show up to our large banquet table of eighteen, and everyone starts to fill out their meal cards. It's like dining at a restaurant hosted by your family and the food is free. I've never felt so high class before. I'm used to budget meals, and weddings that just tell you what you're going to eat.

Dean gets engaged in a conversation with the groomsmen next to him and I chat up Kim, talking about her potentially moving to Georgia as well.

After a long while our food gets delivered to us and I am pleasantly surprised at how good the chicken is. A creamy mushroom sauce drenched all over my poultry. Sign me up!

I look at Dean's salmon and am not particularly impressed. As I've mentioned, I don't like fish so I'm not too disappointed that he eats the whole thing without offering me a bite.

As the waiters are clearing our table, the sound of metal hitting glass starts echoing throughout the room as people are cheering and encouraging the bride and groom to 'KISS, KISS, KISS.' Fred and Emily explode with laughter as they look around at everyone clinking their glasses and then lay a wet kiss on each other to appease the mob.

Soon after, the DJ comes on the speakers and tells everyone that if they want to try to work off their meal they should come to the dance floor and get some moves in. A good amount of people take him up on his offer and before you know it there is a crowd on the dance floor so crammed in that you can hardly see the ground. They must have hired paid actors because weddings don't typically have this many people excited to be the first ones on the dance floor.

There was so much shuffling around of people that I lost track of Dean. Kim asked me to join her and some of the other bridesmaids on the dance floor. I feel slightly hesitant, but also love dancing so I pushed aside the nerves and agreed to follow her. This doesn't follow my typical reserved nature, but not everything about me can be put in a box. I'm a third child that loves to dance.

On the dance floor all the bridesmaids congregate toward each other, and we start moving our hips and arms like a few hula girls on a car dashboard. It's so freeing to have your body sway to the music. Something about your soul and body connecting to your heart and not your head has so much power. If it wasn't raining already, I'd have assumed our dancing was calling the rain to come.

"So, Elise is moving to Georgia at the end of the summer." Kim keeps her feet moving while leaning over to Harper, my bachelorette party couch-mate, to let her know the crazy coincidence. "Just like I've been talking about."

"Oh my gosh, wild!!" Harper says and flashes her big green eyes. "I think it's so cool that you guys ran into each other. You should exchange numbers."

"I think that's a good idea," I say as I swing my arms in the air to the music. "That way we can stay connected while we each look for housing.

Who knows, maybe we'll need another roommate." I lift my palms to the air and keep bouncing them around.

"True. Keep me in mind for sure!" she yells over the next song that starts.

"I will!" I replied.

"The south is so cool," Harper changes the subject. "My favorite part is that when it rains there it's warm."

"No way! Like bathtub water falling from the sky?!" I beam, "That sounds like the best thing ever! I've never minded the rain in Washington, but if it was actually warm water, then I would never leave." I laugh at my own inside joke. "I actually experienced warm rain when I was in Thailand three months ago," I segue into a topic that I've been hoping I could bring up.

"Thailand? Wow. I didn't know you went there. Why were you there?" Kim asks as the song changes, and we all get hyped up and start jumping.

"I went there with a humanitarian group," I bump hips with Harper standing next to me.

"Yeah? Which one?" Kim asks as she comes in for a hip bump herself.

"YWAM. It stands for Youth With A Mission. It's an organization that takes people, mostly young adults, to do mission trips in Southeast Asia," I say through a laugh as I see Juniper and Esther start to make up a couple funky dance moves on the floor.

"Wow. What kinda stuff did you do in Thailand?" Kim brings me back.

This topic gets me amped. I haven't talked about my humanitarian work with anyone since being back. Partly because I'm still processing it all, but also because no one has asked me.

I get ready to start my long-winded speech with a deep breath in. "We were in Thailand for three months. We helped out different organizations reach the women in the red-light district. They help get them out of there and into another trade. It was so fascinating to hear these women tell their stories. Most of them came from the northern part of the country, from small villages. Their parents would tell them to go to Bangkok to meet a nice white man who could marry them and support them. Once they arrive in Bangkok, they get into the sex trade to hopefully find one of these white men, but in fact the white men are only coming for a quick vacation and a short lived, week-long, relationship with a Thai girl. Then they leave and the Thai girl is left devastated and goes back to the red-light district to try and find herself another one. It was an endless cycle. Each woman I talked to was practically telling me the same story.

Their original plan when they left their village up north wasn't to go be a bar girl in Bangkok, it was to be married and have a stable life because their parents in the small village couldn't support them anymore. Now they are basically stuck until they realize the reason these white men came to Thailand was only to have a fling." I realize my dancing pace slowed down once I stopped talking.

"That's crazy! I didn't know any of that," Kim says visibly rattled. "Who would have thought that we'd get emotional and deep on the dance floor?" She purses her lips together and wipes a tear from her eye.

I put my hand on her shoulder because I know the feeling. "I understand your emotions. It was really quite fulfilling work. I've definitely grown as a person by experiencing a completely different culture from mine." I let my hand fall and stand up straighter. I'm feeling proud that at the age of twenty I've traveled and done something with my life.

"Yeah, that makes sense. That kind of experience sounds like it would change anyone." We're halfway through another song and Kim pretends to run a Q-Tip in her ear and throws it away. The funniest dance move I've ever seen in person, she must have seen the movie Hitch.

"It absolutely was and since we got back a little over three months ago so it's all very fresh in my brain." I turn in a circle and sway my hips side to side.

"Nice, will you go back?" Harper asks.

"Not anytime soon. I don't see myself leaving the states for a while." I make a sad face while my arms pretend like they're noodles.

"I totally get it. You have a new adventure waiting for you in Georgia too," Kim responds.

"Exactly," I reply.

The song changes. Just as my group is getting out of this very fulfilling conversation, I lift my eyes to see Dean dancing with some of the other groomsmen. He looks up and our eyes meet. A shiver that I am all too familiar with runs down my spine. I wish I could dance with him, and I feel a prickle of excitement and nervousness as I admit that to myself.

"*Sweet Caroline, ba ba bam, good times never seem so good...*" I see Dean belting out the song as he bounces around and puts his hands up to his mouth to make his voice project. He seems like he really enjoys this song, or he's making a show to be dramatic, I can't really tell. However, he's definitely not self conscious about being the center of attention.

As the song ends the DJ puts a slow song on next and says, "Grab the person you want to spend the next four minutes with and bring them to the dance floor."

I turn to go back to my seat with the rest of the bridesmaids and as I'm almost off the dance floor I feel someone's hand grab mine. I turn around and see Dean looking down at me. "Wanna dance?" he asks me.

"I...umm...yes," I stumble over my words.

He leads me to a corner of the dance floor with the rest of the swaying couples. My wedge heels finally come in handy tonight because they allow me to reach my arms up high enough to place them around his neck. He slides his hands around my waist and pulls me in close to him. Our torso's touch and I feel so weak I could fall over if he wasn't holding onto me.

"I wanted to spend the next four minutes with you," he playfully jokes looking down at me.

"I'm glad you asked. I was kinda hoping we'd get to dance," I bashfully admit as I look away from him and rest my chin on my shoulder.

"You have been on my mind ever since I met you, Elise Berger," He laughs and pulls my chin up to look at him.

"Wha...how do you know my last name?" I ask, completely ignoring his adorable confession.

"I know Emily's last name is Berger, it was on the wedding invitation. Didn't take much to put it together," he admits as he leads me around the dance floor.

"Oh...right..." I look up at him sheepishly before adding, "...and you've been on my mind too."

He smiles down at me, and I can feel his fingers gently petting my back as he says, "Your mysteriousness is something that I feel like I'm slowly solving."

"Oh yea? What part are you solving?" I ask him while swaying to the music.

"I don't know if it's one specific thing. You wanna be a part of a group but it also seems like you're timid in crowds. I think it's adorable. You always look like you're thinking about something funny and interesting and I wish I could hear you say your thoughts out loud. You have the best facial expressions when you think no one is watching." He looks down at me like I'm the only girl in the room.

"Sounds like you've been paying attention. Everything you said is true. I guess I have a hard time in social situations when there's a lot of people around. Being the third child out of four, I naturally grew into the more timid sibling of the bunch. I tend to overthink situations where I know there will be a lot of people, where conversations can be chaotic and I might not have much time to adjust to getting to know someone new before someone else joins in. It's easy to get lost inside my head in these situations," I start to notice how secure he feels under my arms and try not to let that distract me from continuing, "So I guess it makes sense that you thought I'm often thinking of something funny and interesting, I probably was. Sharing it with the class, though...I haven't always felt like I knew when to do so. Like, when is the right time to interject with a funny thought that may or may not be entirely relevant to the topic? Usually, people don't really notice me too much, so I don't really feel like they'd be interested in what I have to say. I'm a little surprised that you noticed, I've never known anyone to pay attention to me so much." I smile up at him and wish this song wouldn't end.

"I'm not just anyone." He eats me up with his eyes. "I've really enjoyed getting to learn these things about you the past couple days."

I look up at him and feel like his words just gave me the warmest hug. "I have too," I blush, then pause and add, "Watching you these past couple days has me getting more and more fascinated by you."

"*The* Elise Berger is fascinated by me? Tell me more." He winks.

"Of course! You have so many good qualities. You seem to see people for the person they are on the inside and you pull that out of them. With all of your jokes you actually bring people out of their shells and make them feel comfortable. It's not just a front you hide behind, it's your way of connecting with people's souls. Your attentiveness to Fred is very adorable. Like you're his golden retriever, you're taking this best man gig seriously. So, your friendship loyalty seems on point."

"Wow, thank you for saying all of that." He brushes the hair off my face for the second time tonight. "It feels good to hear someone else give you good compliments." He smiles.

I lock in on his eyes, "You're welcome. It was nice to have a normal conversation with you and not feel like we only have jokes."

"I told you I have a serious side too. I'm happy that you got to see it before the wedding ends." He spins me in a circle.

"Me too." I come back around from the circle and put my hands back up around his neck.

"This won't be the last time we talk," he informs me.

"I hope it isn't," I respond, and I feel like Cinderella dancing with the prince right before the bell chimes.

We pull away from each other reluctantly after the song ends. As we're looking at each other the DJ comes on the mic and asks everyone to point their attention to the cake cutting ceremony part of the wedding reception. We break our eye contact and move off the dance floor to walk over to the corner of the room that has the beautifully decorated cake sitting on a table.

I stand next to Dean, and this time I make sure we're close enough that our arms have no room to breathe. As I see Fred and Emily grab the knife to cut into the cake, I giggle to myself.

"Wanna share that funny thought with the class?" Dean winks at me, clearly referring back to my earlier confessions.

"Okay, yeah, sure." I feel a burst of warmth spread across my chest as I realize he really did listen, and wants to help me feel more comfortable sharing my thoughts out loud. "Last time I was at a wedding, the ceremony and reception were in the same room. As the pastor was asking the bride and groom to say their vows everyone heard this sound, like a giant amount of slop was falling to the ground. We all looked to our right and saw that half the cake was now on the floor. It looked like one of those fifth grade science experiments showing what a landslide looks like when a volcano erupts. Luckily that bride and groom had a sense of humor and they started laughing about it and told their pastor to keep the ceremony going." I chuckle, and appreciate that Fremily's cake stayed fully intact during this whole day's festivities.

Dean looks down at me with laughter in his eyes and says, "I'm sure it would've gotten an A+ at the science fair, but I'm glad this cake is still in one piece so we can grade it by taste rather than educational purposes."

We break away from our little one-on-one moment as the crowd laughs and cheers when Fred and Emily smash the sweet decadence into each other's face, and Emily pushes it a little up Fred's nose. I bury my face in my hands and a wave of secondhand embarrassment washes over me. Dean leans over to me and says, "That one's gonna mean a trip to the bathroom."

I start clapping and say, "Riiiight! This is my favorite part. I love to see the bride and groom smash cake into each other's faces. Classic." I feel pure happiness as I watch the happy couple finish this moment with a sugary peck.

Shannon moves the evening along by announcing the bouquet toss and the garter toss. Dean and Harper each caught one. I feel a little green goblin rise up as I watch Harper getting to take a 'we won!' photo with Dean, but I just look down at the ground and walk back to my seat at the wedding party table to ignore that green ugliness.

Everyone ends the night dancing for hours. Dean's by my side the whole night. When the reception finally comes to an end, we all send the bride and groom off with bubbles floating in the air and empty cans clanking down the road behind their car as they drive away.

Now comes the worst part about being in a wedding, and especially a family member at a wedding—the cleanup. Everyone in the family and the wedding party get to work breaking everything down and loading it all up in the cars out in the parking lot.

Juniper and I start clearing up the candles and putting them in the boxes that are under one of the tables.

"Man, I hate cleaning up after a wedding," I laugh as I go to another table and grab more candles.

"I remember you saying that a couple days ago. I have to admit, I'm not the biggest fan of it so far," Juniper says, moving to another table close to us to get more candles.

"This is my second sibling that has gotten married, and that's too many. I can't wait to be the one that gets married and leaves the whole mess behind for my family and friends to clean up," I say as I stack candle after candle neatly in the box set in front of me.

"This is my first sibling, so I haven't been jaded like you are," Juniper jokes as she points at the candles she's counting in the box she's about to close.

"I am so terribly jaded. I wish I could just hide in a corner here and not clean up anything else," I admit as a candle falls out of my hand and hits the box below me.

Juniper gets wide eyes after I say this, I can see the gears turning. Then she goes over to a couple chairs. Drags them back to the table we were clearing, sets them down and gestures for me to sit.

"We should just sit down and hold these candles and look like we're doing something but just let everyone else clean up." Juniper opens her mouth wide so I have time to catch up to her idea.

A smile slowly crosses my face. This is the most brilliant thing I have ever heard. "Oh my gosh! Yes! Let's do it. This is the best idea ever!" We both grab a chair and, each with an arm full of candles, we sit down.

"Can you believe our siblings are married?" Juniper asks.

"No. I can't. Emily's no longer gonna go by my family's last name. So strange. Plus, she told me they want to start a family right away. That feels extremely weird." I say as I look around at all the other people sweeping, putting centerpieces away and breaking down tables. Dean looks especially helpful folding the tablecloths and putting them in a box for Shannon.

"They're probably trying to make our future niece or nephew right now," Juniper says.

If I had water in my mouth I would have spit it all out. "Oh my god!" I laugh and do a quick side nod, "You're not wrong." Then a realization hits me. "Holy crap! We are both going to be an aunt to the same kids!" My eyes go wide.

"Yep! I was thinking about that during the reception," Juniper says. "I looked it up to see what we would be called. The internet says we are sister-in-laws, once removed." She tries to point with her finger in the air but, because of the candles, has to wave her elbow in the air instead.

"Oh my gosh, I didn't even think of that, we have a special title. Fascinating," I reply, completely in awe. "I love that we're becoming friends because our siblings married each other. It's just the coolest thing ever." I smile over at her.

"Me too," Juniper says.

"I was also thinking that they'll make cute kids," I say.

"I agree. Two attractive people making blonde hair, blue eyed babies," she says with a dreamy look in her eye. "What's better than that?"

I look to my right and see Dean start to walk towards us. He looks over as if he's going to ask us a question. "Hey guys can you, oh wait…" He holds up his hand, palms facing us, clearly seeing that we're busy supporting candles. "No never mind, you're doing something." He drops his hand and says, "My bad, good job holding those candles. I won't bother you," and then walks off with a smile on his face.

Juniper and I look at each other and laugh. Our plan is clearly working. Dean definitely has a nose for when to play into a joke.

Chapter 10

Past

May

The next morning our two families, in the commune house, pack up to go our separate ways. A little ache in my heart pops up when I realize I'll be leaving this group of people after doing everything together and being in each other's hair for almost a week. I feel like I'm leaving something behind that I never realized I needed in life. I feel like a wishbone missing its other half after being told that it's not supposed to be attached.

I'm going to miss being crammed into this little house with ten people in it. Since growing up with three siblings, chaos is my bread and butter. Too many people in the house is never a point of stress for me. I'd rather shave my head than be without a horde of people in my space. It's when everyone leaves and we are no longer breathing each other's air that I start to feel sad and lonely. I ache for a constant community around me.

I know I am going home with my family so I'm not going to miss my own people. The two parts that are getting me in the feels are, one, I just made a good friend in Juniper and now I won't be sharing life with her and her family anymore. And two, this weekend with Dean I had the most amazing butterflies and that story feels like it's now being cut short. I'm not sure which sadness to cling to more. The guy I'll probably never talk to again or the kindred spirit that I'll rarely get to see. Cue the sad trombone.

I'm bringing my suitcase out to our car in the driveway and after I shut the trunk I turn around and see Juniper coming out of the house, walking straight toward me. "Hey Esel." She puts her hand on my shoulder and asks, "Do you mind if I call you Esel?" pausing for my answer before continuing.

"I love it." I smile. "No one ever gives me a nickname. Esel is so fun and different," I tell her.

"Awesome. You'll forever be Esel to me," she says as she lifts up her chin. "Anyway, I have exciting news." She gives her hands a little cheerleader clap before continuing, "I'm excited to tell you that I'm moving to Georgia too!" She opens her mouth wide and holds her hands still as she says this.

"What!?" I mimic the cheerleader clap and add a little jump in place. "That's the most amazing news! Now I can stop feeling like a sad trombone is following me around. We'll see each other again!"

"Yeah, I've been talking about wanting to move there for a while and my parents decided last night that they also want to move there. So we're gonna be one big happy family renting a house out, all together. Do you and Forrest have a place yet?" she asks and we sidestep to move out of the way as my parents come out of the house to put their suitcases in the car we're standing next to.

"No, we started looking with...Fremily." I smile to myself as that name reminds me of Dean. "But we haven't quite settled on anything," I finish, seeing movement out of the corner of my eye and following it to see an incoming suitcase flying through the air and landing into the trunk. It's

Forrest, who has decided now would be a good time to try his free throw shot.

"Well, you guys should go in on a rental with us. I think Fred and Emily want to join in as well. With how expensive things are these days we all want to find a way to save money on rent. We can all feel crammed into a small space again and live like we're on a family commune for the second time this year!" Juniper says and gives a thumbs up to Forrest, because he did make his shot like a pro.

I pause to let this sink in; this is the best news. Here I was feeling sad about not getting to see my brother-in-law's side of the family anymore, when in fact, they are moving to the same town as me! Plus, if the stars align, we'll all be in a house together. I break my blank stare and give another cheerleader bounce. "Of course, yes! I don't see why Forrest would have a problem with it since it means we'll have cheaper rent, and we all like the sound of that!"

"Perfect. I'll let my parents know," she says, looking over her shoulders to see if they're close by. "They told me to extend the invitation to you and Forrest. Plus, I'm sure Emily will love having some of her family in the house too."

"Here, let's exchange numbers so we can keep in contact throughout the summer." I look down and pull out my phone before continuing, "We can discuss move-in dates and when you guys find a place you can message me the address." I start typing her number as she tells me and then shoot her a greeting text.

"Perfect, got it. I'll have a car too, so if you ever need to use it or need a ride, you're welcome to it," she offers as she turns off her phone and puts it back in her pocket.

"Wow. Thank you so much. I won't be bringing the car I've had for the past four years. It won't make it to Georgia. It's a junker car and actually my guess is it won't make it past Montana." I laugh at the image that popped into my head complete with steam coming out of the car hood. "Speaking of Montana. Kim said she's thinking about moving to Georgia as well. Maybe one of us can reach out to her and let her know we're all getting into a house and possibly she can join to make rent even cheaper?"

"Oh yeah! Good idea. I'll reach out." Juniper pulls out her phone again and shoots off a quick text.

"Back to the car situation. We're taking Forrest's truck across the country. He said I could use his truck if I really needed to as well. So between your car and his truck I think I'll be good to go until I find a job that will help me make enough money to get my own. I really appreciate this," I say with so much joy in my voice my soul might jump out of my skin.

"No problem. Happy to help. It's going to be as hot as the devil's armpit over there and the AC from the car is going to be a welcome wagon from heaven," she says.

I tilt my head back and laugh, "I'll be forever grateful that you aren't leaving me to rot in the devil's armpit." I bury my head in my hands at the thought. "It makes this goodbye a little less bitter." Lifting my head up I continue, "When I was packing, I was thinking about how much fun this week has been, to be surrounded by you and your parents all the time. You guys are so much fun and you just know how to make people feel at ease. I don't think I've met very many people that allow others to be themselves without judgement. Now I get to hang out with you guys even more in the future! I just...gah! I can't believe it." I clasp my hands together and squeeze them tight. Holding in all the energy and excitement trying to escape.

"Ahh. That's so nice of you to say, lady. It's been fun getting to know you and your family too. You guys are a great bunch to hang out with." She opens her arms and pulls me in for a hug.

After everyone else puts their belongings in the car, my dad does a final sweep of the short-term rental house and we start to say our goodbyes.

As everyone shuffles around and gives hugs I remember something I've been meaning to ask Juniper, "Hey umm, how well do you know your brother's friend, Dean?" I lower my voice so no one else swirling around us can hear.

Her eyes look around the yard and she tilts her chin down, asking, "Why?" as she closes the space between us. She can sense I want this to be on the down low.

"Oh, umm, I just talked to him a lot during the wedding and was curious whether he's had quite a few girlfriends?" I look around and rub my arm nervously.

"I knew those interactions at the wedding were fat with chemistry. And I saw you guys slow dance." She shoves me in the shoulder with her hand. "So, wait, are you really interested in him?" she asks with a little too much excitement on her face.

I look down at the ground, still battling with my own thoughts and reverting back to keeping my interests in him to myself. I stammer out the words, "N-n-no. I don't know. He's intriguing." She gives me a knowing side eye, and I feel like I have to admit a little more than that to her, "We had a fun time chatting this weekend and I was just curious about his love life, ya know? Nothing spicy going on here. Just a girl, asking a friend about a boy." I don't make eye contact so I can keep some secrets to myself.

"Absolutely, I want to be a part of the reason you guys get together in the future." She folds her hands together and lets them settle in front of her. "He doesn't have a lot of girlfriends. He does, however, have a lot of girls that are friends. It could be because he only has a sister and just gets along with the female psyche really well," she tells me. This is very valuable information. It makes all of his comfortable banter with me make more sense.

"He actually asked me to be friends on Facebook," I admit to her as I pull out my phone to show her.

"No way! This is the first step. He's got you in his sights now," she says with a laugh.

"In his sights? Damn, that makes me feel like this is a common occurrence for him if you see it like that." I'm hit by a reverse glitter bomb, one that takes away all the sparkle in the air and replaces it with uncertainty. I felt like we had something special but if this is his M.O. then what am I even feeling?

"Oh hun, you're special! I just mean, I bet he's going to do more than just ask you to be friends on Facebook. And I'm here for this. Are you going to message him?" she asks me as she looks down at my phone to see his profile that I just pulled up.

"I don't think so. I'm such a wimp about making any kind of moves on a guy. I know I love his personality, or at least, what he's shown me these past few days, but now that we're going back to our respective States I'm not sure it's worth progressing," I try saying, to dampen the reality of my feelings for him. I look down at his profile photo one last time before I turn my phone off.

"That's a shame. He's a good soul," she says and then her mom calls her name to say they're heading out now. "Oop. It's time to go. Well, have a good drive home. See ya!" We wave as we get into each of our parent-chauffeured cars.

In the car I scroll through his Facebook photos while my dad drives North on I-5. I see a different guy in these photos now that I got to know him better during the reception. I don't see a player, I see a genuinely funny guy who pulls people out of their comfort zones.

We're halfway home and I'm a nap, or two, into the drive. I have my eyes closed and my head is resting against the door when my phone chimes. I look at it and I see an unknown number. The text message says, **"Hi Elise, it's Dean. Miss me?"**

My head jumps off the door frame and adrenaline starts pumping through my body. The biggest smile crosses my face and I reply right away with, **"Oh, hey Dean. What's there to miss?"** I leave my phone open to his text thread and keep smiling while I tap the side of the phone with my finger. I can't believe he got my number. Who gave it to him? I didn't think I'd hear from this guy again and here he is texting me on the same day that I leave Redding. *I will text for love, happy to.*

"Ouch. Excuse me while I lick my wounds." His reply comes in almost immediately.

I giggle to myself at his fake pain and sit up straighter in my seat, **"I'm just kidding. I might have missed you a little. How'd you get my number?"** I ask like a mathematician trying to calculate the Pythagorean theorem in their head.

"From Fred. I had to bribe him if that makes you feel any better. He wasn't going to give it up so easily. Lucky for me, that man will do anything if you give him a bag of skittles."

I smile to myself at seeing his personality still coming through in the text messages.

"Oh, good. I would hope that my new bro wouldn't give out my number to any ole groomsman of his. Even if that groomsman is the best man." I feel giddiness bubble up in my chest. I stare out the window at the grass passing by as I wait for his reply.

I don't have to wait long before my head snaps to attention at the buzz in my hand, **"I'm not just any best man. I was THE best man of the century."**

"Haha! I think it's too soon to claim that. This century has only just started."

"True. I'll have to see how the rest of the population does with their best man titles and rate my experience with it toward the end of the century."

I try to encourage his banter by replying, **"That's wise."**

A few minutes go by and I get another text, **"So how far have you gotten on your drive?"**

I look around me to see if I can spot any traffic signs and see one for Eugene. **"We've gone over halfway. We just went through Eugene, Oregon. What about you?"**

"Fresno, California. We're stopping for gas and food now."

I respond as a laugh escapes my lips, **"I love that for you."** I look up to catch my parents looking back at me, but then continuing their conversation up front.

"Thank you! No one ever appreciates the small things I do in life."

"You're absolutely welcome. Nobody appreciates my sarcasm like you do." I reply to his joke feeling so comfortable, like I could say anything to him and he would find a way to banter back.

"Why are you smiling so much?" I snap out of my little flirting bubble and look over at Forrest who is sitting in the back seat with me.

"Oh, nothing." I turn my eyes down at my phone and then back up at Forrest.

"Suuuuure," Forrest says, squinting his eyes. "Your face can't hide your emotions." He points a finger at me and twirls it around in the air like he's stirring something invisible.

"I'm just texting someone." I admit as little as possible and feel my phone burning with anticipation in my hand as a couple buzzes come through. I can't stop myself from looking down at it, getting interrupted.

"Is it Fred's friend, Dean?" I hear him ask next to me. I look over at him quickly with wide eyes and see him lifting an eyebrow. He's always been good at that eyebrow lift, it basically reaches the moon with how high it can go.

"How did you know?" I ask, my heart starts beating faster as if I got caught in a lie.

"You guys chatted a lot at the wed–"

"We did not!" I cut him off.

"Nice try." He rolls his eyes. "I could see you both really enjoyed conversations with each other. You can't hide your facial expressions," he sends me a look that says, everyone knows this. "And I'm not surprised he got your number." His mouth lifts in a cheeky, knowing grin that looks like he could see this coming a mile away.

So much for keeping my internal world a secret. I put my hand up and touch my cheek. That's two people now who saw us talking at the wedding and noticed there was something between us. "Wow. You're good," I say. "I guess I'm an open book that tries to be a closed book." I chuckle awkwardly. "I really think he's a fun person to talk to, but I have reservations about our current distance from each other."

"For now," my brother says with that knowing grin again. "Just don't self-sabotage this one, he seems like a good egg," he continues then looks back down at his phone.

I stare at him completely shocked. What does he know? For one, I'm pretty sure I'd know if I was going to eventually live in the same place as someone. And two, I don't self-sabotage, boys always end up doing something off putting *or* they break *my* heart.

I look back down at my phone, and my missed messages. All *four* of them.

"I'll always appreciate your sarcasm."

"Should I get the Fritos, or the sour cream and onion Lays?"

"I decided on the sour cream and onion Lays. More flavor."

"What's your favorite gas station snack food?"

Reading through all of those messages I smile, he didn't care that I wasn't responding. He's still wanting to engage no matter what. My fingers start typing my replies.

"Thank you."

"Good choice. Sour cream and onion is way better than boring old Fritos."

"My favorite gas station snack food? Hmm. Probably ranch Doritos or sour cream and onion potato chips."

I finish and start to rub the corner of my phone again, as I blankly stare at the back of the driver's seat waiting to feel the buzz in my hand.

He replies with the cutest response I could have imagined, **"No wonder we get along so well. We have the same favorite snack food. I could never be so comfortable talking to someone who doesn't like a good junk food."**

I playfully nudge him with my words, **"Oh is that the reason? I thought we were both just two interesting people."**

"That too. I like it when you call me interesting ;)"

I notice he sent the typed-out version of the winky face and my nervous system turns to mush and I soften.

"Haha I'm sorry. Should I be keeping these thoughts to myself?"

"No. Never. It's nice knowing exactly what you're thinking. Now that I don't have your face to read, I like when you say things that are to the point."

My shoulders loosen up, **"Oh good. You will always get that from me. Real thoughts, good or bad."**

"I look forward to it."

A smile crosses my face like a whisper that no one heard. **"You're kind! So are you driving by yourself?"**

"No. I'm driving back home with another groomsman. He lives 30 minutes away from me. We've been switching on and off who drives. It's been nice to not have to drive the whole way by myself."

Before I read the newest text I fall deep into the abyss that is my mind and don't register the buzz in my hand. I stare out the window watching everything wiz by, we've gone through big towns, grassy fields and livestock fields. It's mesmerizing.

I feel like Ariel in The Little Mermaid. Plucking the petals off the flower one by one, but instead of asking if "He loves me, he loves me not?" I am asking myself, "Is long distance an issue, or is it not?" At least

Ariel found a way to bridge the distance between them, selling her voice to a sea monster to get a pair of legs. My situation is different, the distance between us is not so easily bridged.

I look down at my phone to see I have a missed message. Then I reply, **"That's cool. I don't have to drive at all. My dad will drive this whole way."**

"Oh really? That must be nice. This is the longest trip I've ever had to take," I'm shocked when I read this because I just got back from a country 7,500 miles away, **"I've got everything I need in San Diego and haven't had a need to really leave the city. Then my best friend goes and finds the woman of his dreams and I'm pulled away from my big city."**

"That's so interesting, my family has always gone on road trips my whole life. When I was 16 we drove all the way to Illinois to visit an aunt and uncle of mine. It must be why I like to travel."

"That sounds ridiculously fun. What places have you traveled to outside of the states?"

"So many! Mexico, Guatemala, Myanmar, Thailand. I hope to add to that list each year." I feel my chest tighten a little bit as I send that text. It seems so small and simple but talking about my travels makes me feel like I'm letting him get to know me a little deeper and it's making me squirm in my seat a little. I've straightened my shirt about three times before I got a response back from him.

"Wow! Those are some pretty unique places. Tell me what you liked most about each one of them in one word."

My heart flips. I don't know what kind of response I was expecting but that one makes my limbs soften into noodles. He unlocked a piece of me with his curiosity, making me forget to tug on my shirt anymore.

"Mexico - the food, Guatemala - the street shopping, Myanmar - the novelty, Thailand - the people."

"Wow. That makes me want to travel further away from my big city. Which one would you go back to if you could?"

I can't stop smiling as I type out my response, "Thailand. The people, gah! So lovely. They also have good food there so it's an all-around win for that country."

"I'd love to go there someday. Maybe I'll find a camera bag to hold there or something, lol."

"Oh my god! LOL! You and your camera bag hobby." I shake my head to no one but myself.

"I'm a very loyal person. To my hobbies and to my people. ;)" There's that winkie face again. Making me melt into Jell-O and prying open my heart.

"That's a good quality to have." I text back appreciating what he's telling me.

"So are you and Forrest getting in any sibling fights?"

His question reminds me that I'm still in the car with Forrest. We've been in our own worlds so much that we haven't talked to each other in a while. I respond, "No actually. Not at the moment ;P I actually get along with him pretty well. We're both just sitting here on our phones and watching the outside world roll by."

"That sounds like me and my sister. We get along really well too." I swoon at his words. A man who is close with his sister is such a green flag.

"Tell me more about your sister."

"She loves surfing and mountain climbing. She is so friendly she could make any introvert feel known in an instant. And she loves plants. **She's one of my closest people. If I do make this move up to Washington I'm gonna really miss her."**

Ahh. He's so sweet. **"I love that you guys are so close. I feel like that's rare!"** I love hearing that he's so close to his family, because I'm so close to mine and I can relate to missing your family when you leave them.

We keep chatting like this for the rest of the car ride. Just getting to know each other. Not wondering if the other person is going to respond, knowing full well we'll get a return text quickly. Knowing we enjoy talking to each other equally. The conversation just flows. It's easy. Nothing is one sided and I can't imagine a future where we aren't talking like this.

A few more hours roll by, along with a few more cow fields, then we make it home. Yelm, Washington. The town I grew up in. With its one street going through the center of town and its two competing grocery stores. Population? 10,000. Noticeably smaller than Dean's city of San Diego. I can't keep track of all those Southern California cities. To me So-Cal is one giant Los Angeles. Like a massive dog pile, not knowing where one town starts and another town ends.

Yelm has got that small town feel where you literally go to school with the guy that bags your groceries. No one wears expensive clothes or gets plastic surgery here. The majority of people are all into nature, horses and rodeos.

As our car goes down the streets of my small town, heading back to my childhood home, I rub the side of my phone and start to daydream about what it would be like to share this town with Dean. I could show him all my favorite spots in my old stomping grounds. The places that made me who I am. I've always wanted to share this side of myself with someone.

We pull into our driveway and I shake my head as I hear the gravel crunch under the weight of our tires. I look down at my phone and see an out of the blue text from my new brother-in-law, **"Stop monopolizing my best friend's time!"** he says, like I've committed the worst crime ever. He has such a dry sense of humor that someone else might think he was serious, but I know he's only joking.

I chuckle to myself. Dean and I have been texting for hours nonstop, and it must have become noticeable to Fred. I shoot back, **"I'm just an innocent party here. We've only been texting...a little."** as my parents and brother get out of the car and I'm left, in my own world, seeing where Fred is going with this.

"Yes, but he won't respond to any of my text messages because you've jammed the communication lines."

He's clearly trying to get me to crack.

"What has he told you?"

I wonder if this means Dean is already talking about me to other people.

"When I ask him why he hasn't responded to any of my texts he replies with just one word, 'Elise'."

I joke as I unbuckle my seatbelt to get out of the car, **"Oh my god, that's hilarious! I'll tell him to stop being so interesting so I won't want to text him anymore. That way you can have more time with him."**

He replies, **"That's all I ask,"** and I can hear his monotone voice through the text.

A smile crosses my face as I start to well up with excitement. Dean must be as enthralled with our conversation as I am, if he's completely ignoring texts from other people.

I change text threads and go back to the one with Dean.

"I just got a text from Fred, he's teasing me about taking up too much of your time lol."

"He's a very protective mama bear. But also, he can't find his house keys and he really needs them before he and Emily take their flight tonight to their honeymoon. I should really respond. lol."

"Haha! Oh my god! Please text him back!" I didn't realize there was actually a serious reason behind Fred texting me. **"This is too funny. I feel terrible now."** I put my hand up to cover my eyes and look around for Forrest to share the hilarious mishap, but he's already inside.

I expect Dean to be busy so I take this time to get my suitcase and head into the house. My childhood home is a four-bedroom, three-bathroom modest space. Knick knacks on the walls, and so much mail piled up on the table that you can't sit at it. My parents are in their room unpacking their clothes as I walk by. I head to my room and get my clothes from this past week out of the budget suitcase I got at a thrift store for $10 and start putting them in the hamper.

My phone chimes halfway through my unpacking and I pick it up mid shirt-toss, and read Dean's text.

"Sorry, just got off the phone with him. I left the keys under the wrong rock at his place. Rookie mistake."

"I hope he doesn't shun you for that." I feel giddy as I set my phone down on my bed and continue throwing dirty clothes into my hamper.

"Nah. I'm like a boomerang. I always come back. So he couldn't even if he tried lol."

"Ha! How long have you guys known each other?"

I have an idea of the answer because of what Sarah told me at the wedding, while we were eating blueberries and almonds, but I wanted to hear it from him.

"For about 12 years. We met when we were 11 years old. A couple of nerdy boys who liked to play the drums and zone out on video games."

Dean's response makes my back stand up a little straighter.

"Wait, you play the drums?? I didn't know that. That's so cool."

I sit down on my bed with my back against the wall and settle in. Dean just gained 10 cool points for that.

"Yeah. I've been playing for so long, it's like second nature. I could be sleepwalking and still be able to drum out a song."

"Haha, you're funny. Were you ever in a band?"

"If playing at church during worship with a bunch of 40-year-olds counts as a band, then yeah, I was in a band."

"Ohhh, gotcha. I would genuinely love to see you play the drums. I wasn't going to tell you this but...you just earned 10 cool points."

I decide to admit to him about his cool point game. In high school, we gave cool points out all the time. It was a sign of appreciation if someone said you did something awesome enough to get 'cool points.' One time I was shooting hoops with some guys at school and the basketball bounced all over the hoop before falling into it. That was the first time someone told me I got some cool points.

"No way! 10 of them! I must be up to 15 now. Yessss! *He says as he punches the air.*"

My cheeks hurt so bad from this permanent smile that hasn't gone away since he started texting me this morning. Best. Response. Ever.

"Haha! 15 sounds about right. Cool points are hard to come by with me. I don't just give them out, they need to be earned."

I cross my legs on the bed and accidentally knock over the half-empty suitcase I was working on minutes ago.

"I look forward to earning more of them ;)"

There's that winkie face again.

Trying to find a way to flirt back, I reply, **"Oh you will. As long as you keep making me laugh."**

"Challenge accepted."

I feel uncontrollably giddy, lay down on my bed and slip a hand behind my head. As I look up at the ceiling I let out a heavy sigh. This feels like the beginning of something I'll remember forever.

Chapter 11

Present Day

January

In the daylight it's easier to make out the shadows of the ceiling texture while lying on my bed. My bones are lifeless so now felt like a good time to ponder my life, my broken heart, my future, my next steps...but I'm getting nowhere.

On the upside I just finished the first book of the *Thomas Taylor* series and have now moved onto the second book, *Hidden Hallway*. This series is clearly going to go by fast. It's been capturing my full attention and I think of nothing else while reading it. Fred was right, it has been a very good mood lifter and distraction. I should thank him later since, unbeknownst to him, his recommendation has really helped me during this period of heartache. I only managed to put the book down just now, apparently having decided I'd rather torture myself with my thoughts than be lost in the magic of the book.

The restaurant adventure with Juniper a few days ago was a nice distraction, but all the feelings are still there as the days pass me by. If I could just flip a switch and turn all these feelings off, then that would make this process so much simpler. Why do I still have feelings for him when he made it black and white? He's not interested anymore. It's never going to be something. Yet everything in me screams for another conversation with him. To be like we were eight months ago, when we were talking every day. *When is time travel gonna be invented, dammit!* My god, this sucks.

Why would he say things like, "I think you might be my dream girl," when he couldn't follow up with a relationship? Why would he tell me, "Maybe we'll be together someday," when someday was never going to come? I'm sifting through all these lies that started out as real life promises. It's gut wrenching that something that gave me goosebumps at first would turn into a never-ending nightmare reel of my broken heart.

I can't ask him these questions to get any kind of closure, because I'm trying not to text him when I get the urge to. The phone call we had when he officially ended things was very one-sided and I didn't get a chance to confront him on any of these questions. If he was slowing down before, he has completely stopped responding to me now. I lift up my phone that is already in my hand, resting on the bed. It's like my hand has a rubber band going from it to my head. I keep pulling up my phone to look at it and then putting it back down. I can't muster the strength to hold it down on my bed, instead of searching the screen for his name, for all that long. I open the text thread with him and just stare at it. Still no response to my extremely casual, **"Hiya toots, how's it hangin'?"** text.

Lying here staring at my last text to him I feel lifeless. Like a forgotten banana peel lying on the ground waiting for someone to slip on, just to remind myself that I exist. I'm a forgotten banana peel. My heart starts racing as I consider sending him another text.

I start to type, **"How's the weather over there? Wear any knitted scarfs lately?"** I stare at what I wrote. That's so cliché. Talking about the weather. I'm going for lighthearted though...Okay, yeah, no, that's good. You can't feel like someone is trying to be clingy if they're just asking about the weather. I should send it...No, I can't. That'll be three texts in a row that he hasn't responded to. He's clearly trying to tell me something. My finger goes for the SEND button, I can't pass up the possibility of maybe, possibly getting a response back, though. I finally touch my phone screen and the text whooshes off. I lay my phone and my hand back on my bed.

Hearing a knock on my door, I stay in bed and yell, "Come in!" When I hear the click of the doorknob I lift my head up just enough to see that it's Emily. Then I flop it back down on my pillow.

"Hey sis, whatcha doing?" she asks as she steps into the room to sit on Juniper's bed.

"Just laying here...thinking," I say, having a conversation with the ceiling, not making any eye contact with her. I like living in this house with all of my family around to run into. It's nice not having to pick up the phone to call them, but instead getting a knock on the door and in they come. It makes falling into a hole of broken heart depression harder to do.

"Yeah, how's that going for ya?" she asks with concern in her voice.

"Umm. Ha! I don't know. Fine I guess," I say, trying to give her an answer that I don't have.

Just then Fred pops his head around the corner of my doorway and says, "So you're...freaked out, insecure, neurotic, and...emotional?"

With that I started bawling for the second time this week. Why do these people know exactly what to say to me to bring up all these emotions that I'm trying to control! I look back and forth between them, one on my roommate's bed and one in my doorway. Through tears I say, "Yeah. There's probably something to that. Ugh! Apparently. Since I'm crying over it."

I've been trying not to bring up the Dean topic with them. We've had so many conversations over these past four months about him that it's starting to feel like they don't want to hear about it again. They probably want to put me in beat-a-dead-horse subject jail.

"I only meant that people who say they are 'fine' usually aren't really fine." Fred tries to save himself as he slowly steps two feet into my room.

"It's all good. You hit the nail on the head, or more like, hit my heart with that nail," I reply with sinister sarcasm.

Fred lets out an uncomfortable laugh. "Sorry."

Since Fred and Dean have been close friends for so long I felt like he would be the BEST person to help me get into the head of Dean so I could have some understanding about why Dean is acting the way he's been acting. But Fred has kept his conversations with Dean close to the chest and I'm not getting any clear information about what Dean is thinking. I don't blame him though, he's in a tough spot.

I can see it from Fred's perspective, Dean has been his best friend since childhood so they're practically brothers, and now, he is also my brother-in-law. In terms of loyalty during our break-up, or break-up adjacent situation, it can't be easy for him to navigate both our feelings. I get that he wants to respect Dean and his privacy, I do, it's just...I wish I could get some answers to stop the spiraling, and Fred feels like my only chance at getting them since Dean isn't talking to me.

So, as Emily and Fred are here with me, I decide to be honest and I tell them, "I'm still having a hard time getting over Dean. I know I have to, but it's just...it's just hard." I throw one arm over my eyes like the pathetic teenager I'm embodying.

"I get it sis. You want to find your forever person and he wasn't it. That's super disappointing." Emily crosses her legs in front of her to get more comfortable.

I lift my arm up and say, "Yep. It is." Then rest it back down over my eyes.

"Well do you need anyone around to help you keep processing it?" Emily asks, and I feel like my heart is opening up.

"If you don't mind?" I cringe at the need to talk this out even more.

"Absolutely. We're here for ya, sis." Emily waves her arm for Fred to enter the room and sit down next to her.

I take my arm off my eyes, look over at them and start explaining my heart, "I talked to Juniper about it a few days ago. I guess I still need more time to process, to get closure for myself. I can't seem to talk it out as much as I want to. It's completely draining me, but I don't want to stop talking about it."

"Yeah, the feeling of closure can take some time to kick in," Emily says.

"My heart hurts and I just want to either love him or forget him," I say slowly, looking over at Fred who is looking down at the ground. I feel uncomfortable admitting I still have a thing for Dean in front of Fred.

"That makes sense. Both options are closing the chapter to your broken heart. And closure feels like the only way you can move on." Emily shifts her feet around.

"Exacly. I'm just ultimately wondering one thing that keeps spinning circles in my head, why do you think he officially ended things?" I look right at Fred when I ask this. I need to hear from him. He could know more than I do.

Emily looks over at Fred too and leans in his direction. "That question is for you, babe."

"Oh," he looks up, "Umm. I don't think he meant to hurt you. I think he just got confused with all the feelings going around, that he just had to take a step back and not string you along anymore."

My heart feels like it's been punctured and is now oozing invisible blood, "Is he scared of feelings?" I ask.

"Not that I've noticed. But maybe he needs time for himself right now. To get his own mind straight." Fred looks at the hairs of his arm, not making eye contact. I can tell he's uncomfortable.

"Do you think he'll ever be interested again?" I ask the second looming question that's been running through my mind ever since that last phone call with him.

"Umm. I don't know. I don't want to answer that for him," Fred says, trying to protect both me and his friend with his answer.

I turn my head back to the ceiling. "Ok." I breathe out.

"Are the *Thomas Taylor* books helping?" Fred asks me, changing subjects slightly.

"Yes, actually. I like being brought into the magical world of *Thomas Taylor* and feeling my heart heal, even if just for the short hours of reading." I smile up at the ceiling at the thought. "Thank you for the recommendation, I wouldn't have thought to pick it up myself, but I'm really glad I did."

"That's great!" Emily says, reaching across the room to pat my arm. "So how do you think you will start healing and moving on?"

"I think I'll just have to hold space for the moments that bring up the heartache but let myself fall into the moments that bring me joy. Slowly I'll be able to move on. This one just hurts more than the other ones have." The honesty vomits out of me because it's the only way I know how to be.

"That's very real, and normal, and human. You got this girl. I'm here for ya Ellie, if you need anyone to listen again," Emily says using her childhood nickname for me.

"Thanks Ems," I reply using my nickname for her.

They get up and walk out the door. Fred turns around and gives me a cheesy grin with two thumbs up as he exits. This attempt to try and make me laugh but also try to lighten the mood cracks my 'Wrath of Elise' facade and makes me smile. I can always count on my bro-in-law to keep me smiling even if I don't feel like it.

I've got to get out of this funk. Fred's cheesy grin reminds me of that. I want to laugh, be happy, be free and I know I used to have that. I need to find that part of myself again. Okay, here we go. From this moment on I'll tell myself it just wasn't meant to be, and that, if a relationship was supposed to happen then it would have. Alright, I'm ready. Happiness starts...NOW! I squeeze my eyes shut, clap my hands really loud and then just lay there. I start to slowly open up my eyes like a newborn kitten but I feel the exact same. Well at least I'm starting somewhere.

Buzz, buzz. My phone goes off. I lift my phone hand up so quickly you would have thought it was being pulled by a magnet. My eyes dart around the screen taking in all the information as quickly as I can. I gasp. It's from Dean. He responded and said, **"Nothing but white skies for days. The only neckwear I've been sporting lately is a tie."**

My heart is beating so fast I can't decide whether I should respond right away, because clearly he has his phone in his hand right now and maybe he only has ten minutes to respond and I shouldn't waste this opportunity in time, or...should I play it cool and wait a couple of hours to respond? My lack of patience takes over and I start typing, **"Haha! Oh yeah, how's that boring office job going?"** I hit send right away.

I so badly want him to respond again and put us back into, at least, the category of friendship.

He leaves me wanting. I get no response for the rest of the day. As I sit down to my bowl of mac and cheese with hot dog bites, I realize I feel so emotionally drained from this tug-of-war we keep playing.

What a waste of emotions. After getting no response for a whole week, I got so excited to finally hear back from him that my adrenaline kicked in. I felt giddy for a total of ten seconds as I quickly responded back to him, then I was left unsatisfied with no response back. Again.

I'll be waiting with bated breath for another full week to get one more lame response. It's like I'm a junkie getting a hit. Then when the high is over I'm grumpy and exhausted.

The excitement of hearing from him always takes over. Now I'm kicking myself for not waiting an hour, or even a whole day, before responding. He isn't giving me anything, so why do I respond back to him like we're the closest of friends? I'm not picking up what he's dropping. He's clearly telling me something that I'm not getting. Ugh. Now it's like I'm starting from ground zero, as I have to start taking all this time to let go and process this mess of feelings again.

Chapter 12

Present Day

January

I wake up on Wednesday morning thinking about what I am going to do for the day. It's been a week since Dean's didn't respond to me, now for the fifth time. Today is *not* going to be a day where I think about Dean, text Dean, or have any conversations about Dean. I will be a mime in training today if I have to.

No one in this house of nine people has an actual nine-to-five job. Sarah and Mitchell are retired but the rest of us work college-age jobs at places like pizza restaurants, coffee shops and warehouse stores. So sometimes a few of us have our days off all at the same time. Today happens to be that lucky day.

Last night Emily, Fred, Juniper and I realized we were free as a bird today. We decided, while watching Seinfeld reruns, that we should all do something together. So this morning we started brainstorming.

"What about a walk?" Emily asks with an open smile and eyes wide. She might be the only one in the house that enjoys walking or running. I'm more of a team sport athlete.

"I don't want to exercise on my day off, I'd rather eat bacon and butter on the couch," I look at her as I scrunch my lips, and mouth the word 'sorry'. She nods her head accepting my response.

"What about clubbing?" Fred jokingly asks as he rubs Emily's back. I feel a pang of sadness hit my eyes at their physical touch. I look down to lessen the burning sensation. Dammit, I wasn't supposed to think about Dean.

"What about finding a river or a lake?" I chime in so that my thoughts can lead somewhere else instead of...him. I start fiddling with the corner of my book so no one can see my eyes.

"To walk!?" Emily asks, still holding onto hope that someone will want a little bit of exercise along with her.

"Oh, umm, I just wanted to stand in it and throw rocks or something," I cheese.

"What about flying to Europe?" Fred asks as he shuts the fridge door after getting a sparkling water. I forgot how similar Fred's humor is to Dean's. I shouldn't be surprised since they grew up together.

Shoot, Elise, think about something else.

"On who's dime?" I ask with a laugh at his antics.

"What about exploring a part of Atlanta?" Juniper chimes in.

"What about hitch-hiking to get there?" Fred says with a cheeky smile. There he goes again, putting up suggestions that aren't real.

"There! I think you nailed it. That's what we'll do, Fred. We'll hitch-hike to Atlanta!" I play along.

Just then, Josh walks in and goes to the fridge. I see him make eye contact with Fred and then say, "Sparkling water," with a nod, then he walks back out of the kitchen.

Josh is a down-to-earth dude from New Mexico. If you had a fish or a deer in your backyard, he would be the right person to call. Ready to walk you through all the steps of gutting the animal. He doesn't talk to me much, he stays to himself. I've gotten to know him as much as

I've gotten to know the cottage cheese in the fridge. Some insight—it's molding.

After a few more ideas get thrown around between the four of us, plus a few more fake ones from Fred, we finally land on exploring a part of Atlanta. We haven't been in Georgia very long, and Atlanta is so big, it's an easy place to go to and explore new sites. Atlanta has a mix of old time feels and new hipster style to it. We can even walk the bridge where the Atlanta Ripper preyed on his victims back in the early 1900s if we wanted to, but not today.

We look up some places to go eat in Atlanta before we head out, all feeling a little peckish. A nice light coffee and pastry sound wonderful. We pick out a cafe and grab our bags, load up in Fremily's car and go on our Atlanta adventure.

The traffic isn't too bad for most of our ride, since it's a Wednesday in the late morning hours. Definitely not rush hour time. Which is a relief because we didn't have to break the law and use our fake police siren this time. I jest. The downtown streets are so busy, though, we had to claw our way through to park a few blocks down from our destination. The city can be such a complicated place sometimes, especially when you're used to small town vibes, but the reviews of this cafe reassure us that it will be worth every impatient driver who took our parking spots.

We walk up to the cafe with a spring in our step. It's a cute little French cafe called Café Intermezzo. What we massively overlooked was how popular they are. So popular, in fact, that we had to put our name on a list and sit outside until a seat was available for our party of four. We hadn't expected to have to wait an additional forty-five minutes just to be seated, but I guess that's normal in the big city. It gave us an opportunity to catch up some more.

"How's work going Fred?" I ask as I take a seat on one of the waiting benches outside.

"Nothing too exciting going on with it. The meat is still red and the floors still need cleaning every day," he says while patting the seat next to him for Emily to sit down.

For someone who likes to make jokes at every turn this is an odd response from him. "How mundane. That's so unlike you," I reply.

"I've got to mix it up sometimes. Can't lead an exciting life all the time or else everyone would be too worn out by my stories," he says as he goes to grab Emily's hand in a sweet 'couple in love' kind of way, and I feel a gut punch at my loss. They have one of the healthiest relationships I've ever had the pleasure of witnessing. Living with them and having them around these past four and a half months has really inspired me to look for my own partner that I can grow with and learn more healthy ways of coping with the hard parts in relationships.

"That's a bummer. I'm only friends with you because your stories are so good, though. This might have to be our last interaction." I look over at Emily and shrug, as if to say, sorry it had to come to this.

"I reject that implication. I was never good at telling stories," he says with a deceivingly straight face.

The group of us roar with laughter at the lie. The other cafe-waiting-patrons look at us and my cheeks go red.

"How's your work going, Juniper and Els?" Emily asks us as she crosses her legs.

"Good. I like the job a lot. It covers three of my love languages; making coffee, reading books, and interacting with the customers. Plus, I like how chill our bosses are," Juniper says as she watches the people passing in front of us.

"I agree!" I say. "I've never loved a workplace more."

"Any interesting things going on in the coffee world?" Fred asks.

"Oh! I have a story," I say as I sit up straighter and wiggle to the end of my bench. "The other day someone came in and asked for a Venti Caramel Macchiato, which is a traditional Starbucks drink, not a common 'every coffee shop has this menu item' kind of drink," I explain with a heavy eye roll. "You see, the traditional café macchiato, or espresso macchiato, is a shot of espresso with a splash of steamed milk foam thrown on top. Whereas the Starbucks Caramel Macchiato is layered and not mixed; caramel, milk, and espresso. So, it's basically a latte that's not mixed up. I badly want to explain that to the customer but I can't be so direct about it, we might lose business. So instead, I just make them the Starbucks drink they asked for and send them on their way" I finish and reach down for my phone that's in my bag but stop halfway and fight the urge.

"That's very big of you," Fred says with raised eyebrows. He looks like he's trying to figure out what I'm talking about. It's hard to understand the frustration every non-Starbucks barista experiences in this world.

"I've had a run in with those people too!" Juniper throws her arms in the air. "It would be so satisfying to explain the difference to them. You know, give them some culture in the world. Although I can't blame them, the overly-sweet-cold-milk-barely-any-coffee Caramel Macchiato is one of my deep dark secrets. It's a fave of mine at Starbucks, but I know better than to order that at a small coffee shop around the corner. I'm sure they'd make it for me but I would feel the judgement of ruining a classic drink deep in my bones." she says, having my back with equal frustration.

"I've actually never had one from Starbucks. I just know about them," I admit the shame of my coffee virgin history. Meanwhile, my hands feel awkward on my lap without my phone.

"Me either," Emily and Fred reply in unison. Emily is now rubbing Fred's back and my heart feels like it's bleeding out by a thousand tiny little paper cuts, just watching two people be in love.

"I recommend it. It shouldn't disappoint. It's one of their popular drinks. Unless you have the taste buds of a lactose intolerant nun," Juniper says as she fiddles with a couple of rings on her finger.

I laugh. "I'll have to try it next time I'm there," I say, fully excited to enjoy all the lactose I can in my future.

Thirty minutes later the hostess finally calls the name for our table. We get up and follow her as she leads us through the front door and to the left, then down what looks like a breezeway to the bathroom but it's lined with a single row of tables and chairs on both sides. This section of the cafe feels like we've been exiled to the grunt tables. The hostess points at two different two-person tables on either side of the hallway, puts our menus down and says, "Please be seated. Your waiter will be with you shortly."

Fred and Emily sit at one of the tables on one side of the hallway, then Juniper and I sit at the table on the other side.

I look around me and feel so strange. We're seated with our party but not at the same table. I feel like we're a couple of kindergarteners that made too much noise and are forced to sit apart, but there's not enough space in the classroom for that so we can still talk. The space that separates all the tables down the hall is big enough for one person to walk through with, only a little leg room.

I have to admit, though, eclectic seating arrangement aside, the atmosphere here proves that it was worth the wait, because once we're seated we're transported to the streets of Paris. As if this cafe came straight out of the French city itself. There's stripped awnings, hanging plants and twisted wrought iron fences inside.

As we wait for our waiter to come take our order we start talking.

"So, how is everyone liking the town of Tyrone?" Juniper clasps her hands in front of her and leans forward, bouncing her eyes between our two tables.

"Yeah, it's good," Emily says, tickling Fred's hand. "Reminds me of Yelm." She smiles over at me as she brings up the town we grew up in.

"I'm a fan," Fred says, smiling over at Juniper.

"Umm. It feels too small for me," I admit plucking a piece of lint off my forearm.

"Oh, really? What part feels too small?" Emily asks, looking at me like I'm pointing out the strangest flaw in our Georgia town.

"I've only ever lived in a town that has 7000 people in it. This is the third town of this population I've lived in. I want to live somewhere that has so many restaurants, coffee shops and shopping centers I won't know what to do with myself." I sheepishly look at Emily with a grin. Admitting this means I may move away and I don't want to make her sad.

"I understand. I actually feel the same way," Juniper says across from me with the same sheepish grin.

"I had no idea you guys felt this way!" Emily exclaims, her mouth falls open as if to show us she is completely dumbfounded.

"Yeah, I know I haven't been here for long, but I already feel pulled in a different direction. The last place I remember feeling like myself was

Thailand." I rub my arm and keep explaining myself, "The city, those people, the food, the culture, every part of it made me feel like I was who I'm supposed to be." I almost feel like I have to convince them to see what I'm feeling.

A large group of people walk in front of us, and we bob our heads to move around the hallway passers to keep eye contact with the other table in our group. As if we are little kids lost in a crowd and the tall, stranger grownups are blocking our view.

"You really did have a great connection with the people there," Emily replies, trying to show sympathy for my side while still bobbing her head around the people.

"Exactly. I don't know if I'll actually go back to Bangkok, but I know I need to go somewhere that has the bigger city feel." I look up and see the waiter finally making his way over to us. Feeling a little relieved to see him, because talking across the little hallway feels like everyone is listening. Like those dreaded nail salons. Nothing is a secret when twenty strangers go silent and you are the only ones talking.

We order and I decide on a Heavenly Lemon Torte and hot chocolate since I'm not the biggest fan of coffee. It's ironic since I work at a coffee shop. People do ask me why I work there if I don't like coffee and I say, "I'm there for the smells." Most people nod their head with understanding. They get it. Who hates the smell of coffee?

Juniper orders a Tiramisu and a cappuccino. Now, Juniper is a lover of all beverages. When she used to work at a tea shop she knew all about the teas. This is no exception now that she is a coffee barista. She knows all about the different ways coffee can be made and she enjoys every last one of them.

"Do you think you'll leave town, Juniper?" Fred asks his sister, his face sporting the same look Emily was giving me, hidden sadness at the idea of his sibling leaving town.

"I've been thinking about it. I feel so out of place here. Too many people gawk at my full tattoo sleeves. The people in this little town don't seem to like others who are different," she says, tracing her finger on the blue and purple flower tattoo on her wrist.

"That must be hard," I say. "You deserve to feel like you aren't being stared at by everyone and their brother just because you have tattoos. That's so silly." I reach across the table and pat her forearm with the face of a lion on it.

She shrugs as if to say, 'that's life sometimes', then she replies, "I appreciate the support."

"We all deserve to live somewhere that makes our heart come alive." I nod my head with a smile, having my heart come alive has been something I've been thinking about lately.

The waiter brings us our food twenty minutes later. I look over and see Fremily sharing a cheesecake slice. My head buzzes with vertigo as I watch them enjoy their food in blissful silence.

I'm trying so damn hard to enjoy these moments and not think about Dean. *At least you thought about him a little less today, that's progress.* I feel some sort of power coming back to me because more days have passed since I've texted him now. The urge to check my phone hasn't gone away, but at least the urge to actually text him has become more manageable.

We finish our food and enjoy the last moments of Paris before we have to step outside into the mild Atlanta winter to head home. I pull my phone out of my bag without even thinking and open my text thread with Dean. Old habits die screaming, apparently. I stare at it as I follow my family down the street to our car. I hover my thumbs over the screen to start a text, but I've made so much progress not being the 'girl who's still clinging to the guy that told her he's over her.' *See, manageable.* I lock my phone and put it back into my bag. I'm really glad we came out and did something today. *This is definitely what I needed.* I wait as Fred unlocks the doors and we all lower ourselves into the car. It's been seven days since I've texted Dean.

Chapter 13

Past

June

Dean and I have been texting non-stop for a week now. We text about what we're doing throughout the day, and ask each other 'get to know you' questions. I've learned that he likes the color red and hates the texture of octopus. I've told him that my favorite color is yellow and I can't stand when people crop dust in public.

When he said he liked the color red that reminded me of the tie he wore at Fred and Emily's wedding. Emily had picked out 4 colors. One color for two pairs of bridesmaids and groomsmen.

I'm making myself a sandwich when I text him to ask, **"Didn't you get to wear the red tie at Fremily's wedding??"**

Bringing up our inside joke, he says, **"Yeah. They actually gave me the choice. Since I'm the best man of the century after all."**

I smile as I respond, **"Haha! Still tooting that horn, eh?"** I tease him as I take a bite of my PB&J.

"I just don't want you to forget that I was the cool best man." He continues his side of the banter with a splash of charm.

I take another bite and type, **"I won't forget. You made history."**

"I appreciate you saying that. Being noticed by you is all I care about these days,"

My cheeks warm at his admission.

"You're always flattering me." I smile down at my phone, and before he has time to respond I send another text, **"But actually, I just remembered, I got to pick out my color too."** I remembered that Emily asked me a couple of days before the wedding which color I liked better between yellow and orange.

"Oh yeah, it was yellow." He says with no question mark, a confident statement.

Oh my god, I start walking to my room in the back of the house to get ready for work. I can't believe he remembered.

"Umm yes...it was yellow..."

I don't know what else to type except a confirmation of his statement and a gazillion periods.

He replies, **"I was paying attention. Maybe a little too much."**

And I pick up the cheeky flirtation in his text.

"You keep making me blush."

It's weird, whenever he talks about noticing me, I always feel a mix of giddy-school-girl and uncomfortable. It's the wallflower in me fighting between 'happy to be noticed' but also 'wants to hide away.'

He replies with, **"No one will match my awareness of you."**

I finish my very jammy sando, text back, **"Haha I do believe that is true."** and break away from our texting convo to start getting ready for my shift at the local grocery store. It's my first day back since the wedding. I work in the deli and have a six-hour shift to *not* look forward to. They don't let you have your phone on you, which has practical reasons for it but, man, it's like leaving my arm behind in the locker. Which unfortunately means I won't be able to text Dean for a whole two hours, until my first break. That will actually be the longest we've gone without texting each other, since Fremily's wedding. I begrudgingly get my uniform on—a sloth could have moved faster than me—then head outside to start my car.

When I arrive at work I go to the break room, look at my phone one last time and see his text, **"So how is that small town of yours doing?"** I quickly reply with, **"Still small. I feel like I've only known small ideas and small world views, even after having traveled, it just seems so deeply ingrained."** I put my bag and phone in my locker and go to the deli department. If I could find a way to sneak in my phone I would, but my boss is a very good manager and will notice a big block sticking out of my pocket.

I've only been working here for a month, and I've already realized that Deli Clerk isn't my dream job. I'm not used to standing up for hours at a time, my feet get tired so quickly. My manager keeps jokingly telling me that I'm too young for my feet to be tired and I should stop complaining. It's hard to hear her say that because I want to be a good employee for her.

This department is full of people who have been working five plus years at the grocery store. There's Trish, the department manager. Whan, who cooks the food for our hot section. Nancy, who has the most seniority and works up front. And then there's me, who works in the back doing the grunt work. I applaud them for their work ethic. I can't wait to find the job that keeps me from wanting to travel off to new places.

"Did you prep today's pasta yet?" my manager, Trish, asked me fifteen minutes after I arrived.

"Not yet. I was getting the rotisserie chickens ready to put in the oven because they take longer. I was trying to be as efficient as possible," I say as I look down at my hands, hoping she'll see that I'm trying my best as a newbie at the job.

"Oh. You're right. Good job Elise. I love seeing your efficiency." She smiles then says, "Well, when you're done with that, the pasta will be right here. I'll set everything out on the prep tables to help things go faster for you," she says to me and then she turns to walk away.

"Thanks," I say with a shoulder shrug. It feels good to hear her say that. I've always wondered if she liked me as an employee or not.

I love setting up the rotisserie chickens. It's like playing that Operation game, you want to go slow and not touch the side walls or you'll get burned.

Trish helps Nancy up front when it's too busy for one person to handle. Most of the time she asks me to come up front if someone needs a sandwich made. Trish hates making the sandwiches, so I get the pleasure.

I was halfway through mixing up the Mediterranean Orzo Pasta when a big rush hit us and Trish came into the back to ask if I could help up front. I walked straight to our Signature Sandwich area and got to work.

The first customer asks, "Can I get the turkey panini melt with extra pesto?"

"Do you want tomatoes?" I ask as I'm laying the turkey down on one side of the bread.

"A little," the customer says.

I finished making this sandwich and the sandwiches for the other two customers in line then head back to prep the rest of the Mediterranean Orzo Pasta. I'm more of a baker and not a chef. I can whip up a couple of muffins, pies or cookies like a magical fairy whose one gift is baked goods. However, learning these pasta recipes is really upping my cold foods game.

I've lost track of time because as I'm thinking about what to do next, I see my manager rounding the corner and she tells me to take my break.

Oh phew! I can't wait to get back to my phone and talk to Dean. I take off my apron and head to the break room. After I grab a quick snack and my phone from my locker, I sit down at one of the tables and start my 15-minute break.

I smile when I open Dean's text thread and see how many texts he has sent me.

"I like that you have an innocent small-town outlook. It makes you less jaded than the rest of the world. You come across very trusting."

"Have you ever been hiking? I just started doing it more."

"I'm checking out a new trail today. Wish me luck."

"Hope your day is going well."

"I'm up here at the top of a hill looking down at one of my favorite bridges."

"Hopefully I make it down without dying. If I don't reply, assume I've fallen and lost my memory."

I put my feet up on the empty chair next to me and start my replies. I'm delighted to have all these texts to respond to. Of course, my OCD for responding to each text as they came through kicks in.

"You do? I would think that compared to your big city life it wouldn't be very exciting. I am trusting! Maybe a little too much?"

"I've walked down our country road to the local gas station LOL! Does that count?"

"Good luck! I hope it's everything you ever wanted."

"My day is going good! I'm at work right now. Haven't been able to respond as often."

"How did you fare in the great outdoors? Was it pretty on the hill with the bridge in your view?"

"Oh my gosh! LOL did you make it down safely?!"

I sit there waiting, pulling my feet down and then back up on the chair, a little anxious for his responses. I doubt he lost his memory like he joked about, but there's always that possibility. That would cut our texting fun short, real quick.

I hear the buzz of my phone and grab it quickly. My feet fall to the ground because of my speed.

"Hey Elise! Long time. Missed ya!"

Oh phew. My texting-Dean-smile returns.

"No. The big city life isn't all it's cracked up to be. I'd love to learn more about your point of view. I think being trusting is something to be respected."

"Haha! Sure. I'll let you have the win. Country roads are basically hiking trails that are paved. ;)"

"Yes! It was amazing. It's so sunny and green right now."

"No problem."

"Thanks for asking. The bridge was gorgeous. It would be even better if I had a pretty girl by my side."

"Yes! I made it down without any memory loss. Your exclamation marks make me feel honored that you care so much."

The way he's responding to each of my texts makes me smile, it suggests that he might have the same OCD tendencies. I start my second round of replies.

"I've missed you too ;) not texting you for a couple hours feels so weird. I'd love to say it won't happen again, but sadly, I'm only on a 15-minute break."

"Ahh. That's so sweet. I like to hear you say that. Well, a couple of my points of view are; you don't know who needs a smile today,

people might be stressed out at life and not you, understanding is free so learn how to give it."

"Thank you!"

"Sounds gorgeous."

"What pretty girls do you know that would go with you? ;)"

"I do care. I'm so happy to hear you didn't lose your memory, just as I'm getting to know you."

I take a bite of my protein snack that I grabbed—and bought—from aisle 7 and read his texts as they come in.

He texts, "Elise, you have me smiling. I'll have to understand then. We can't always be talking, I guess. Even though I would like that." Clearly not aware of the effect his texts have on my face.

"Wise words from a pretty amazing small-town girl. I had no idea you had such depth."

"You're the only pretty girl I know."

"I would hate to cut our time short."

A little flutter runs out of my chest and through my limbs making everything feel wobbly.

"Dean, you have me smiling."

"I'm soooo deep! That's what runs laps in the head of a girl who stays quiet."

"I'm the only pretty girl you know!? Stop being so sweet to me."

"I would hate that too."

I look over at the time and realize I have to go back to work, then I get another text that makes me push work off a little longer.

"Quiet girls are hidden gems...and I'll die on that hill."

I look up from the phone and stare at the microwave across the room, questioning how I was ever uninterested in him at the wedding.

"I'm blushing."

I pull my feet down and off the chair they were resting on then send another text.

"Hey, I gotta go back to work now. I am only on a break. I hate cutting this short, but I'll talk to you in a couple hours!"

I put my phone back into my locker, without waiting for a response and head back to the deli. When I enter my department, I see a long line in the hot food area and Trish making the kind of eye contact that could burn a hole in your forehead. I can see the desperation in her eyes, like a lost kitten that needs help. I put my apron on and join her, filling the customers' orders. There are two types of people in this world, we got our typical orange chicken with Chow Mein customers and our fried chicken with Jo-Jo's customers. And both types of people deserve to be fed.

Ping ponging between helping Trish out with customers up front and prepping food in the back, my next few hours go by fast. When I go on my lunch break and look at my phone I have a text. Welcome back butterflies.

"Ok. Talk to you later." was his reply to me from a couple hours ago.

Twenty minutes ago he texted, **"So when you get back to your phone, how is your shift going?"**

Standing in front of my locker, not even thinking about how hungry my stomach is, I reply to him, **"It's going pretty good. Today has been steady work and that's been nice, it makes the time move along fast."**

After sending the text message, I head to the coffee shop that's in the grocery store to get myself a muffin and a coffee. Well, I'm getting the third cousin of a coffee, a blended mocha with whipped cream on top.

You can barely taste the coffee, just the way I like it. I have 30 minutes to kill and I'm hungry, so I order fast to satisfy my stomach gremlins. Then sit down in the seating area and wait for my food. My phone buzzes...

"That's amazing! The faster you get through your shift the faster you get to tell me what they do with all the food left over at the end of the night. Do people take it home or do you throw it out?"

"Haha we actually don't get to keep the food at the end of the night. They don't technically let us take the extra food home. We have to 'throw it in the garbage'...I shouldn't be telling you this, but we secretly take something that we want home but don't tell upper management."

I admit the trade secrets to him and hear the sound of the blender that's making my frappuccino stop.

"What?! You can't take home the food that you are already going to throw away. Make it make sense!!"

I smile at his supportive frustration.

"It's a true outrage! I would much rather give the food to the homeless or someone that actually needs it and not just to the trash."

I hear my name being called and walk up to get my order.

"You have a good soul, Elise."

His reply comes in as I take a big bite from my muffin.

"Ahh shucks. Thank you. What else have you been up to today?"

A coworker walks up to me, interrupting my texting. We chat for a few minute about the new apron policy and then when we're done I look back at my phone to finish reading his texts.

"I've just been sitting here playing Call of Duty."

"I started playing it when I got back from the hike up that hill."

I like talking to him. I still have fifteen minutes left on my break and I don't want to waste any of it blushing.

"Now that you mention it. I didn't realize I've been playing for 3 hours. Man, time flies when you're defending your country's honor."

I smirk at his joke.

"So I've heard."

"The country doesn't deserve your services."

"I can actually never figure out how to twist the body and move the feet at the same time. LOL!"

"My brain seems to be stuck in the 2D world of Nintendo Mario. One story line. Get the coins. Jump on the mushrooms and turtles. Kill the boss. Done."

I had to break my thoughts up into four texts.

"That's cute. Do you want to learn?"

I text back between drinks and bites, "Nah. Not really, I don't have time for video games."

"That's fair, you like reading and TV shows. That probably takes up enough of your time."

My eyes go soft as I read his text, I feel so seen, "Lol. Exactly. I don't need to defend our country's honor when I can be sucked into a world full of romance or fantasy."

"People who read are smarter than the rest of us."

"That's quite the compliment!"

"It's the honest truth. I admire people who can get sucked into a book and live in the world of fiction. You guys have better memory, emotional intelligence, spelling and comprehension. I admire that."

This text makes me feel relaxed. I've never felt so understood and admired by someone before. The person he is showing me is not the first impression jokester, who also looked like a player, that I met at the wedding. I like that I was wrong. I hope I can make him feel seen someday.

"No one has ever made me feel so normal before. Thank you!"

I hit send and take a peek at the time. Damn, time goes by way too fast. Before he can respond I send out another text as I get up and throw my trash away.

"I'm sorry. Gotta go back to work again. Chat soon."

He replies almost instantly, "Get back to work you slacker."

I respond, "HAHA!" before I put the phone back in the locker-cage it's been banished to.

I clocked back in and went back to work. This part of the shift isn't as busy as the first part. We don't do as much prep in the evening part and there's less of a food crowd waiting to be served. We get into a rhythm and end the night with me doing the dishes in the back while seniority employee, Nancy, cleans the hot and cold display cases up front. And unfortunately, all the food went into the garbage. Such a waste.

I drive into the driveway around 10:15pm and I'm beat. I just want to pass out in bed and sleep all night. I park the car and walk inside. My bedroom is clear in the back so I have to walk through all the living rooms to get there. As I pass my parents' room I knock on their door so they know I'm home. They've asked me to do that ever since I got this job. Now that they go to bed before I get home it gives them a sense of peace and I respect that.

I get dressed into my pajamas, brush my teeth and flop under the covers in my bed. I conk out within minutes and I'm peacefully dreaming about hanging out with all my YWAM friends in Maui when a loud bell rings and all my friends are trying to figure out why a bell is going off in the house. We look all over when…I wake up to the sound of my phone ringing and I'm all disoriented because it has pulled me out of my sleep.

"What the heck?" I think. *"Who the hell would be calling me right now?"* My toxic trait is that I get so grumpy when I'm disturbed in my sleep. Reaching for my phone, I see Dean's name flash across the screen. *Ugh. I wish I had the energy to talk right now but I'm not answering that.* Why is he calling at such a late hour? It has to be like 2am. I hit the side button on my phone which declines the call. Then I look at the time. It's only 11:10pm. Wow I was in such a deep sleep I felt like I had been sleeping all night and not just an hour. I turn my phone off so he doesn't try calling back and wake me up again. *"I'll text him in the morning,"* I think to myself as I drift off to sleep again.

Chapter 14

Past

June

I wake up as the sun begins to rise as if I'm Cinderella, but without the birds singing to me or the mice getting me dressed. Although—I tilt my head—I wish. As I'm rubbing the sleep out of my eyes I remember that last night I got a phone call at the lamest hour. Man, I wish I didn't hate being woken up so much when I'm sleeping.

I reach for my phone and remember that I turned it off. I power it back on and see a text message from Dean.

"Hey, sorry I called you so late. I assumed you had just gotten off work and thought it would be a good time for a phone call. Hope I didn't wake you in your sleep!"

It's hard to be mad at him, now that he's so apologetic. And it was really sweet that he wanted to talk to me after my shift, like he had been waiting for the right time to call so he could give me enough time to get home. So instead of sending a sassy text about it, I'm more reserved in my response.

"Hey, morning! No worries. Yeah, you did kinda wake me up, but that's ok. I turned my phone off and went back to bed."

I get out of bed and start my morning routine. I got a text back from him an hour later.

"I'm so sorry!! I didn't realize you'd be sleeping. I'll log that away in my brain...Elise, sleeps before 11pm."

I'm glad to be making light of this because last night I was grumpy about it.

"Haha I was just so beat last night after work, I passed out. I don't normally need an hour or two to wind down after work. I can just change, brush my teeth and go to sleep." So many friends I've talked to tell me that when they work a late-night shift they need to come home and watch a movie or chill out before going to sleep. Even if their shift gets them off at 1am. I must be lucky to be able to just fall asleep within minutes of getting off a late shift.

"Gotcha. I like learning things about you. I'll remember this."

I decide on a little more transparency to avoid being in this situation again, and admit to him, **"Sorry, I turned my phone off after you called. I didn't want you to call back and wake me up again. I didn't want that kind of wake up. I prefer to be slowly annoyed by the gentle sounds of flutes."**

I figured if he wants to learn about me then I should be honest about my forever annoyance with nighttime awakenings.

No one is home as my family have all left for work, so I sit down to my breakfast of a bagel and cream cheese at my table for one.

"I don't blame you. I'm so sorry I annoyed you. I don't ever want to do that again."

"No worries! You didn't know."

"Are you available to talk tonight? Only real friends talk on the phone."

"Yeah, I'm available. We really need to cinch this friendship and do it right. Can't have people thinking we're not committed. I get off work tonight around 10pm. I'll call you when I get home."

"Excellent!"

The day whizzed by like an uncontrolled freight train. It felt like an identical twin to yesterday. I was actually looking forward to this phone call with Dean to shake up the normal-ness of it.

I like phone calls. When I was younger and we only had a landline, no cell phones yet, I would want to chat, and chat, and chat with my friends. My parents would put a 15-minute cap on the personal phone calls because they didn't want the phone lines to be held up for hours with their 4 kids having personal calls all night long.

Once I got my own cell phone, I'm glad to say, I've finally got some freedom from that.

After I got home and readied myself for bed, I grabbed my phone to call Dean.

"Hey Berger, nice to hear from you. It's been too long."

I can hear the smile in his voice as he calls me by my last name. I lay down on my bed and say, "Hey Ludwig, I agree. It feels like ages since I last talked to you," even though the last text between us was 10 minutes ago.

"We can't ever let it go this long again," he says, playfully teasing.

"Oh, I agree. Friendships die with this much time between conversations. It won't happen again." I chuckle at our playful banter. "So how was your last video game sesh?" I ask him knowing that he has been playing all night. While I was at work, he mentioned a couple times that he was having a hard time on a mission.

"Oh, good. I played 'Call of Duty: World at War – Zombies' today. Got a new record, you might like to know," he says and I can hear the squeak of a chair over the phone, like he's rocking in it.

"I would like to know, yes. Did you make it to the next level?" I ask, indulging him as I play with the corner of my pillowcase with my free hand.

"Yes. I moved onto another mission. Unlocked a new map even. Secured my place as an excellent player in the gaming world."

"Good work. You saved the world from having 100 more Nazi Zombies today. On behalf of America, I appreciate your service," I say with an inflection in my voice that I hope is interpreted as a smile over the phone.

"Happy to help. It feels good to be appreciated. It's hard out there." I can hear the clicking of the video game controller as he says this.

"Combat from the couch is so hard." I laugh out loud as I roll over onto my side.

"You have no idea," he returns his own equally sarcastic comment.

I know nothing about the latest video games that these gen Z men seem to waste their entire day on. I shouldn't judge though, if I were to be put in front of a Nintendo with some 2D Mario I would play that for hours as well.

"So, I never asked you, what do you want to do with your life?" I change subjects.

I hear a heavy sign escape his mouth on the other side of the phone, "If I am being completely honest, I would love to travel the world and check out as many new places as I can," he says.

I sit up in my bed and lean forward, "Oh my gosh, that sounds amazing. That is exactly what I want to do! What about that idea draws you in?"

"I have always been interested in other peoples culture. Doing something outside of my normal routine to remind me that I am not the only human on this earth and all the ways that I do things are not always the right way. Even though I've never traveled out of California, I hope to someday go somewhere exotic for my first trip."

"I love that perspective. It is so good to be reminded that our American culture isn't the only way things are done. And, I highly recommend Southeast Asia for your first trip. Those people are some amazingly humble people. Inviting you into their homes without hesitation."

"I'll keep that in mind. I loved hearing you talk about Thailand while we were at Fremily's wedding. It has definitely put that country on my top five list."

"Good." We sit in silence for a minute as the reality of us having a similar goal in life sinks in.

He breaks the quiet to say, "When I was younger my parents would take my sister and I to little corners of Los Angeles that had culture. Like; Little Italy, Little Tokyo, and Chinatown. Whenever we went to those places my little brain really thought we had traveled out of the country. It wasn't until I got older that I realized it was just a little drive from our house. But I always wished it was the real deal."

"Ahh that's so sweet. Did your parents travel a lot before having kids?"

"They went to Europe a few times. We always had little trinkets in the house that we couldn't touch, mainly because they had too many memories attached, and my parents didn't want us to break them."

"Ahh, that's so cute. How fun that they traveled so much! They sound like my kind of people. I think I would hid away my little trinkets from my kids while they were growing up too. Traveling is such a treat and not something you can always guarantee will happen again."

"Yea, I guess you're right. I never thought of that."

I smile at his words. He sounds so innocent and humble when he talks about his family. I like that.

To change subjects I ask, "So how is that insurance office job treating you?"

"It's better than you'd think. I get to sit in a chair all day and wear a button-up shirt. That's the dream." He's clearly trying to make light of a job that just gives him a paycheck.

"Wow. Do you wear the kakis like Jake from State farm?" I laugh at him while I ask this.

"I wish. They won't let us wear khakis. We have to wear black or blue slacks," he informs me.

I get up and walk to one of the paintings on my wall. As I look at the different colors that make up the grass in it, I say, "What a drag."

"I know! I've started a petition. I'm getting signatures on it next week. If we don't win then we'll start a protest rally in front of the building. All 4 of us. They won't see it coming," he says and I can hear the clickity clack of the video game controller in the background again. Multi-tasking between killing zombies and talking.

"You should have a sign that says 'Down with the SLACKS or you'll get SHACKS'." I pause and start to feel awkward that he didn't understand so I explain, "because they'll lose business and...oh, never mind." I laugh at having to explain my joke, it was too far of a reach but I was trying to think on my toes.

"Good one!" He's just humoring me, it wasn't that good. "I'll have a sign that says, 'Jake from State Farm had it right, give us the khakis or you'll have a fight," he says back.

"Love it!" I'm actually serious, he did better than me on the fly. "Haha! You'll really get them with their trousers down. Bahaha!" We both erupt with laughter now.

"So do you like it there?" I ask, wiping away the tears from my eyes, no longer able to see the painting that I've been stuck looking at, as my brain switches from my conversation with him to the random items I have in my room.

"I actually do. The people are nice. The pay is good. The work is a little mundane for my taste but there's worse things in life," he says.

"Totally. The people are really what make a place fun to work at. My manager and coworkers are nice and there's no drama. They are twice my age, though, and I can't seem to relate to them very much. What's the age of people at your job?" I ask, now able to see the objects in my room, they no longer look like a blurry Monet painting.

"Oh, they're our age. Just a bunch of kids in their twenties trying to make enough money for gas and food. No one really wants to be doing this job forever, but they'll stay here until something else comes along." Then, out of nowhere, he exclaims "Got 'em!" and I can only assume it was another zombie. "Ok. I'm turning the video game off now. I feel rude to be playing while talking on the phone. I just wanted to finish that mission."

"I appreciate that," I feel thought of, "I hope to do more with my life than just a job that is heading nowhere. I hope to work with the less fortunate more permanently someday, but it's a little dream of mine, tucked away into the far reaches of my mind." I keep giving him information that I don't normally tell anyone else. I feel so comfortable with him I would probably give him my measurements too if he asked.

"No way, Berger! You're a fountain of surprises. That humanitarian work in Thailand really left a mark huh?" he asks.

"Yeah..." I twirl a strand of hair between my fingers. "I can't stop thinking about my time there. It changed me. It changed the way I view the world. I feel like I'm more accepting of others now." I don't tell him that I have a hard time accepting myself. That feels too deep right now.

"Wow. That's so cool. I love hearing you talk about it. Tell me something else that you like."

I can hear the rustling of sheets, as if he's laying down on his bed.

"I like surprises. Whenever someone brings me something that I didn't ask for, I always feel loved." I smile at the ground.

"I'll have to keep that in mind."

"I also like when people keep their word and actually do the things that they say they're going to do. I feel like too many people in this world don't follow thru."

"You're right. I've noticed that with a lot of my guy friends, actually. They often tell me something they are going to do, and then when they don't do it I'm left a little confused. Like, come on man, don't tell me you're going to visit or go for a hike, if you're not actually going to."

"Exactly! My biggest pet peeve is when people cancel plans on me. I get so excited and hyped up for a good hang-out and then it all gets dashed when I receive the dreaded text that tells me 'something came up'."

"We've definitely got to get better as a society at this. I blame social media. Quick reels that keep our attention for ten seconds and then we're onto the next thing."

"It's definitely social media. I'd love to see people interacting more, without their phones in their hands."

"Same. I like that we both can agree on this," he replies.

"Me too," I pause, then say, "Well...to talk about a lighter, extremely random topic, something else I like is the word is rhythm. It's just so cool that it has only consonants." I go to sit back on my bed.

"No way! I never noticed that !" he exclaims.

"Yep! Write it down and see for yourself."

I hear silence on the other end while I assume he is taking the time to write out the word, "Wooow. I see it now. What a random thing to like."

"What can I say, I like to live on the edge." I chuckle as I lay back on the bed.

We started talking about politics a little bit. More so about how 2024 was his first year ever voting and he felt really proud of it. I told him that 2028 will be my first year. I think it'll be fun to be a part of something big for the country.

Our phone conversation flows even easier than our texting conversation. We just go from one topic to another seamlessly. No pauses or breaks. Neither one of us falls asleep. We just talk, enjoying each other's company.

I can feel my heart be pulled even more toward him. A smile crosses my face whenever he tells me a story about his dad or his sister. I really like that we can go from being serious to playful all in the span of 5 minutes. It feels like something real is developing between us, but that also scares me.

"So tell me something else about yourself, something serious," he asks and I pull my legs up into the fetal position, resting my arm under my head.

"Like what kind of serious?" I ask as my resting heartbeat starts to amp up for a marathon.

"Like, tell me what calms you down when you feel upset."

His voice sounds so soothing, I'm instantly at ease.

"Hmm," I take a minute to think. "Ok. So, this is going to sound weird. But, when I was younger we always had milk in the house. So now as an adult I always grab a glass of milk when I feel sad or need to process something."

"That's cute," he says.

"Cute?" I ask as I roll onto my back.

"Yeah, drinking milk when you are sad is the closest form to innocence I can think of. I like how innocent you are. It's refreshing. I don't meet very many girls like you."

"Oh. Well, I'll take that as a compliment," I say beaming up at the ceiling. "So now tell me something I've been wondering about, have you ever had a girlfriend?"

He stays silent for a second before he responds to the question that is making my heart flutter the most. "I have. I had one in high school that didn't work out for more than a year of classes. We were just too different."

I stay completely silent on the other end of the phone as I feel like we're falling into a good conversation.

He continues, "Then I had a relationship that ended a few years ago. I dated her for two years and we were serious for a while, until she decided that our relationship was too easy and she ended it out of the blue and it broke me. It took me a couple years to process and get over it, but now I can happily say that it was for the best."

"Oh man, I'm so sorry that happened! What a terrible feeling to have someone completely pull the rug out from under you like that." I sigh heavily and scrunch my lips to the right side. "That would break my heart too."

"Thank you," he pauses and we sit in comfortable silence as we both process his story.

After the tension of his story begins to wear off, he asks, "So what about you? Have you ever had a boyfriend?"

I don't know why I didn't expect this question back but the air catches in my throat. "I actually, umm, haven't." I pause for a minute to see if I want to continue with my emotional experiences with men, but decide to elaborate more since he did the same when I asked. "But umm, I kinda had a similar situation to you. The closest I've gotten to a boyfriend was when I was seventeen. Me and this guy would talk on the phone every day, and sit with each other during school, and chat every chance we had. Then after six months of this he told me he wanted to go back to his old girlfriend and date her instead of continuing whatever we were building. It broke my teenage heart so much I sometimes feel like I haven't gotten over it." I'm holding all this tension in my body as I finish my last sentence and try to relax my arms with my brain power.

"Ooooph. That sounds terrible. I'm sorry you had your heart broken like that." He breathes out a loud breath. "I wish that never happened to you. You didn't deserve to have your heart broken like that."

I feel a warmth build in my chest, "Thank you. It feels good to hear that from someone. Especially you. I think because of that I've had a hard time accepting myself," I admit the deep thought I had three hours earlier at the beginning of our conversation but now that we've fallen deeper into a trust circle I feel comfortable saying.

"I always want to make sure you feel taken care of," he tells me and I can't stop my heart from trying to thump its way to the moon, "and if I can play any part in you accepting the amazing woman that you are then I would feel like I accomplished a great thing in life."

"Ahh. You're very sweet." I want to keep talking about this, but also don't know how to have such deep conversations for too long and my brain is telling me to change the subject. I settle on asking. "So why didn't your family come to Fred's wedding?"

"Previous work engagements. Stuff they couldn't get out of," he says. "But they sent Fremily a gift! So that's something."

"Ahhh. That's nice of them. What was it?"

"A salad spinner."

I burst out laughing. "Well...everyone needs a salad spinner," I tease.

"My family likes to do little pranks. They were banking on Fred finding the humor in it since he knows them. Every family event we have, we each pull little pranks on each other. This one time, my mom replaced the sugar container with salt," he says with a little chuckle.

"Oh my god! Your mom sounds hilarious!" I put my hand up to my mouth. "Too bad they didn't get the happy couple a chip and dip bowl."

"No, I got them that," he says.

My little chuckles have now turned into a full-blown laugh which I can't control. He's sitting on the other end of the phone just listening to me as I try to stop the laugh and I have to pull the phone away from my face to calm down. Once I get it together enough to form sentences, I hear him laughing too, then I say, "You're kidding me! That was too good! Knowing a little bit more about you now, that tracks." I try to stifle any more of my laughter.

"I'm glad you find the humor in it. And I like your laugh," he says.

167

"Thank you. Yours isn't too bad yourself."

"Ahh you're too kind. So how can I gain more cool points?" he asks me seriously.

"Hmmm," I make a noise as I walk over to the light switch and turn it off. There's no point in keeping my room illuminated because I'm not going to get up and inspect any more random items in it. I'm just going to lay on my bed in the dark while we chat into the night. I take a couple seconds to think of something, then the perfect thought comes to mind and I say, "You could come up to Yelm for a visit." I say it half jokingly, but also as serious as a plane crash because I want to see him in person again.

"I'd love to."

My eyes get wide as he says this, I didn't expect him to agree with it. It was just a girlish hope and here he is thinking about it. "I'll have to ask for those days off work. Then I can fly up there, but I won't have a car so you'll need to come pick me up. I could be there for a weekend and then fly back home," he says and I'm floored because it sounds like he's already thought of it.

"Oh my gosh, you would do that!?" I say, unable to contain my excitement. "I would love that! I could show you around my town and all my favorite spots! This little town is what made me who I am and I'd love to share that with you!" I say with so much enthusiasm I can hardly contain myself. "If you came to visit me you would get 100 cool points and you'd automatically make it into the triple digits."

"That's everything," he laughs and I join him. "I'll have to figure out the perfect time to go. Our summer is usually the busiest time of the year so I can't take time off until after the summer. Once we get closer to that benchmark we should start looking at the calendar and choosing a good weekend," he says. "I've actually been thinking about this for a few days now. It's nice to hear you bring it up."

"You have? Aww. I'm glad we're both on the same wavelength. This is such a fun idea. I can't wait!" I say. I have all these ideas of places I want to take him. I'm going to start writing up a travel itinerary right now so I can make sure we hit all the spots that I love about my little town. I'll be his tour guide, and I'll act like he's on a tour bus. I beam with excitement that only my bedroom furnishings can see. It's going to be so much fun!

"Me either," he says.

He starts to tell me about all his favorite places in San Diego and, if I ever came to visit him, the places that he'd want to show me. I'm buzzing even more off this idea, if that's even possible. The two of us visiting each other would be adorable! Like a real adult friendship. Relationship? It's a something-ship and I'm here for it.

I glance over at the time to see how long we've been talking and I gasp. "Oh my god, Dean, it's 2:45am! I can't believe we've been talking for 4 hours already!"

"Wow! Has it really been that long?" he asks and I hear rustling in the phone like he's moving around to look at the time.

"Yep." I pull my phone away to look at the time lapse on it. "Holy crap. Yep. 4 hours and 27 minutes. I've never talked on the phone this much before. I guess we both know how to keep the conversation going," I say as I move myself to the ground with a pillow and a blanket.

"You know, I don't talk this easily with everyone. I've only ever talked to my family this way," he says.

"No way! I'm flattered." I pull the blanket up to my face and hug it. "I feel honored to be one of the people that makes you feel comfortable enough to talk and let time pass so quickly." I can't stop the body goosebumps from popping up all over me.

"You should feel honored. It's not every day you find someone like me." He laughs and adds, "I'm joking. I'm not trying to sound cocky, I'm just so surprised to have such easy conversations with someone."

"I am too! I don't want to take this for granted," I say and pull the covers down to look at the black ceiling. I realize this is one of those people that you get to have in your life once or twice in a lifetime.

"Good," he says and we sit in comfortable silence for a minute. "So have you ever done any cow tipping up there in ye'ole hick town of Yelm?" He breaks the silence with a stereotypical image.

"Ha! No, actually I've heard of people doing it when I was in high school, but I wouldn't dare. I feel like they'd chase you and kick at you if you weren't strong enough to tip them over. That's not the pastime for me. I'll stick to my reading or watching TV. What's your favorite movie?" I roll over to my side.

"Oh man, probably Best in Show and Drop Dead Gorgeous. They both have this dry sense of humor that is really great."

"I've never heard of them."

"You're missing out. They are so funny I could watch them on repeat. They're kind of old movies though. From probably 1999 and 2000."

"Oh geez. Those are old movies. Sometimes I can't watch them when they're that old. I just don't relate to the characters."

"That's such a bummer. You're missing out on some movie gold." He laughs and continues, "Have you watched any good movies lately?"

"Oh my gosh, yes! I'm very much into the romcoms. Don't judge. I really liked Bridget Jones Diary. And they just came out with a new one last year!" I pause to hear his reaction as I roll over to my other side. I like lying on the floor, but sometimes it has its drawbacks. Hip pain.

"Mmmhmm."

I hear a little chuckle come out of his mouth.

"Did I just hear a laugh?" I purse my lips and squint my eyes in the darkness.

"Maybe. But I can see it. I can see the appeal for some people," he lets me have the win.

"Then there's Holidate. That one was my favorite," I continue.

"Oh! Mmmhmm. Yeah, that one looked promising," he says, still unable to contain all of the sarcasm coming from his mouth. I can hear him choking on a laugh over the phone.

"Don't laugh!" I wave my hand in the dark. "These movies are really lovely!"

"I'm sure they are. Continue please," he nudges me along.

"The last one I'm gonna say is a little older and it's, Penelope. So cute." I finish with confidence as I rub the itch from my nose.

"Oh, yes, I've heard of it, pig face girl who falls in love, who wouldn't enjoy that. So good." He sounds like a pig as he's holding back laughter. "Hits all the right notes you want in a movie." He's now laughing so hard and I join him because it is quite funny when you think of it that way.

I pull my hand away from my mouth after my laughing stops. "Here's how I see it. I adore that they portray true love as being blind. Someone can love you despite what your face looks like. And you only have to love yourself first and beauty will come. Plus, there's a bit of magic and who doesn't love that," I say, with all the confidence I have left in my movie choices.

"Ok. I'll give you that. We all love a bit of magic. And loving someone for what's inside is a great quality."

That strikes a chord. I've been judging him so much on his looks from the beginning that I keep forgetting it's what's on the inside that counts. If I wasn't looking at his exterior, I would've easily admitted that I liked him from the first time I talked to him.

"I love a good moral plot in a story," I say, realizing my own failings. Realizing I'm living one myself.

"It's why we watch movies right? We can't resist the transformation arc."

"I guess so. Huh. Interesting." I get lost in that realization.

"Yep." he leaves time for me to think that through. Then he says, "Just don't say you like any Nicholas Cage movies. I despise them."

"What do you mean? Why? Are they bad?" I ask, wanting to be enlightened because I really do love his movies.

"The writing is terrible. The acting is terrible. Everything about them is so bad. I have never understood why so many people like his movies." I hear a crinkly bag open up as he says this.

"Guilty." I scrunch my nose.

"No! Elise! No!" I hear him crunch on a chip.

"I love National Treasure. It's so fun to watch him uncover all the clues. And the cute leading lady. Not to mention the cute nerdy guy that tags along. It hits all the right topics for me. I love mystery and clues. You know Clue is my favorite board game?" I say changing the subject because I don't want him to put me in the 'she's lame for liking Nicholas Cage movies' category.

"Mine too! I could play that game every day for a year and still not be bored."

"It's like you're reading my mind. I would happily join in on that!"

"It's a date," he says and I feel happy at the thought.

The conversation continues from nieces and nephews to our high school experience to past crushes we've had. Nothing is off limits. Everything gets talked about. I don't hold back or get embarrassed by the things I'm admitting.

We change topics. We both realize we like pepperoni with pineapple on our pizza. He tries to convince me to watch Drop Dead Gorgeous.

"I'm holding my breath, it's that serious," he says.

"I promise. I'll watch it this year." I make a mental note to watch Drop Dead Gorgeous.

"Thank you!" he says.

We continue talking like two old friends that haven't talked in ages. Despite my heavy eyelids I find myself still captivated and unable to succumb to the sweet rhythms of a daily night coma. Our lives are open books to each other. We're devouring all the information we can about one another and enjoying every minute of it. We talk about candles and junk food and best friends. We laugh so hard we cry a few tears...again.

"My eyes are really starting to feel heavy," I finally admit when I look over at the clock again. "Holy crap, Dean, this time it's 5am! Oh my god. We really need to get off the phone now," I say realizing that the sun will be up in just one hour.

"You're right. My eyes are starting to get heavy too," he says and I hear him yawn.

"The sun is gonna come up in less than an hour. This is crazy! But I had a fun time talking to you." I manage to get out right before letting out my own yawn.

"I had a fun time talking to you too. I'll talk to you tomorrow. Sweet dreams, Berger," he says.

"Sweet dreams. Goodbye," I say and we both hang up.

I can't believe how late it is. I've never talked on the phone with someone for 7 hours before. I take a deep breath in and slowly breathe it out. THAT WAS AMAZING! It's like all those times I got cut off at the 15-minute mark by my parents when I was a teenager were all made up for right now in this conversation. I fell asleep on the floor with just my head poked inside my closet. I'm hoping the walls of my closet block the sun from waking up Cinderella.

Chapter 15

Present Day

January

It's been over a week since our trip to Paris via Cafe Intermezzo. That was a fun distraction for me. I need to find more things like that to do. Something that will take my mind off how I wasted my time with Dean. Or worse, the fact that I would give up every Saturday from here until eternity to give him more of my waste-able time.

I also can't stop thinking about the amount of days that have gone by since I last texted him...and, ugh, from a text that he hasn't even responded to. I wish I could stop thinking about how I almost had it all with him. I feel lonely being a girl, who liked a boy, and hasn't gotten over him since he's backed off and left her wanting. I can't help it but I feel desperately in need of his attention and conversation still.

I'm walking to my room when Kim asks me, "Hey, are you going to take a shower right now or can I?"

She shatters my glass room of thoughts, and I feel ripped out of my reverie like a time traveler unexpectedly going forward in time and having to figure out where they're at. I recover quicker than expected and say, "No. That's ok. You can have the shower."

"Thanks," she replies. Kim is a true Montanan. She is always wearing cowboy boots and her blonde hair is always perfect, not one hair is out of place on top of her head. I've gotten to know her more in these past four months of being housemates than when we were bridesmaids together. She oozes country. Whenever you talk to her you feel like you ate a cupcake. So sweet it hurts your teeth.

I stand in her doorway and we chat about my new job for a few minutes and then turn the subject to her new job. We work opposite shifts so it's nice to catch up when we're both home. When she walks into the bathroom I walk into my bedroom and sit on the bed.

I look at my alarm clock. That was a nice little 15-minute distraction from my current emotional state of being. Heavy sigh. They say pain gets better with time, but how much time is it going to take for the ache in my heart to get better?

Just then Juniper walks into our room and says, "Hey girly, want to go clothes shopping at Lizard Thicket?" with a little valley girl pep in her voice.

I'd like another distraction, one that lasts longer than 15-minutes, so I say, "Yeah, I'll be ready in five minutes."

After I change my shirt and go downstairs, we meet in the foyer then head to Lizard Thicket. This little clothing boutique has the most adorable clothes ever. Every time we come here I always want to buy everything I try on. Unfortunately, I don't have that kind of money so I just buy a couple items off the clearance rack and live my life in these few beautiful items. I told Juniper in the car that I want to try to add to my wardrobe and get dresses that make me feel like a new me.

"Ooooh, this one's cute," I say as I hold up an adorable knee length baby doll style dress with a cream colored, fitted bodice, and then a quilted bottom made of cream, yellow and orange squares with floral designs on each of them. I tilt my head side to side to take it in and imagine myself dressed in it. This one could help me change my style from just jeans and a shirt to an adorable, new woman.

Juniper nods her head up and down a few times and says, "Oh my god, yes. That one's happy!"

Her enthusiasm gives me the confirmation I need and I throw it over my arm. "I really like it, I'm gonna try it on." I smile and continue perusing.

Shopping isn't normally my kind of time killer but today it feels very therapeutic. I flip through the sea of fabrics shaped into dresses to find ones that perfectly fits my personality, and the *new me* I want to become. Going through the motions of clothes shopping is keeping my mind off...everything.

"Look at this number," Juniper says, holding up a strapless, flowing, silky, floral dress.

"Yes! Love! That fits your style perfectly," I say as I nod my head in agreement. I love her style. It's so Bohemian, free, and eclectic.

"I love the clothes here, but I would hate to work here." Juniper lowers her voice to whisper, "It seems extremely boring. You have to help people find clothes but if you don't have any customers come in then what? Sort the clothes? It's never busy here so I could see them being bored all day."

I look around for the employees to make sure I'm not offending anyone. Then I lower my voice to match her whisper, "I agree with you. I much prefer the coffee shop as a job because when we're busy the time zooms by. Then if we aren't busy we get to sit and read our books. I love that part of it!" I say to contribute to her thought.

"Same, I love the book reading perk of our job," she said, "Oh hey, speaking of books, what *Thomas Taylor* book are you on now?"

"I'm on the third one! *Locked in Alozic*," I say.

"That's a good one. You have so many books to look forward to. I wish I was reading them for the first time again," Juniper replies.

I pull out an all-black dress that has a couple of cream colored accents on the bottom fringe and put it over my arm, then reply, "I love that Thomas Taylor starts to feel confident about himself and stand up to his aunt and uncle right at the beginning of this book. He doesn't seem too upset about potentially losing his magic because he's an underage wizard using magic outside of their school, Stiltsen. Ha! Shrinking down his uncle's brother. Although he deserved it because he clearly is a jerk."

"I agree, total jerk. I like when Thomas gets saved by the Shadow Bus," Juniper says while she pushes hangers of dresses past her one at a time on the clothing rack next to me.

"Yes! After he escapes Boring Drive and gets picked up by the emergency transport service for 'stranded witches and wizards'," I say. Regurgitating the words from the book, I could almost taste the paper. "So clever. Thomas always finds a way out."

"He's a wily one alright," she says as she's holding a dress up tilting her head to the side. "What about this dress?" Juniper asks and she turns it around for me to see. It has a fun islander floral design, cuts off at the mid-thigh, strapless with a stretchy bodice to fit any size chest.

"Yes. That one is winning! It's perfect to go over a pair of leggings!" I say, eyes wide.

"That's exactly what I was thinking!" She smiles as she puts it over her arm and continues her search for another great dress.

We continue talking about books, movies and tv shows. I hold back my thoughts on Dean. This is a happy place, I don't want it stained with the sadness of my unrequited something-ship. We continue looking at all their clearance items, devouring every cute dress in our path like a caterpillar eating a leaf.

I get to the end of my last clearance rack and suggest, "Let's try on the few items that we found. I have three. How many do you have?"

"I have five. I think that's good enough. Or at least a good start if these ones don't fit well." She smiles and follows me to the changing area.

We head to the back part of the store. They really have made it feel fancy here. The lighting is soft and the changing stalls are so big you have enough room to do kicks in the air, unlike the changing room at big chain clothing stores that only leave you enough room to take one step away from the little mirror they have in there. Lizard Thicket clearly didn't try to cram in the changing rooms back here, they wanted it to be an experience. An experience that will convince you to buy as many of their expensive clothes as you can.

We get settled into each of our changing rooms and try on our first outfit. "Ok. I'm done. Ready to show each other?" I ask.

"Yep!" Juniper yells from the changing room next to mine.

Then we both walk out and ooh and ah over each other's dress. "I like it," and "It looks good on you," and "You should buy that one," were being thrown back and forth across the red carpeted changing area.

We repeat this two more times like the characters in a Cuckoo clock dancing in circles. Then Juniper tries on her final two outfits without showing me. I end up picking the all-black one and the quilted looking one. A fresh look for a new me. Juniper ends up getting two out of her five. All in all it was a successful trip. Plus, it gave me two more hours of distractions. *Thomas Taylor* and pretty dresses. That's my new secret weapon to getting over him, I guess. It's been eighteen days since I've texted Dean.

Chapter 16

Past

July

I had to get out of the house because I've been doing nothing but texting Dean and going to work. So I decided to drive over to my friend Kyla's house before my next shift. I haven't hung out with very many friends since I've been back from my humanitarian trip and I thought it would be good to catch up. Kyla actually used to be my boss, but we bonded while I was working for her. It was the end of my senior year and my overly trusting teacher told me I could choose to do my photography elective outside of the classroom. So my title became 'apprentice' at a local photography studio.

Kyla and her husband, Ashton, have been family friends for as long as I can remember, I feel like I've known them forever.

I learned so much from working at their studio. Photoshop, angles, poses, editing, photo-book making etc. They must have seen potential in me because once I graduated they asked me to work for them permanently and my title was upgraded to Office Manager. I was with them for two years before going off to do humanitarian work with YWAM.

When I came back from my six months in Hawaii and Thailand, I asked them for my job back, but they said they couldn't me. They hired someone new, Karen, and she is really fitting in with them. I understand, sometimes the timing isn't there. So, I had to go find another job and that's how I landed at the grocery store. The perfect summer job before leaving town.

Visiting Kyla will be fun. She went and had a baby eight months ago, while I was gone at YWAM. I haven't met the little bundle of joy yet and am really looking forward to seeing the little squish in person. When I knock on her front door I stand on the porch rocking on my toes and heels for a couple minutes before she answers.

I hear the click of the latch unlocking and she opens the door. Her straight, long red hair is falling over her shoulders and she has her son, Roosevelt, on her hip. "Hiiiii. Good to see you! Come on in," she says a little out of breath, but her words still sound like the cutest 90s cheerleader.

I open my arms wide as I step into the house and she gives me a bouncing hug. I ask, "Hello, how are you doing?" Each word coming out individually with her bounces.

"Good! Really good!" she says, adjusting Roosevelt on her hip.

"Hi, little guy, nice to meet you." I reach out and rub his chubby little hand. "Have you been working much with Roosevelt around now? I can't believe the last time I saw you, you were pregnant and now you have this bouncing baby boy!"

"I know! Isn't it crazy! This little guy here has us soooo happy!" She looks down and nuzzles his nose with hers. "I'm not going out on photoshoots as much now that we have Roosevelt, but I work in the studio sometimes with the editing and the billing." She gives a half smile as if she is trying to be ok with backing off from a job that she loves. "We have Karen now and she has a knack for photography." She taps my shoulder as she adds, "Just like you do." She gives me a princess level smile.

"Oh nice! I'm glad Karen is working out for you," I lean into her hand on my shoulder. "I'm bummed that I couldn't come back to my old job, but happy that you guys aren't lacking any help."

"I completely understand, you were amazing to have around," she gestures for me to come further into the house, leads me to the couch and motions for me to sit down. "So how have you been?" She leans down to put Roosevelt on the floor to crawl around.

"I've been surprisingly good, for being in a perpetual state of transition." I watch Roosevelt crawl over to a bunch of stacking rings and pull them off of their post. His movement makes me pause, I never stopped to realize that between all the places I've lived in the past year I haven't stayed somewhere longer than three months. "The humanitarian work was amazing. Doing something for others has really changed my life."

"Tell me more. What kind of work did you do?" Kyla asks as she takes one of the rings that Roosevelt brought over to her.

I smile at their interaction and answer, "After living in Hawaii for three months I got to go to Thailand for three months and work with the nightlife workers in the Bangkok red light district. Those women didn't know what they were getting into when their families sent them from Northern Thailand to Bangkok."

"I've actually heard of them. Expecting to find husbands, but only finding men who want flings." She says with a shocked face that ends with an open mouth.

"Yeah. Exactly. They are sweet ladies that just want to be loved and the world is taking advantage of them." Now I take the red ring that Roosevelt is handing me.

"Will you ever want to go back?" She asks and I sit there in silence, not expecting this question but thinking about what my heart would want.

I look down at my hands, then look up at her and say, "I would absolutely love to," searching her face to see how she'll respond.

"If that's where your heart wants to be then you should listen to it." This is the first time in a long time that I've seen her face get serious.

"Thank you for the encouragement, but I can't think of that right now." I sit back further into the couch and let it eat me alive. Being devoured by soft pillows isn't a bad way to go.

Kyla laughs. "Fair enough. What have you been up to since being back?"

"I've been working at the local grocery store and that's been fine."

"Oh yeah, sorry about that." She shows her teeth and sucks in some air. "So what's next for you? You mentioned being in a perpetual state of transition?" She changes the subject.

"I'm actually going to Georgia in three months. I've been reading up on things about Georgia, and I can't wait to check it out. I love going to new places and I'm so excited to explore my new town and be in the South. Their culture can be a little different from ours and I can't wait to figure out all the ways it's different!" I say beaming and giving my arm a scratch.

"I've always wanted to visit the south! You'll be a Southern belle!" She bounces a little on the couch with her hands on her knees.

"Honorary. I'll have to be accepted as one of them first though." My laugh gets overlooked as I try to pull myself out of the couch.

"They'll accept you, they'd be silly not to." She waves her hand in my direction. "So, meet any guys while doing your humanitarian work?" She tilts her head and leans toward me, not looking away.

"Actually I *have* met a guy, but not through humanitarian work." I break eye contact and say, "His name is Dean, he lives in Southern California, and we talk and text on the phone every day."

"Wait, what!" She shakes her head like she's getting rid of cobwebs, "Is he a friend or something more? How long has this been going on? Where did you meet him? Do you like him? Tell me everything!" she erupts with a volcano of questions.

I bring my shoulders to my ears and scrunch my nose. "Okay, okay," a smile crosses my face, "His name is Dean. We've been talking for two months now. We get along so well, our humor matches up and our understanding for each other's interests match up. He's turning into one of my closest friends." I point my eyes up as I try to remember her next question. "I met him at my sister Emily's wedding last month. He lives in Southern California though. Which is a drag, so I don't get to see him in person, but we FaceTime when we can," I take a deep breath to continue answering all her questions. "We talk all the time, I really enjoy his personality. He has this tall, dark and handsome look that I've never been into before because they've always looked like a player," I pause to take in her facial expressions, "I've started to go from immense fondness to actual feelings." I put my face in my hands and shake my head. I sit like that for a few long seconds as I bring up my next thought. "The worst part is that I'll be on the East Coast and he'll be on the West Coast. Long distance doesn't seem like it'll be successful."

"You seem to be doing it for the past two months though. You could always see how long distance goes," she brushes off my comment as if it was a pesky fly that didn't matter. "Some people do that and it's successful."

"Yeah. I actually heard a statistic on that recently. Did you know that only 25% of people who date long distance stay together? I've heard it's hard." I put a hand over my mouth before I continue, "I don't wanna think about it, though. I'm really just enjoying our current some-thing-ship. Whenever I think about how much this guy seems to like me, I start to feel all over the place, sometimes I'm very giddy and then other times I feel very uncertain."

"I understand, it's hard when you don't know what the future will look like. This is so exciting though! You know, Ashton and I only dated for six months before he proposed. We knew right away that we wanted to be together forever," she says with a smile that reaches her ears as she recalls her own dating relationship.

"I love that for you guys. It's beautiful. I guess I need to just keep leaning into this and see where we end up."

"That's very wise. Ultimately you need to follow what brings you the most peace. Just don't self-sabotage this one," she says as she reaches to pick up Roosevelt who just lifted his arms up for her.

My mouth drops open. "What makes you say that?"

"The two years that you were with us I saw you go through crush after crush. Sometimes it wasn't a good fit, but other times you would see something wrong with them that was never there and you couldn't explain it." She presses her lips together and gives Roosevelt a bear hug.

"I didn't know that I used to do that!" I'm aghast. I remember feeling like something was off with all those guys, but the way she's describing it makes it sound like it was all on my side and not theirs.

"Yeah, at least that's what it looked like from my perspective." She holds up one free hand and turns it into a half shrug.

I stare at her with my mouth hanging open like a wide mouth bass. She can't be serious. Is this real life? "I uh...I don't know what to say," I reply and furrow my brows like I'm trying to complete a complex physics question.

"That's okay. Just being aware of it is the first step." She stands up and rests Roosevelt on her hip, "Anyway, want to come see the studio? You haven't been in there for almost a year!"

I nod, stand up and follow her out, still processing this eye-opening information. I walk behind her as we go outside and walk around the corner to their studio that's on their property. It is a detached three car garage that they converted into an office space on one side and a large studio on the other side. I'm itching to go inside, so much that my skin could fall off. I know I won't be working here ever again, but it still feels weird, like I'm saying one last goodbye and it's the end of an era.

I walk through the entrance door, and the nostalgic smells hit me at once, followed by a flood of memories. My heart lifts with happiness and I look around at the modest studio office. I loved working here and dealing with seniors, weddings, newborns and boudoir clients. I handled the office work for everything. From the booking to the billing. I miss it terribly. Even the office mascot, their little black dog that hangs out in the studio and likes to bark when someone walks in the doors. I smile at him and give his head a little scratch.

Karen is sitting at my desk, I mean my old desk, and looks up when we enter the studio. "Hi Karen, Elise came to visit today," Kyla says, pointing her thumb behind her, at me.

Karen waves at me and says "Hi, Elise!" then turns to Kyla, "Ashton is in the back doing some senior portraits." I politely wave back to return the greeting.

"OK. No problem, we won't go back there." Then Kyla shows me that they've added a fresh coat of paint to the walls and a nice little Keurig coffee bar for people to enjoy while they come into the studio.

"That is so fun! I love that you're offering that now. Makes it feel less like a dental office and more like a welcoming photography studio." I say as I peruse the coffee, tea and cocoa options they have on display.

"Then we added a couple more colors to our back drops in the back there, but since Ashton is in a session I won't show you that." She waves at the white door acting as a veil separating the office from the studio.

"Yeah, no problem," I say. "It's so nice to be back here again. Who knows, this is probably my last time too," I say with a side grin, knowing that my move to Georgia is probably going to be a permanent one.

"Don't say that. You're welcome to come hang out any time you want to," she says as she flitters one hand into the air as if to sprinkle fairy dust on the situation to make reality sparkle more.

"I appreciate that." I cross my arms in front of me and smile.

"Oh!" Her back springs to action as if being pulled up by a puppeteer. "Let me show you what we did for fall photos last year, while you were gone! We still have it set up! It's so cute." She turns and walks out the front door to head outside, still holding Roosevelt.

"I only have a minute before I have to go to work," I tell Kyla and she nods. I turn to Karen, "Bye, Karen. Good to see you." Then as I'm turning to the exit Karen replies in kind before I walk outside.

Once outside I follow Kyla to her backyard which is nicely manicured. Behind that nicely manicured lawn is a fence and beyond that is a giant field of tall brown grass. We go through the gate of the fence and we start walking toward an old rusty 1940s Ford F-100. The Ford is perfectly poised in the middle of all the tall grass. It has a couple of hay bales strategically placed on the bed of the truck and on the ground to the side of it for people to pose on.

"This is adorable. I love it!" I say truthfully, and I walk around it, as my inner photographer takes in all the angles. I can see right away that this would be a hit with the senior portraits.

"Thanks! Everyone loved it last fall. We did have some sunflowers hanging out the window, but those all dried up. We'll use it next school season too and I'll get more sunflowers to add a pop of color," she informs me with a flick of all her fingers. One arm momma style.

Staring at the old rusty 1940s Ford reminds me of a guy I made out with when I was nineteen. He owned one of these old trucks and he would pick me up to go out to eat and we'd end the night making out in his truck. I ended things with him because I felt like he liked me too much and that made me feel uncomfortable. Hmm. It's interesting now that I have Kyla's words in my head. Maybe I just self-sabotaged that relationship and it never became anything more because of...me.

I scrunch my nose at the memory. "I'm sorry to cut this short but I gotta run."

"No problem!" she says as she turns to lead me back to the driveway. Her and Roosevelt wave to me as I start my car and pull onto the road heading for work.

Once I pull into my job's parking lot, I look at my phone and see some texts from Dean.

"I hit a bird today while I was driving. It was tragic. The little guy flew over the hood of my car and landed on the road behind me."

I smile at how random his text messages can be.

"**Oh my god! That's awful!**" I type back with wide eyes. "**I've never hit a bird before. I probably wouldn't know what to do if that happened to me.**"

I don't have to wait long before he sends a text back saying, "**I had to keep driving. His life was already taken. There's nothing that could be done.**"

I reply, "**Poor little guy.**" Then, still sitting in my car, I sent him another one right after, "**Hey, did you ever figure out what was going on with your car?**" Bringing up a conversation we were having earlier this morning. I like that we talk a lot about nothing. All of the mundane things that happen to us.

"**It was the radiator hose. It kept slipping. I have to drop my car off at the mechanic in a couple days so they can fix it. In the meantime, I shouldn't be driving it so I'll have to find a coworker to pick me up and help me get to work.**"

"**Oh man what a drag! I'm so sorry.**" As I show my teeth to my phone in an unflattering way, then ask, "**Is that expensive?**"

"**It'll be quite a few hundred dollars I think.**"

"**Ouch. That sucks.**"

"**I agree. It'll be a third of my paycheck.**"

"**Oooph. That's the worst! Hey, I'm sorry to cut this short. I have to go to work now.**"

"**No problem. Talk tonight?**"

"**Yes, of course! I'll talk to you then.**"

"**Can't wait,**" he says.

I put my phone in my bag and walk into the grocery store. I can't stop grinning as I fix my signature messy bun. I think it's the coolest thing that I have a boy that likes me so much he wants to talk to me on the phone. I ignore the uncomfortable feeling that wants to vomit up out of me.

We've been talking every other night for the past two months. I've got another six-hour shift ahead of me and another night full of hours talking to a boy.

Chapter 17

Past

July

I have to fully prepare my brain, my senses, and my hands as my family and I get ready to go on our annual, week-long camping trip. The campground doesn't have any cell service, which is great if you want to unwind and unplug from society. It's not great if you have an addiction to texting and calling a guy back in the real world.

My family goes to a lake in Republic, Washington, every year called Curlew Lake. Curlew is a man-made lake surrounded by hills and it has a campground on it that's well kept. The campground looks like a field of grass that has been sectioned off into individual camping spots.

My family has tried going to other campgrounds, but they're all useless, made up of concrete and gravel. Who dreams of grey when they seek an escape from normal life? Curlew gives us grass and trees while we spend our time outdoors. The lake is murky and you come out of it covered in little algae blooms, but we don't care. There's so many other positives to this recreational haven.

The no cell service part is probably the only drawback. The one place I have ever been able to get a couple cell service bars is on the swings at the community area of the campground, which is clear on the other side of the campground from my family's sites.

The upcoming week feels bleak as I think about all the hours of the day I won't be able to chat with Dean. On the upside, the small town of Republic is just a short 10-minute drive away and I could be back in society with access to my calls and texts if I get desperate.

This hilly site has been my family's yearly gathering spot for 4 generations now. For the seven days we are here, my *entire* family goes. I'm talking about grandma, grandpa, siblings, parents, aunts, uncles, great aunts, great uncles, first cousins, second cousins, thirds cousins, nieces and nephews. The WHOLE crew! We take up half the campground with our horde. We're not a rowdy bunch, just a group of people that want to stay connected.

I love my extended family, but I get so overwhelmed with having all these people around at once. So I lay like a chameleon blending into the hammock I call home. Hoping to be seen, given a gentle smile, but not spoken to.

Every year I wish I could take a significant other here so I can spend the time boating, sunbathing and generally relaxing hand in hand with a boyfriend. This year my far-fetched whimsy is still screaming at me. I tried to convince Dean to come so I could fulfill my lifelong daydream, but he couldn't make it because this was the same weekend his work was honoring him for some award. *Damn, why does he have to be so accomplished?* So, I spend my days with no extra hand in mine. Flying around on the family boat and lying in the sun, as lonely as an alley cat.

After a few days of camping and no texting I'm jonesing for some conversation with Dean. I did warn him that I would be camping and out of cell service so he doesn't think I'm ignoring him. I'm hoping he's just as desperate for conversation with me as I am with him. So, after three days of lounging, reading, and tubing behind the boat I go to the swings with my phone to see if I can get one bar of cell service.

It took a few minutes of walking in little figure eight sequences in the small ten by ten area before I finally get it. I stand frozen like a human statue who's busking on a big city street, afraid to move or I'll lose my one bar of hope. Some texts came through. They were from the man himself.

"Hey stranger, hope you're having fun living with the mosquitoes and grass." The timestamp is from yesterday morning.

He sent, **"I guess this means I'm thinking of you."** only a few hours later.

A smile crosses my face. He really has been jonesing for me too. I start sending my replies.

"Hey stranger, it's been fun. I've made friends with the mosquitoes this year. I haven't been bitten very much."

"I've been thinking of you too, more than ever. I hope the award ceremony went well."

I hit send and don't dare move an arm or else I risk the bar of service going away. I wait around for a couple minutes. My attempt at standing like a mannequin doesn't help because the one and only bar that I get isn't sticking around. It's playing peek-a-boo with me. I look up and start thinking about going back to the campsite after ten minutes of standing still waiting for a text to come back, when my phone chimes.

I turn my head back down to my hands. He responded.

"I'm sure your skin is relieved."

"You saying you're thinking of me too brings life to my bones. I'm beaming, Elise. Beaming."

I smile at my phone as I read.

"The ceremony was so small it was almost not worth my time. They gave me a little plaque and we had cake. I'd have rather come camping with you in hindsight."

I swear I can hear music in my ears. I look around for the sound but soon realize that it's just my own happiness.

"Ahh! Beaming! :D"

"I'm so happy to hear that! It would have been fun to have you here! My extended family is so nice. Plus, it's warm and with the lake so close by it's a refreshing place to vacation."

I hit send and feel an itch on my forehead that I force myself not to scratch.

He replies, **"That sounds too good to be true."** and I start to feel an ache in my chest for his live presence.

"You have no idea."

My favorite thing about texting him is that I don't have to ask a question in order to get a response. I can almost guarantee that I'll get a response even if my texts don't have very much content. It's like being carried on a cloud of confidence.

I hear my phone chime again and look at my screen.

"Been out on the boat a lot this trip?"

"Yes! We've been out every day. I typically go tubing with my siblings. Esther is the one who drives the boat for all of us. It's very kind of her since it means she's out on the lake all day long. I'm sure she gets tired of it though."

I shift to my left foot to give my right one a break. I like that he's met all my siblings at the wedding so I don't have to go into too many details.

"Wow. She's a rockstar!"

"I agree! Rockstar is a great way to describe her."

I smile at his kindness.

I hear my name and lift my head to see Esther coming right for me. "Hey El, we're getting ready for dinner." I nod at her and say, "Okay!"

I look back down at my phone and start typing, **"Oh shoot! I need to go back to the campsite for dinner. So I won't have cell service again. It was nice to feel normal again and be texting you!"**

I wait just a minute to see if I can get a quick text back and I'm not disappointed. He responds with, **"I agree. I've been feeling like a piece of me is missing without texting you. I can't wait to talk to you soon!"**

I get goosebumps all over my arm as I turn off my phone and run to catch up with Esther.

The next couple of nights fly by with all of us finding different ways to relax during the day and then everyone coming together at night to eat and play card games.

While we are playing cards on our fifth night, we all talk about going into town tomorrow so we can get some end of the week items from Anderson's grocery store. After five days of camping we've run out of a couple of things. We always do a grocery run at least once during the trip. I want to try and call Dean tomorrow during our hour in town, so when Emily suggests driving down tomorrow, I yell, "I'M IN!" with a little too much enthusiasm that it made a few people jump around the card table.

After breakfast we load up as many of us that can fit into our cars and head into Republic. The drive there is an ordinary backcountry one. Fields of brown grass with cabins or manufactured homes tucked in the back. You might see a single cow, horse, or goat, but no big farms with large amounts of grazing animals.

This town feels very similar to Yelm. Two small competing grocery stores. A hardware store. A couple mom and pop restaurants. My favorite place to go in town is the ice cream shop. When we arrive we park in Anderson's parking lot and disperse. Mom goes into the grocery store to get items we ran out of. Dad and Forrest go to the hardware store to get more fishing equipment. Fred and Emily go find a coffee shop that they can relax in as adorable newlyweds. Then Esther, Michael, and I go to the ice cream shop.

"Hear from Dean at all?" Our walking silence is broken when Esther turns her head to ask me this. Her and Michael are ahead of me on the small-town sidewalk.

"Yes, we were texting a little bit the other day," I say to the back of her head.

"Oooooh. What about?" Esther asks while turning her body sideways and crab shuffling up the sidewalk now.

"Just that he's thinking of me and hoping I'm having a good time here." I try to give her the best part of our texting convo.

"Ahhh, that's sweet. The few interactions I had with him at the wedding, he really showed his genuine side. And then you two dancing, gah, I could really picture you together," she says as she holds up her hands like she's putting a picture frame around me.

I turn my head down and look away from her, then say, "I'm starting to like him a lot. It scares me."

"Why would it scare you?" she asks.

"Because what if he breaks my heart, or worse, decides that he doesn't like something about me? I've been told lately that I push guys away when there's nothing wrong with them, so I'm trying to really process what the meaning behind that is." I sheepishly grin at her.

"Oh yeah, you did that with Luke and Beau in high school."

"Not you too! Ugh." I look down at my feet. "I had no idea I was doing any of this. Those guys just all of a sudden made me feel uncomfortable with how much they liked me, and I didn't like it so I stopped being friends with them. Is that what I've done with every single one of these guys in my past? Pushed them away because their feelings for me made me feel uncomfortable?" I squint my eyes trying to figure it out. "That can't be. Can it? No, it can't be. Why would I do that though?"

"It sounds like you're onto something. I'd really think about it because if Dean is ever going to be something then you don't want to push him away before he can be." She turns to walk into the ice cream shop before adding, "I hope the story of him has a happy ending."

"I kinda do too." I grab the door from her to walk in.

Once inside we crowd around the ice cream in the glass top freezer, like kids around a tv, to read all their flavor options. My favorite ones are chocolate chip cookie dough and anything with chocolate and peanut butter. The ice-creamologist serves us pretty quickly and I walk away with the beginning of a sugar rush, thanks to my chocolate chip cookie dough in a waffle cone.

I walk outside to open my phone and call Dean.

After two rings I hear, "Why hello, good to hear from the best volleyball player on the planet."

"You flatter me," I reply as I take a lick of my ice cream.

"I started to think you forgot about me," he replies.

"I don't think that's even possible," I say as heat enters my cheeks. Either from the sun I'm standing in or from my obvious flirtatious compliment, it's hard to tell.

"Have you guys played volleyball yet? I know you said that you normally round up for a game during your camping trip," he says and the red cheeks stay. He remembers everything I tell him.

"We actually have!" I light up. "It was fun. We played boys versus girls. Which in hindsight might have been a bad idea because all the boys in the family are super athletic and competitive, so they play to win. They were hitting the ball down at us so hard we were blowing up. Unfortunately, we just weren't fast enough to return the ball back to them in any aggressive way. So we lost," I say as I step into the shade of the sideways awnings, because this heat is turning my ice cream into the wicked witch of the west and I want to enjoy it myself, not feed it to the sidewalk.

"That's too bad. I wish I was there to help."

I lean against an exterior wall of a local business and smile down at my ice cream. "I would have liked that. Hey, there's always next year," I say before I can stop myself. I don't know what life will look like next summer and inviting him to something a whole year out has me sweating now.

"I'll be there!" he replies emphatically and I wish I could reach out and hug him.

"Ahh you're so nice!" I say licking two trails of ice cream sprinting down my waffle cone like they're trying to win a race. "What have you been up to?"

"Working, hiking and playing video games. My three favorite pastimes." He chuckles. "I've actually been thinking a lot about coming to visit you." He pauses and I stay silent holding my breath. "Do you think I could do that next month? I was thinking the end of August?" he asks.

I can't hardly control the bubble of indigestion now stuck in my throat, or is that excitement? My adrenaline kicks in and I start shaking a little. I try to make it sound like nothing is actually happening on my side of the phone and ask, "Are you serious?! You really want to visit in August?"

"Yeah, if you'll have me," he replies.

"I would love for you to visit!" Emphasis on the word LOVE. I bounce on my tippy toes as I continue, "No one has ever come to visit me before!" I stop bouncing. "I need to confess, I have actually been planning an Epic Yelm Tour in hopes that you were actually gonna follow through with what you said, and make a trip to me." I clench my teeth and hold my hand up to my nose where my ice cream is now an inch from my forehead.

"Elise, you're making me swoon like a surprised maiden. I would be honored to be driven around in a tour you created for me of your hometown," he says and I can hear the smile in his voice.

All the clenching in my body releases as he says this and I do a happy dance in the middle of the sidewalk. "You always find a way to flatter me while you're being flattered," I say, starting to bite into my waffle cone now.

"You deserve to be adored. And I'm just the man to do it," he says and I smile and squeeze my eyes shut to let that sink in. I don't think I've ever wanted to lean into a boy liking me more than I do with him.

"That's sweet. Thank you." We sit on the phone in silence for a minute while I collect my hopeless romantic self, then I ask, "Have you beat your next mission of zombies?" Changing my attention to him.

"Yes, actually! Those brainless, heartless wannabes don't know what hit 'em." He made a grunt sound like he was punching the air. He clearly has a vendetta against supernaturally undead humans.

"Go get 'em!" I push my ice cream cone fist into the air just as Esther and Michael walk out of the shop. Esther nods her head gesturing to the direction that they are starting to walk and implying that I should follow.

I'm walking when Dean asks, "What are you up to now?"

"Oh, we just got some ice cream and now I think we're meeting up with the family again. Not sure what we're doing next." I take another bite of my cone, no longer inflicted by the running events that my ice cream was trying to play.

"Thank you for thinking of me during your outing. Don't forget the mosquito repellent. I've heard that area is a mosquito circus," he jokes.

"Nothing but elephant tricks and lion tamers around here. We've got you covered for all your entertainment needs," I say trying to tease him back.

"I wouldn't expect anything less from the company you keep," he laughs.

"I have a reputation to uphold," I say laughing back. We get back to the parking lot and the rest of my family is waiting around for us. "Oh sorry, looks like we're about to head back. I lose cell service a minute out of town, so I'll have to hang up now. It was good to hear your voice! I can't wait to see you at the end of August! And I'll text you when we leave here in a couple days," I say as I'm getting closer to my family.

"No problem! Thanks for calling. Have a good end to your trip. Don't miss me too much," he flirts.

"I can't promise anything," I flirt back. Then we say goodbye and I put my phone back in my pocket.

When I reach Fremily's car to load up, Fred says, "Monopolizing my friends time again?"

"Who's asking?" I throw the final piece of waffle cone in my mouth.

"His mom texted me," he jokes.

I nearly choke., "Tell her I'm sorry and that he's available now."

"She appreciates your mindfulness." He smiles back.

I laugh and then get into the car. As we drive back to camp, I watch the fields roll by and think about Dean visiting me in a month. I'm excited to see him again. His awareness of what kind of person I am and his personality has me falling.

The next couple of days go by with potlucks, dock jumping, and boat trips on the water. I've had fun but I'm ready for it to be over by the time our last day comes. Not having cell service has been so hard. Especially since I've become accustomed to texting Dean all day, every day. We pay for our trip and drive out of the only place left in America that doesn't have cell service. I look down at my phone to see text messages starting to come through from Dean. He's missed me. I smile and start my replies.

Chapter 18

Past

August

"**I**'m catching the 7am flight from LAX and I'll be landing at 8:25am in SeaTac. I shouldn't get lost finding baggage claim, but send in reinforcements if you don't hear from me.**"**

I'm already wide awake in bed when my phone buzzes at 5am. Today is the day he's going to visit and I couldn't sleep at all last night. I felt like the energizer bunny.

I grab my phone to read his text, then smile as I respond, **"Got it. I'll be the one in the Red Ford Explorer. LOL. I haven't told you yet, but I've had plastic surgery so you won't recognize me. I look completely different."** I hit send as my shoulders shake with small giggles.

He texts back, **"Ok! I'll be the tall one with brown hair and a goofy grin on his face. Hopefully I get into the correct Ford Explorer or else I'll be having a weekend with someone completely different than I expected to LOL :P."**

I laugh out loud and respond, **"Could you imagine?"**

"I don't want to. LOL"

"Haha! Did I mention yet that you coming to FINALLY visit me is adding those additional 100 cool points I've been hanging over your head? Your total is officially up to 185 now LOL."

Throughout the past few months of talking and texting he's earned himself quite a few invisible status symbols.

"I've been thinking about this for weeks. I'm excited to officially get those cool points. It might be the driving reason that I'm showing up today."

I wiggle with giddiness in my bed.

"You've earned them."

"Can't wait to show you around my old stomping grounds. I finally get to show someone my favorite parts of town!"

"I can't wait to see it all for myself. You've talked about your life there enough that I've created an image in my head. I'm curious to see if it matches the hype." he texts back.

"Oh, it will. Or it will disappoint you to the same extreme and give you the perfect story to tell your grandkids someday."

"That's all I ask."

"But hey, I've got to finish getting ready and head to the airport. I'll text when I land." He sends one text after the other.

"Sounds good!"

I can't wait to see him. I finished creating my Epic Yelm Tour last night. Complete with stops that make up who I am. I've written it out in North to South order, so that we don't have to double back. It feeds a level of my OCD by being very efficient. I'm so curious if we'll get through all of it today or if it will be filling our time between the two days that he's here.

The wait is horrendous. I've tried to speed up father time, but I couldn't busy myself enough. I cleaned the dishes, wiped down all the countertops, even started vacuuming each room.

I finally had to stop when I remembered that no one was awake and the vacuum was probably not the most pleasant way to wake up. Before leaving I remembered that I had to pack something as a surprise for Dean halfway through my tour. My brother-in-law, Michael, helped me get this part ready and I can't wait to see the look on Dean's face when we stop at number eight on the list.

I head to SeaTac and my ever-reliable invisible bugs start fluttering in my stomach. I've been daydreaming about what it will be like to see him again. Now that we've developed a close something-ship I can't imagine it being a bland one. Just being in his presence will probably be satisfying enough.

I look down at my speedometer and see that I've caught the lead foot disease. I lift my foot off the gas to try and slow down. All this excitement has me anxious to get there fast. I reach out and turn the radio up. Sweet Caroline is on and it makes me smile. Thinking about how he belted out that song back at Fremily's wedding has turned my butterflies into ants crawling on my skin, I'm vibrating.

I'm just coming up to his airline's sign when I see him come out the doors, more handsome than I remember. I stop the car right in front of him and throw it into PARK. We lock eyes instantly and he walks quickly to the car while I hurry out the driver's side door to meet him on the sidewalk.

He throws his bags down on the ground and our bodies slam into each other as we hug. We stand there holding on for the longest time. Like two souls finding each other again. I feel his big hands wrapped around my back, holding on tight like he's never going to let go. He lifts me up into the air so he's not bending over anymore, and my feet dangle six inches from the ground. Our breath is the only thing I'm thinking about. We start to breathe in sync with each other as we're on the sidewalk wrapped in each other's arms, daring anyone to tell us to move along.

He's the first one to pull away. He puts me down and I look up at him and start to feel sweat behind my knees. He's so tall. He smiles down at me and grabs my face so we can look into each other's eyes. A rush of electricity runs through my body as I think he's going in for a kiss. We stare at each other for a few minutes before I put my hands on both of his wrists and just hold on. We're both smiling at each other when he steps back and says, "Let me look at you." I'm thrown off balance but I'm a good listener so I do a 360-degree turn. "Yep. Just as I remember you. You're the person I've been talking to this whole time. I'm glad I wasn't being catfished."

I go back in for another hug and we sway from side to side while I laugh so hard I shed a tear and say into his chest, "Could you imagine Fred playing the biggest trick on you and not letting you know it was never my number that he gave you!"

"He'd owe me his firstborn if he ever did that." He rests his chin on my head. "I'm so glad he didn't though!" he exclaims as he squeezes me tight. This is actually the first time we've ever hugged. At the wedding we danced and had a couple of electrifying arm grazes that were out of this world but never really became friendly enough to pop our hug bubble. After one final squeeze we both pull away and I help him get his bags into my car.

I start driving us back to Yelm and he says, "I'm also glad you didn't get that plastic surgery you mentioned."

I make a squawk sounding laugh and say, "Oh, that's right, I did mention that this morning." I cover my mouth with my hand and look over at him before talking through my fingers, "I'm so sorry I did that.

I only slightly wanted to stress you out. Turns out, I was lying." I shrug my shoulders and lift my palms up to the ceiling before putting on hand back on the steering wheel and the other one on the gear shifter.

"What a relief," he says and his hand moves toward my right hand resting on the gear shifter. I catch my breath, but he moves right past it for some gum in the center console. I could turn on a light bulb with the electricity coursing through my fingers. I steady my breath and try to find another subject to talk about. "So, umm, how was your flight?"

"Pretty uneventful. No turbulence or delays. There were a couple of babies on board that sang a duet with their cries. It lulled me right to sleep," he chuckles.

"I love that!" I laugh, "Baby duets are the best." I smile at the image. "So, I know you just got off a plane but I want to start your tour of the town right away. I brought my tour list that I told you I was making," I say as I pat my pocket. "You ok with that?"

"I'm your captive for the weekend."

"You can't see where we're going, but what really matters is that I'm having fun the whole time and you'll be along for the ride." I laugh a little, trying to continue sharing my clever thoughts with the class and hoping he finds me funny.

"Anywhere you want to take me, I won't protest." He licks his lips.

"You don't know what you just agreed to," I say with a sinister laugh.

We drive in silence for a while and I feel completely at ease. I don't think we need to fill the silence in order to know that we're enjoying ourselves.

As we turn off I-5 and head down Nisqually Road we're surrounded by evergreen trees that line the road on both sides, so dense, with barely any houses around. It feels like we've entered the forest. No more city life. No more tall buildings. Just the open road and green foliage for miles.

"Hey, what mountain was that off in the distance when we were leaving SeaTac Airport?" he asks as he points behind him.

"That was Mt. Rainier."

"Oh, wow. That was pretty."

"I agree. There's this spot in Yelm when you're driving down the road and the trees perfectly frame the mountain on both sides," I say, keeping it to myself that I will bring him there on our tour today or tomorrow. "Fun fact, there is a town called Rainier close by. Its boundary lines actually border Yelm's."

"No way! That's really cool. How do you keep them straight?" he asks.

"If we're talking about the mountain we'll say Mount Rainier, but if we're talking about the town then we just say Rainier," I say as I merge the car onto a roundabout that feels out of place in these woods.

"I'm happy to learn the ways of the locals to fit in."

"Good. Don't call the mountain just 'Rainier' or you'll be an outcast." I squint my eyes and point my finger at him playfully.

"I wouldn't dare," he says as he holds up his hands to surrender. This weekend is going to be fun having him around.

Once we reach the top of Yelm I turn to him with a flourish of dramatics, chin down, eyes wide, and ask in a low voice, "Are you ready?"

He lowers his chin and responds back, "For anything and everything, Elise."

"Alrighty!" I sit up straight. "We're hitting our first stop," I say as we pull into the parking lot of a school. "What we have here"—I nod to the building in front of us—"is Southworth Elementary. This was the first place I ever went to school." I park the car and proceed to get out. Dean follows suit and I walk him toward the school.

"I spent only one year here. My worst year of school, kindergarten. The year you get weaned off your parents." I smile and look down at my feet. "I remember my mom dropping me off at my classroom and I was so scared to go into the room by myself that I ran back to her when I realized she wasn't coming with me." I point at one of the classrooms across the pavement. "She held me somewhere over there until I was ready and then the teacher walked with me into the room to show me the cool coloring area. My mom waved at me from the window and with tears in my eyes I waved back and gave into the experience."

"What a good mom," he pauses and looks at me until I lift my head to make eye contact. "I can see little Elise at the window waving to her mom with tears in her eyes and excitement in the coloring table." He gestures toward a cluster of windows, asking, "Do you still like coloring?" as he winks at me.

I smile at his question, happy to share more of myself with him. "Hmm, I guess I do still like coloring." I tilt my head and look up at the roofline. "That might be why I was so drawn to photography. I prefer landscape over portrait photography, but those jobs are hard to get." I lead him between two buildings and walk down a breezeway. "Do you like coloring?" I ask him.

"I'm a regular dude. I don't pull out my coloring books anymore." He puts his hands in his pockets and shrugs.

I laugh. "Fair enough, I'll appreciate coloring for the both of us. But this is a good segue becaaaause"—we round a corner—"there is this giant map of the World on the concrete." I open my arms wide as if to reveal a big prize. The world map has every state colored in like a rainbow.

My childhood heart sings at the sight of it. "This used to be one of my favorite things to do during recess."

He looks around in silence to take it all in. "I love it. This looks like a dream play area for little Elise," he says and he holds his hand out for me to take it.

I grab his hand and he pulls me close to him and starts swaying.

"What are you doing?" I ask.

"Dancing on the world," he replies as he tightens his arm around my waist.

"Little Elise never thought this would happen." I sway with him to the non-existent music.

He brushes a hair out of my face. "I'm sorry you were sad when your mom left you on the first day of kindergarten."

I smile at how soft his touch is, "Thank you, no one's ever cared enough to sympathize with me about it," I say as a whisper. Then we sway back and forth, already starting my tour off right.

After a few minutes I start to feel out of place, so I pull away and step back to say, "Well this is it. The first stop on the tour," and I tilt my body from side to side as if I'm a hula dancer on the dash of a car.

"Epic," he says, standing there like a towering tree ready to shade me with his love.

I smile and scratch my arm as I say, "Now let's head back to the car and continue our tour."

We walk close to each other while we head back to the car. Not quite touching but almost. I can feel the electricity coming off his arm.

I pull back onto the road and show him the next three stops. Explaining how each one weaved into my childhood. After explaining to him that crazy-lizard-conspiracy-people live here I ask him, "Has this town surprised you yet?"

"Abso-freaking-lutely." he looks behind us to get another view of the building now in our rearview, "I wanted to make sure that actual lizards weren't coming out of the ground." He wiggles his hands in the air like he wants to avoid something spooky.

"Don't worry, they won't getcha." I laugh at his fake discomfort.

"Good." He turns back around and adjusts the strap to his seatbelt.

I giggle and turn the car into another parking lot, this time for the local high school. "Here we are. We've arrived at my favorite spot during my high school years. The sports fields," I say as I put the car in park and open my door to get out.

"Is this where little Elise turned into teenage Elise?" He looks around in awe. "I can picture you playing soccer just dripping the ball down the field," he says as he starts to kick his feet around with an imaginary ball.

"Jokes on you because I didn't play soccer." I cross my arms. "I threw the shot put in high school track and field." I stick my tongue out at him.

"Ooooh, color me impressed. How far could you throw the shot put?" he asks as he steps back and his eyes look me up and down.

"36 feet, 6 inches." I hold my head high and puff out my chest a little.

"Is that good?" he asks.

"It made me place 8th in State in my senior year. So it's up there." I shrug my shoulders and start walking him toward the track.

"Whoa! Nice work. Looks like Elise has more to her than just coloring. You're a combination of sporty and artistic. I like that in a woman."

"Thank you," I pause on the track and put my hands on my hips. "I've got many layers." I pretend to toss my hair with a smile, even though it's pulled up in my signature messy bun.

"So, did you bring a shot put today to prove it?" he asks as he pretends to look around us for a round metal ball.

"Ha! That would have been a nice addition. Unfortunately, I did not. You'll just have to take my word for it." I lift an eyebrow at him.

"Can you be trusted with telling the truth?" He winks.

"Oh, yes," I pause. "Trust me." I wink back.

"I believe you actually."

"Good." I push his shoulder because I've now regressed back into a teenage girl. When all he does is rub his shoulder and look down at me with a smile I say, "I played volleyball here too. Let's walk that way and see if we can peek into the gymnasium. I doubt it but let's try." I start to skip and lead him toward the gymnasium.

"You're doing a great job with the tour by the way," he says as he speeds up to keep pace with me.

I look over at his eyes and smile. "Thank you. I've been thinking about this for ages, so I've carefully picked out all my talking points." I feel tingles run to my stomach.

"I'm enjoying it. Keep it up." He brushes elbows with me, and I forget how to walk.

"Why thank you," I say as I remind myself that one foot goes in front of the other.

We weave through all the buildings until I find the one that I know is the gymnasium. "So this is the gym where I played volleyball," I say as I turn to face him and gesture with both arms up at the building like Vanna White on Wheel of Fortune.

"It's amazing!" He opens his mouth in a wide smile. "Looks like the outside of every gym I've ever seen."

"No way!" I exaggerate. "I thought this would be something you've never seen before." I wink at him and wave my arm for him to follow me. "Let's peek in."

We walk up to the little window in the door and as we both lean in our cheeks touch. I point to the right. "Look at those white lines on the ground, those are the volleyball boundaries." I try to steady my breathing and hope my cheek doesn't sweat.

"Ooooh, and you played right here for a crowd of people?" he asks, not moving away from my cheek.

"Yep. A crowd of one hundred would stare at us in our cute volleyball uniforms as we passed a ball around." I laugh and my cheek bounces around against his face. *I wish he would turn and kiss me.*

"Elise, a cute little volleyball player. Do you miss it?" he asks and stands up.

A little disappointed that he broke the physical contact but not wanting to show it, I stood up at the same time and replied, "I do. I loved being a part of a team. It's like you get to see your community of people every day at practice. I get sad when I make a group of friends and then we have to part ways because life moves on. If I could lasso all my favorite people and make them live in the same town, I would." I look down at the ground and feel nervous that I just admitted to him something I've only ever thought in my head.

"I like that you just said that. I've often had that thought myself." He reaches out and puts his hand on my shoulder.

I put my hand on his hand and look up at him. "Really? That makes me feel less naive."

"You're not naive. You're honest. I like that." He starts moving his fingers under my hand to rub my shoulder.

"You're sweet." I mimic his action, stroking his fingers under my hand. We stand there staring at each other, neither of us making a move. My head starts to spin, and I feel uncomfortable sitting in limbo. I take my hand down and say, "Let's head back to the car and go to our next stop."

"You're the boss," he says and we walk back to my car.

We continued on to the next three stops which included lunch at a local Japanese restaurant.

On our way to the eighth stop, I ask him, "Impressed so far?"

"Not surprisingly, yes. This town is a little bigger than I thought it would be." he smiles over at me in the front seat.

"Wait till I bring you to Rainier. That's probably gonna meet *all* your expectations." I lift my eyebrow a couple times like I'm keeping a secret.

"I can't wait. I've never seen a tiny town," he replies and I see his arm move closer to mine on the center console. I glance down without moving my head to see that only an inch is separating us. I try not to stare at our arms for too long, feeling like a fish that can't blink. "Where are we headed?" Dean asks.

"You'll see," I say with a cheeky grin.

I take a right and pull into a gravel parking spot. "Here we are, stop number eight." We both look at what's in front of us.

"Your local skate park?!" He asks with enthusiasm and turns to search my face.

"Yep!" I say. "I have a skateboard in the back just waiting for you. Michael is letting me borrow it so you can grind the pavement," I tell him, smiling with joy at this surprise.

"No way!" He beams. "You thought of me during this tour? This is the nicest thing ever." He turns to the back and looks down at the skateboard on the ground with a jacket draped over it. He grabs it and we head over to the concrete area with all its metal bars and ramps.

"Thank you, Elise," he hugs me before he runs a quick few steps and puts the skateboard under his feet to start doing skater dude tricks.

I found a seat on one of the concrete walls bordering the skate park. Watching Dean makes me remember that I used to love going to the skate park with a boy to watch him skate when I was in high school. I've always been a skater chick at heart even though I don't know how to skate at all. I smile as I watch the enjoyment on Dean's face. I'm trying to remember how that friendship ended. *Ahh man, that was probably me who ended it.*

After a while he glides my way. He quickly hops off his skateboard like a gazelle, stands in front of me and looks down so our faces are level with each other. With a warm breath on my face he asks, "Do you wanna learn?"

I grin up at him and slowly say, "Yes." I pop up and let him lead me over to a corner of the skatepark that doesn't have anyone.

He puts the skateboard on the ground. "Okay. Let me go through a little of the beginner skills," he says. "First, you have to put one foot on the board and push off. Second, you have to stay on the board," he teases.

"Oh, is that how skateboarding works? I didn't know," I tease back.

He smiles then gestures toward the skateboard on the ground. "Now put one foot on the board and leave one foot on the ground."

Then he takes my hand and tingles race up my arm. He keeps his eyes on my feet and the skateboard and says, "I'll help you balance as you push off with the foot on the ground to get yourself to go." I adjust my foot in the middle of the skateboard and push off with my left foot as he keeps holding my hand to lead me in a straight line. I think this is the skater equivalent of someone teaching you how to golf and walking up behind you, wrapping their arms around you and showing you how to swing the club at the ball.

He looks at me with pride in his eyes and says, "Good job. Now let's turn around and go back. This time push off and try to put that left foot on the back of the board and just let the skateboard glide under you. Use your arms to balance and bend your knees a little."

Still holding my hand to keep me balanced, he watches me as I push off and place my left foot on the back of the board. I wobble a little bit and the board flies out from under me. I almost hit the ground, but he catches me around my waist with his other arm, leaving my nose an inch from the pavement. I can feel his arm hold tight as my body is parallel to the ground. Slowly, he lifts me up to steady me as I get my feet back under my body. I turn around to face him and his arm is still wrapped around my waist. I look up into his eyes, and we stare at each other for what feels like hours. Neither one of us is moving. My face feels flushed and my heartbeat increases.

I decide to awkwardly break the heart pounding moment by saying, "It's so hard to let it 'glide under me' as you say because all I can think about is how it could have a mind of its own and slip away, leaving me landing on the concrete." I look around and then up at him, still wrapped in his arms and give a nervous half laugh. "Exactly like what just happened."

"I get it. Your first time can be difficult," he says and his hand slowly unwraps around my waist, feeling every canyon of my back before he drops it to his side. "It's cute to watch you try though. Would you like my help balancing again or do you want to try it by yourself?" he offers.

I don't really want to stop holding his hand, but I want him to see that I can push myself in a task. So I tell him, "I'll try by myself." I feel a mix of regret and discomfort when I get back to my starting point and push off.

Running through all the tips he gave me I try to execute them as gracefully as possible. I have to harness the power of the gazelle like he does. I start wobbling and the board slips out from under me, but I catch myself before hitting the ground.

I look up and he's running over to me. "Are you ok!?" he asks, getting down on the pavement with me.

"Yeah, I just need to learn how to balance on it better," I reply.

"You'll get it," he says as he reaches for my hand to help me get up. If only all these hand holding interactions didn't have to leave me with scrapes.

"Thanks. I think I'll try one more time and see how it goes," I say, wiping off the dirt from my pants and collecting my confidence.

I turn the skateboard around and put all I've learned to the test. I go slow, keep my balance, and make it twenty feet without falling.

"I did it!" I say as I hop off the board. "I probably went elementary-school speed, but I didn't fall this time. That's a win!" I do a big jump in the air. "I'm done though," I say as I rub my butt that is starting to bruise. "Thanks for showing me how to do it!"

"You're welcome," he says. "I'm done here too. Let's head to the next stop, Miss Tour Guide." He leans down to grab the board off the ground, and we head back to my car.

Chapter 19

Past

August

The next five stops are quick drive-by's. I show him my favorite back road, a bunker house built into the side of a hill, and the photography studio where I used to work. We finish our day by looking at what movies are available to watch tonight. We land on Happy in Holland and head back to my house for dinner.

At the house he puts his bag in the spare room and we go out to the living room to hang out with my parents and brother before dinner. None of my other siblings live at the house anymore. They're both married. So it's just Forrest and I left, and once we leave for Georgia my parents will be empty nesters. Kinda strange since this house has always been full of people running around in it. Growing up is a strange and wonderful thing.

"So what did you two get up to today?" My dad asks from his recliner.

Dean and I look at each other and then I say, "I drove him around town to show him some of my favorite spots here."

"Yep. She showed me a couple of her old schools and her old job. Then we had some lunch and went to the skatepark for a bit. It was a pretty good day," Dean sits down on the couch next to me.

"We're going to go to a movie tonight after dinner to finish off the day. I want to show him what our cute little theater looks like." I wiggle in my seat.

"I'd love to get out of the house. Can I tag along?" Forrest looks over at me and asks.

I snap my head at him and give him a look. "Umm. Actually I forgot. I have to finish a project I'm working on. Darn. Maybe next time, Dean." Forrest stands up and pats his back before heading to the kitchen to hide.

It seems like everyone caught on to what just happened, even my mom in the kitchen paused, but we all moved on with our conversation like an elephant didn't just walk through the room. Thank God my brother can read my mind, or else I would be going on a sweet little date with Dean and my bro. Not quite what I was picturing.

"No problem, Forrest," Dean responds with a grin.

My dad continues chatting with Dean about his plans. Dean fills him in on his move up to Bothell after the New Year. My dad makes a couple jokes about the people that live in Bothell and the surrounding areas. Dean looks like he's genuinely laughing at every punch line.

Then my mom calls us all over for dinner at the table. We chat about my dad getting some new clients added to his handyman business. My mom is starting a new job at a Private School in town. Forrest talks about him going to the school in Georgia along with me. We're like the perfect picture of a cordial family.

We finish up dinner and Dean goes over to help my mom with the dishes. I watch him make small talk with her as she passes him dishes to dry. I smile, he really is a genuine guy, I can see us having a future together.

When we start driving to the movies he says, "I like your family. They're pretty easy to chat with. Your mom is very sweet and your dad is a hoot!"

"I hear that a lot. About both my parents. When I was growing up I always wanted my dad to stop talking so we could leave, wherever we were, and go home but he has charisma and people love talking to him," I say with a chuckle.

"My dad is the exact same way," he replies.

A shocked look crosses my face. "No way! I love that we have that in common." I stay silent the rest of the ride. I really like this guy.

When we get to the theater we get our tickets at the ticket booth and buy popcorn. We find the number eight theater and settle into our seats. There's not very many people in here with us, which feels like a bit of foreshadowing of what this movie is going to be like.

The movie is about a woman, Teagan, who goes to the Netherlands to find herself. In the midst of finding herself she falls in love with a handsome Dutchman.

The movie doesn't keep my attention though because I'm constantly looking down at our hands and see that they are almost touching, but not quite. I don't know why he isn't trying to hold my hand. It's distracting me from the movie more than the actual act of holding hands would. I can't keep track of where Teagan went to and why she's alone with her handsome Dutchman in a run-down cabin. It's all a big, jumbled mess in my brain because I want him to HOLD MY HAND. But I'm not man enough to do it myself. This is every woman's nightmare. Having great chemistry with a guy, being put in a romantic setting and not getting to feel the electricity of a good handhold.

When the movie finishes, we throw our half full bucket of popcorn away, because I didn't hold up my end of the jumbo size bargain. I was too busy focusing on how little attention my hand was getting.

As we start to leave, I look through the floor to ceiling windows that lead outside, and see that it's raining. This is when I realize I completely forgot my jacket at home. Rain isn't typical in Western Washington in the month of August, but you should never make assumptions about the weather here. We have two seasons, rain and sun, and you should be prepared for both at any given time.

Dean notices I don't have a jacket and takes his off to cover us both from the rain. He puts his arm around my waist and pulls me in tight to his hip to make sure we're close enough to fit under the jacket. Finally, a move that didn't come after me falling on my bottom.

No surprise to anyone, this is a better move than holding hands. This feels like a perfect fit. He's so tall my shoulder fits right under his armpit, I can practically smell his deodorant.

We walk slowly to the car, even though it's raining. Our steps are in sync with each other, both savoring this moment. Almost like we don't want to let it go too fast. We've built up this insane chemistry all day that anyone with a needle handy could come over and pop it like a bubble. When we get to the car, I see that it's the only one left in our section of the parking lot. I didn't realize we walked that slow. I smile thinking about it.

He walks me to my side of the car, and I reach for the keys in my pocket. I sense his tall, warm body and realize he's standing really close to me. I look up to see him looking down at me. I turn my shoulders to face him square on. "There's something I've been thinking about doing for ages," he says and he slowly reaches his hands down to grab my face.

He pulls me close to him and sweeps me into a kiss. His hands hold onto my face, and his lips move over mine. I lift up onto my tippy toes to reach his height while my hands hold onto his waist.

Talking on the phone for hours every day is like getting to know someone on steroids. All you have is talking, all you have is getting to know each other. I feel like we've known each other for years and not just months.

I've wanted to know what he tastes like, smells like, and feels like ever since he saw Juniper and I sitting in the chairs at Fremily's wedding trying to look like we were busy doing stuff and he noticed our ploy.

Our mouths keep exploring each other's as we continue to kiss in the dark under the flickering light of the parking lot lamps. His hands move from my face down to the small of my back and he pulls me into him as tight as he can. I feel the hard muscles of his stomach against mine and my arms reach up to wrap around the back of his neck, fingers in his hair.

His hands are dangerously close to the top of my butt, and my senses are firing off explosions of electricity. *Will he touch my butt?* Before I can finish that thought one of his hands goes down the whole way and gives my butt a soft squeeze. Then the other hand doesn't leave the second cheek out for long and it follows the contours of my back and gives the second one a twin squeeze. I pull his face closer to mine as if to close any gap left between us.

When we finally break away, we realize the rain had stopped at some point but couldn't tell you when. I come down off my tippy toes and land my feet flat on the ground. As if my feet now realize they are no longer flying. "Your mouth tastes nice." He leans his head down and we touch foreheads. "I think you might be my dream girl," he says and we close our eyes, breathing heavily.

When I finally catch my breath I say, "We finally broke the ice." I breathe him in. "There's always been this tension between us. I'm glad we're finally past that."

"Me too. I wanted to do that ever since this morning at the airport but didn't know how you would take it. After such a thoughtful day you planned for us the timing finally felt right," he said, eyes still closed.

"I agree. I'm glad you pulled the trigger. I was waiting for you to hold my hand during the movie, but it never happened. I could barely pay attention to the plot." I pull away and look him in the eyes.

"You didn't miss much," he says with a laugh. "For the record, I wanted to hold your hand too." Then he bends down to kiss me one more time. I fly up to the clouds for the second time tonight.

When we finally come down, we get in the car and drive back to my house. Holding hands like a couple of penguins.

The next morning I wake up and realize none of it was a dream. Dean has actually come to visit. Dean has actually seen my hometown. Dean has actually made out with me and touched my butt in the parking lot of our little theater!

This weekend has been better than I hoped. It is, however, already coming to an end. Dean takes a jet plane home tonight and who knows when the next time I see him will be.

I have a few more things to show him today but hopefully it won't take up most of the day and we can just chill with Esther and Michael for the rest of it.

I walk out of the bedroom and see Dean in the kitchen. "Good morning, Dean," I say to him and he returns the greeting, "Good morning, Elise."

"My family left the house for the day already?" I ask, wondering if we can act like a couple of teenagers.

"Yep," he replies and saunters over to me, wraps his arms around my waist and pulls me into a kiss. One I willingly fall into. We start to make out while he rests one hand lightly on the top of my butt, this time more comfortable than sensual and the other hand is holding me tightly to his chest.

I smile up at him when our lips part. "How did you sleep?" I ask as he's holding me like I'm a pillow he never wants to let go.

"Like a baby," he says looking down at me from his tall perch, the trees are practically in his face. "Not a care in the world."

"Same," I say and then slap his arm to move onto our day at hand. "Excited for another day of adventuring?"

"Am I ever! Whatcha got for me Berger?" he asks and releases his arms.

"There's a few places on the list that we didn't get to yesterday and I'm dying to point them out. Most of them are drive-by's so it should go quickly," I say clapping my hands softly as if a giddy schoolgirl just took over my body and replaced me.

"I'm dying to see them," he replies and my face softens.

I tilt my head and say, "Ahhh, you're sweet," as I hold my hands clasped up at my heart. He's making me want to push past my new realized tendency to push guys away. I want to stick around and fight for this one, even if the long distance is hard.

"Now! Let's make some quick pancakes and fry up some sausage patties, then head on out!" We both get to work on breakfast, this time the space between us is not noticeable under a microscope. Our hips touch the entire time we tandem cook. I look over at him flipping the pancakes and realize how confident he seems. At the beginning I saw it as cocky, but I had it all wrong. He just knows who he is.

We get done eating breakfast and I take him to four drive-by spots. My favorite railroad sections, a road that looks gorgeous in the fall, where I was able to live out my basic girl dreams as a senior in high school when I took photos there in my cowboy hat.

He grabs my hand when I start driving him to the next stop, where Mt. Rainier is perfectly framed by some trees. I look down at our intertwined fingers and the center console with the gear shifter underneath our hands and say, "I feel like there's something between us."

He laughs so hard I might have seen a little tear form on the side of his eye. "You remembered! Good one, Berger." He gives my hand a squeeze. I look over at him and smile, proud of myself for bringing a joke full circle.

I look back at the road and say, "Okay. So, coming up is the spot I mentioned yesterday where the trees frame Mount Rainier perfectly. But you have to be paying attention because the Bob Ross, picture perfect scene, passes by really fast." I drive for a few more seconds and go, "Okay. Ready...ready...ready...Right here!" I point ahead of us as the trees frame the mountain and then move out of frame as the car keeps going.

"Oh my gosh, I saw it. That was so beautiful. You live in a mountain scape photograph. Can we stop so I can take a photo?" he asks me as he releases my hand and grabs for his phone.

"Absolutely. I was hoping you'd want to," I say, way ahead of him because I was already slowing the car down to find a safe spot to pull over. He gets the picture and we move onto the next stop.

About a quarter mile down the road I pull into a parking lot. "This here is our local entrance to the Nisqually River. Get ready to see another Bob Ross painting. The trees line the river and the water moving over the rocks will make you want to find a button up shirt and search for oil paints," I say with a laugh and throw the car into park.

We get out of the car and I lead him toward the water. There is a small opening that breaks the tree line and points you to the river. You can hardly see the river from the parking lot if it wasn't for this opening, like a giant neon sign from nature. We walk up to the five-by-five square feet of beachy sand, that's native to the shoreline, and see the magnificent Nisqually River rushing by us. White caps crest the water as it moves over rocks and tree debris underneath it.

"Wow. It's nice here. Watch out, I'm feeling the urge to skip a rock," he says as he looks down, finds the flattest rock he can and throws it sideways over the rushing water.

He gets four skips out of it before it plummets to its icy grave. "Good one!" I say, impressed. I'm impressed by anyone that gets more than two skips out of a rock. "Every summer we would bring our inner tubes here and float down the river. It only feels good this time of year because the air is hot outside and it takes less time for the cold temperature of the water to become bearable."

"Cute! I can picture little Elise floating down the river having fun with her family. I love how close you guys are!" He looks over at me, and his smile reaches his eyes. "I feel like I've learned a lot about your childhood. Thank you for sharing."

"I'm glad you've liked it." I smile back.

Then out of nowhere he starts to take his socks and shoes off. "I really want to see how cold it is."

"As long as you don't mind having numb feet for the duration of your time in the water. The river is made from mountain runoff so it's freezing," I say teasing him, but it doesn't deter him from his pursuit.

"Actually, I'll join you." I add, "I love putting my feet in the water. Even icy death water," and start to take off my own socks and shoes.

"Ooooh, that's pretty cold!" he says and I can see the hairs on his legs start to stand up a little and his shoulders go up to his ears with tension. "Okay. Okay. It's not bad after a couple minutes though," he says as his shoulders start to come back down.

I join him in the river with my bare feet and experience the biting cold followed by the refreshing contrast of hot air on cold skin. He starts to walk deeper into the water all the way up to his knees where his shorts start. I put my hand up to my mouth and giggle at him as he tries to hide his squirms caused by the fresh cold water touching his dry legs.

"So, you're not the type of person to shy away from a challenge huh?" I say seeing his mouth open like a silent wide mouth bass, but he still keeps going further. Not only are his knees submerged but the bottom of his shorts are in the water now too.

"What do you mean? This is the warmest water," he says with a deceivingly straight face now.

"Have fun in there. It's before noon. I'm not gonna join you when the temperature isn't at its highest of the day," I bait him into coming back to shore.

"Oooph. Oooph. I don't know what you mean. I could live in this water." He tightens his fists, giving away his discomfort even when his face tries so hard to hide it.

I stand on the shore, proud of my decision not to go any deeper into the water. Watching him squirm is satisfying enough. He takes one final step in and I can see that it's now reached the middle of his thigh and that seems to be his last straw because then he says, "You know what, good point. I'm coming back." He wades through the water as it gets lower and lower on his legs until he's finally back standing next to me on the shore where it's safely ankle deep. "That was a wild ride though. This water is freezing. Does it ever get warmer?"

"Not at all. The outside air just gets hotter so you kinda get tricked into thinking the temp is okay," I tell him from experience.

We stand next to each other soaking in our time together as if it was our last. He grabs my hand and holds it with both of his, then turns to face me and says, "Elise Berger, this has been great. I'm sad to see the weekends over but I do love that you were able to show me around your small town and share with me a little part of who you are. I'll always cherish it."

"Ahh. That was very sweet. Thank you for saying all that. Also, you're welcome," I say smiling up at him, inching closer to see if I can close the gap between us. "So now that's the end of my tour! I hope you liked it!"

"Yes. I absolutely loved it," he answers and then leans down for a kiss. He holds my one hand onto his chest and wraps his free hand around my back to pull me in. I fall into kissing him. Trying to remember every move he has, every pause he takes, every tongue flick he uses. Searing the memory into my brain so that when I miss him I can recall this moment with ease.

"My pleasure," I say, answering his comment when we finally pull away from our cloud nine.

Hand in hand we walk back to my car as the heat of the pavement starts to burn our feet. We put our shoes on in the car and I reluctantly drive back to my house. This weekend was everything I hoped it would be. I'm sad to see it ending.

When we arrive home, we go inside to find that Esther and Michael are already here. "Hi guys!" I say as we enter the living room. Esther already had lunch made and we sat down to eat.

After our meal we play a game of Clue, both of our favorite game. Dean won, and after we congratulate him I realize it's already time to head to the airport.

"Thanks for the board game. You had an honorable win," Michael says as he shakes hands with Dean.

Then Dean turns to Esther and gives her a hug. "Good to see you."

"Hope you had a fun time in Yelm," Esther says.

"I did. I really did," Dean says as he turns to me and gives me a side smile.

"What was your favorite part?" Esther asks.

"Umm, probably going to the movies." He looks over at me and winks, which Esther saw and I know I'm going to get questioned for after this. "And the river," he finishes.

"Nice! Those are solid hangs here on the old Prairie," Esther says.

Dean looks over at me with confusion on his face. So I chime in to explain, "Yelm's nickname is the Pride of the Prairie, so a lot of things in town are named after the prairie. Our yearly parade is called 'Prairie Days Parade', a couple of streets are named 'Prairie Park' or 'Prairie Lane'.

"Ahhh. I get it now. The old Prairie was a treat to me. I hope to come again," he says as they say their goodbyes.

Esther grabs my arm and says, "You're going to explain that wink to me when you get home." I nod and wink at her as Dean and I head out the door.

When we start driving I tell him, "I have a surprise! One final drive-by, a place we talked about but I forgot to take you. It'll add an extra zing in your step. Plus twenty minutes, but that's ok, we have time."

"I love surprises! Count me in!" he says. "I'm trying to think now about a place we talked about, but I haven't seen yet."

I head North and look over at him. "I can feel the anticipation that's written all over your face," I say with a laugh, elated that I know where we're going and he doesn't. Also, that I get to show him one last thing. We drive for a few more minutes and pop into a tiny town with a sign that reads, "Welcome to Rainier."

"Oh Rainier! This is awesome. This is the tiny town. I can't wait to see it," he says.

"Don't blink or else you'll miss your chance," I say with a laugh.

We pass by the iconic deer silhouettes that sit at the beginning of the town. Then a gas station. Followed by a cookie shop. Then the final gas station and convenience store, and then finally, we head out of town.

"Wow. That is exactly what I expected your little town of Yelm to be. A small one street town that has nothing but a couple stores," he says looking behind us to get another glimpse. "That did not disappoint."

"Well, I have to turn around and go back through the town to get to I-5 so you'll get another chance to soak it all in," I say with a laugh.

"Amazing," he says.

We drive back through in silence, and he seems genuinely interested in seeing this small town of Rainier. "How many people live here?" he asks.

"About 2,500," I say.

"Brilliant," he says.

I continued our drive up to the SeaTac airport. The time went by so fast. We agreed we'd keep talking just as we have been with texting and phone calls. Then we made plans for after New Years. I would be home for the holidays and he would be moving to Bothell.

We pulled into the SeaTac airport, and I followed the familiar blue signs that lead me to his airline. I parked the car and got out to help him with his bags. We stood on the sidewalk for a couple minutes, hugging each other just the way we did when he first arrived. I wasn't ready for this to end but definitely glad we made such great memories this weekend.

"Oh wait! I have something for you," I say as I turn back to the car and grab the item I have been waiting to give him for months now. I didn't tell him about it, just secretly knitted away at it so I could give him the gift of warmth. He wanted me to make him something and since scarfs are the only thing I know how to knit I finished a perfectly adequate, long, neck covering rectangle.

I turn around and hold the scarf behind my back. I saunter over to him and smile up at him as I say, "I told you I would make you one someday." Then I pull the scarf to the front of me and show him my creation. "A scarf!" I exclaim with as much zest as I can for a boring item of clothing.

"No way! *You* actually made me one?! And it's red and black. My two favorite colors. You get me." He grabs the scarf and rubs it against his face. Then he twirls the scarf around his neck. He looks down at me and puts my face in his hands. "Thank you. You've made this weekend so special. I'm sorry I have to leave now and we don't get to spend more time together."

I smile up at him, feeling known, and then I say, "Me too."

He pulls my face close to his and we fall into each other as our lips meet. Our mouths move slowly and rhythmically as we say goodbye for the last time, but without any words. We don't pull away for a few minutes. Once we do, we look each other in the eyes and end with one final peck on the lips. Releasing each other from our grasp, we submit to the distance that we have known before.

He bends down to grab his bags off the ground and says, "Goodbye, Berger," then turns around and walks toward the sliding glass doors that will lead him to his flight. He looks back at me with a final grin and a wave. I wave back and he keeps walking forward. As the sliding glass doors shut behind him, my eyes fill with tears and a single drop slides down my face. I hope I see him again, I know that with long-distance stuff you are never guaranteed anything.

Chapter 20

Present Day

February

I can't believe it's been a month since I've texted Dean and I still feel like I'm looking at my phone every minute to see if he's texted or called me. There were so many nights where we would talk on the phone for 6-8 hours and wouldn't realize the time until it was 4am and then we'd force ourselves to get off the phone so we could sleep.

What I wouldn't give to see his name pop up on my phone and hear his voice again. *"Hey Berger, I've been thinking about gardening lately. What are your thoughts?"* He always brought up the most random topics that were so interesting to talk about, and we had such an easy back and forth about everything. I can't believe I let go of a good thing when it could have so easily been mine. Someone who gets you and can carry a conversation, without making it feel like pulling teeth, is so rare.

As a thought crosses my mind, I pop out of bed in one fluid movement. I want to ask Juniper if she wants to take a day trip to Savannah today. We both happen to have the day off work again at our coffee shop job. Luckily for me, she always seems to be up for spontaneous adventures.

I leave the comfort of my room, my GLOOM room as it's been called in my head lately, and walk down the stairs. I find her in the kitchen making some breakfast. We're the only two awake right now because we're used to such early mornings with our job.

"Hiya toots, how's it going?" I ask as I bounce into the kitchen. I'm really jazzed to give her my idea and see if she's up for my distraction. I haven't felt this kind of excitement in a couple months. I've been so contemplative and boring.

"Good. Just making my morning-unfertilized-baby-chick. What's up with you?" she replies with her morbid sense of humor as she moves her spatula around the frying pan.

"Ha! Thank God, it's unfertilized. Umm, I was just thinking about what I want to do for the day." I put my hands on the countertop and place all my weight on them. "Do you feel like going to Savannah today? We've been talking about it for ages but haven't really been motivated to do it yet. I would really love another distraction from my phone and the lack of activity there." I move the weight off my hands and put my elbows on the counter, resting my chin on my fist. I'm feeling antsy as I continue, "Like when we went to Cafe Intermezzo. That day really took my mind off Mr. San Diego." Hopefully she can feel my sense of urgency.

She looks over her shoulder at me and says, "You know what, that sounds like a great idea! I haven't been on a spontaneous adventure lately and it's sort of depressing me." She turns back around to flip her egg. "A lot of people have been telling me about Savannah lately and I've been really wanting to go there. So yeah, let's get after it!"

"Awesome!" I lean my weight back to my feet, and with my hands clasped in front of me, I bounce a little on my toes. "I can grab a bowl of cereal and throw on an outfit and I'll be ready in fifteen minutes," I say, proud of my ability to be ready in a flash. I grab a bowl out from the upper cabinets and find some cereal in my food section of the pantry.

"Brilliant. Me too," she says as she puts her egg on a plate.

We both scarf down our breakfasts and throw on our spunkiest outfits, then hit the road. It's a four hour-drive and Juniper's got the best tunes. We jam out for a good hour or two with The Beatles, Queen and Floggin' Molly. We throw in a bit of the Wicket Witch soundtrack to mix it up with the upbeat sounds of a few rival broadway witches and wizards at school.

I held it off for as long as I could, I've tried now for a couple hours to keep him off my mind but the topic just bubbles up out of me like a fountain that has dish soap in it. It can't be stopped, you can only ride it out until all the feeling-bubbles are gone. I think I just need to keep letting myself process it and not try to shove it down. If I don't let myself process it all out then maybe it will still be something that affects me twenty years from now. I definitely don't want that. So I take in a deep breath and start a conversation about...you guessed it...Dean.

"Juniper, do you mind if I talk about Dean again?" I ask as I put my feet up on the dash.

"Of course you can. I want you to talk about it anytime you need to," she says as she turns her head to meet my eyes and smiles.

I nod. "I'm racking my brain, trying to figure out what went wrong. I mean, I know I was to blame initially, but I tried to make up for it by explaining myself to him. It didn't seem to help. I don't know why it didn't change his mind." I look over at her and search her face for an answer I can't figure out myself.

She stares ahead at the road and asks, "Do you think you broke his heart too much?"

I look down at my hands in my lap as I consider what she just asked. "Maybe..." I let out a heavy sigh. "Ugh. I wish I could've seen the self-sabotaging before it happened!" I put my face in my hands and say, "I hate that I did that!"

"What feels so hard about letting it go and forgiving yourself?" She scratches the top of her hand and then puts it back on the wheel at ten and two.

I feel like she took a bazooka to my heart, which now has a gaping hole that I'm looking down at. "I..." The air catches in my throat. "Uh..." I keep looking down. I dig deep and say, "I don't like the feeling of doing the wrong thing and then being rejected." I drop my head with that admission.

"Do you think that maybe, you want what you can't have?" she asks and I cringe. "Do you think that if he hadn't closed the door on his side, you would be feeling this way?" She looks over at me and presses her lips together as if to say, I had to ask the tough question.

"Gah! The questions are so painful," I pause, then realize what a gift this is. "I appreciate being given the space to look internally." I sit there for a minute thinking about what she's asking me to answer. "I know I had feelings for him at the start. The middle just got all muddled because of how big the feelings got, and then I realized I liked him deeply once he pulled away too."

"That's good for you to admit, babe. At least you have that answer." She slows down at a stop light as we come into a little pass-through town. "So, now why can't you let all of him go?"

"I think I'm still holding onto hope that this person, this some-thing-ship I built with him can become *something* again. When I look back at the story of us in that chapter of life, I realize that I did actually have what I wanted and I pushed it away. I'm scared I won't find it again if I let it go. I'm scared someone else won't find me as interesting and fulfilling as he did. Or what if I do find someone who falls for me, but I don't reciprocate because they're simply not Dean, a constant reminder that I let the one for me go because of my own self-sabotage." I lean my head against the window of the passenger side door.

"Ahh. Yes, that makes perfect sense." I don't look at her, but she pats my hand as she speeds the car up again and she continues, "Your heart wants to be known like that in the future. I get it, Love. It's hard to accept a different future than the one you saw with him, or with anyone for that matter. But you will find that again." She's always been so good at validating my emotions.

"I think ultimately I'm mad that I can't be the couple I thought we would be." I say, still leaning my head against the window. Finally admitting the one thing I have been thinking about for weeks. The one thing that makes me sound like a desperate person who can't move on. Allowing all the emotions to flood back into my mind and soul, I've lost the strength to hold my head up. "What I miss about us is that we knew how to listen to each other, made each other laugh and appreciated the little quirks. Conversations were so easy. How can I let that go!?" I say that last word a little louder than I expected. Rain starts to hit the window and I feel like the weather is matching my mood.

"I hear ya. It's depressing. Those are big feelings. Having to rewire your brain to tell yourself it's over even though you don't want it to be over is a tough thing to think about and wrap your brain around," she says as she turns on the windshield wipers.

"Yes! Exactly! I don't want to rewire my brain! I just want to be 'us' again." I close my eyes and let myself feel the pain of that reality. I want to be 'us' again...but it will never be 'us' again. Deep porcupine quills hit my heart as I'm allowing myself to admit my deepest desires. Everyone wants to make you feel better after a 'breakup'. Everyone wants you to be happy again, it's a rare friend that will let you sit in the pain and feel all the feels.

Another wave of thought hits me like I'm being crushed against the rocks in the ocean, "I ruined it, Juniper. I ruined it by being my dumb, over-emotional self." I breath out my biggest insecurity, then I slowly shake my head. "I ruined it. I've always been told that I'm too emotional and too sensitive. I bet he didn't want me back because I showed him too many emotions when I was 'trying to get him back' and I was all over the place!" I put my hands on my face and pull my cheeks down as I whine.

"Hey, babe, stop that. Don't ever get down on yourself for being authentic and true to your feelings and emotions. Those things are what make you uniquely you. I would hate to have a friend that was a robot. Having you as a cyborg is not my jam...actually," she pauses, then shrugs and continues, "That would be cool, but that's not the point!" She points her finger at me. "When you show emotion, and you are vulnerable, it's the realest thing to witness. Not very many people are like you."

I feel like her words just wrapped me in a big hug, but my insecurities get the better of me. "I can't help it when it's truuuue!"

"No, it's not true. Don't put this all on yourself. Just because some boys weren't man enough to handle your emotions, doesn't mean you are too emotional and too sensitive. All those other people in your past that told you that you were being too emotional can go scratch their eyes out with a grapefruit spoon," she says with a little hit on the steering wheel.

I chuckle at the grapefruit spoon comment, I love her. I continue riding the insecurity train and say, "I want to think that way, but it's just happened too many times that I fall for someone, show them how emotional I can get and then they back away." I look down into my lap and tears start leaving my eyes instead of just sitting in the corners of them. I've been thinking lately that once I fix myself, he'll want me back.

"Why do you think that if a few people say something dumb that it's actually true?"

I look over at her with tears chasing each other down my face, almost ready to do the ugly cry but instead I answer, "It's easy to believe someone when you trust them with your heart. After I showed the people in my past my heart, I was ignored. My only choice was to believe them." I look back down at my hands now catching my tears.

"*They* are the ones that are emotionally stunted. Not you! And Dean didn't say this to you, did he? For all we know he's just trying to protect his own heart from being broken again," she says, looking over at me.

"I don't know how to like myself! That's probably why I pushed him away and self-sabotaged. It's hard for me to accept other people liking me so much. I'm having a hard time seeing Dean's rejection as anything other than proof that I'm just...not good enough." I grab at my collar bones and start to ugly cry. There it is. The truth behind all of my pain and anguish.

"Elise Berger, you are a beautiful soul. You are a rare beauty that will help the world see we need to be more real. You have so many fun and interesting things about you that anyone would be lucky to be your friend or lover. You have so much emotional rawness, it's refreshing! It's a priceless quality. Don't let anyone take it from you!" She rebuts with so much confidence I realize I need to start breathing in what she is saying to me.

"Damn, that feels good to hear." I wipe the tears off my face, then squeeze my eyes shut as more tears keep flowing. I take a deep breath then hold it in without exhaling. This feels like truth. This feels happy. This is the first time that I've owned up to my side of the situation. Now that I have, I can stop blaming myself for something I didn't realize I was doing, and projecting that onto Dean because it was too scary to admit.

"Good! Listen to me, Miss Mermaid Hair," she says looking at me with her eyebrows raised, referencing my lush golden locks. "I know it's the dumbest most cliche thing to hear but you *will* find someone who doesn't care about the emotional mistakes. If it's not Dean it will be someone else. You now see your own pattern of behavior for what it was, so you can go into your future relationships with a clean slate. Instead of letting the insecurities take over, you will show them your true, beautiful, emotional self, unapologetically. Instead of running when they fall in love with you, you will grab that love with both hands and hold on tight, because you know you deserve it, just like I know you deserve it!" She keeps looking between me and the road, I give her a side grin, trying really hard to accept what she is saying, "I know, I know, it's so dumb to hear, but it's the truth! He is out there and you *will* find him," she finishes.

"You really think that all of my feelings and emotions are normal?" I shake my head. "I just can't wrap my head around that. Probably goes back to childhood, as everything does. I've always felt like I wasn't allowed to have feelings. I was always crying over things, and my brother and parents would always want me to stop. No one knew how to help me navigate them, so I just learned that they were unacceptable," I admit. Going deep is the recesses of my brain for a reason to my madness.

"Really? They would tell you to stop crying?" She tilts her head down and looks over at me with wide eyes. "I could scream. That's awful."

"Well, they would say, 'you're ok, you're ok,' and tell me how I should feel instead of asking me what I was feeling. I would go out into the horse field and cry on the hills out there, because I didn't feel like anyone wanted me crying around them." I stare out the window at the trees rushing by. I forgot that this happened when I was a teenager. My family is so friendly and fun to be around, the one thing they've always lacked is the ability to hold space for someone to have big feelings.

"Sounds like a group of people who don't know how to manage their own emotions, so they just stomp out the emotions of people around them. Don't let those experiences stop you from expressing yourself freely." She speeds up the car to pass a slow driver in front of us. "I will beat this horse until it's dead, your emotions are healthy, Elise. You actually expressing them makes you way healthier than the people that push them down and act like everything is okay." She gives me a gentle pat on the shoulders to make sure I'm picking up what she's dropping.

I look at her through a second rain of tears, her words washing over me like a clean drink of rainwater. I give her a smile and stay silent. I turn to look out the window for another minute then turn back to her and say, "Thank you." I push a smile onto my face. "You are making me feel safe to be myself. All of this pain from Dean is actually making me be a healthier person by processing out these thoughts and feelings with you. Your friendship is invaluable!"

I close my eyes and open them again, "I'm *going* to believe you. Today starts my healing journey." I massage my chest as I feel the little cracks on my heart start their first layer of healing. I made a mistake and I own that now. I want to allow myself to make this mistake and learn from it. I'm also allowed to have emotions. I'm allowed to want deeply and feel deeply. Anything that tries to make me think otherwise can be run over by a stampede of pigs!

"I'm here for ya, Love. Anytime you need to talk. There's never such a thing as too-much-processing with me. I'll talk this out until we are black and blue because I value your mental health." Juniper gives my shoulder one final pat and returns it to the steering wheel.

We sit in a comfortable silence while the Broadway performance of Wicked plays in the background. The world passes by the window in a flash and, as I'm listening to the soothing vocals of Iliana Ortez, I'm feeling light-hearted for the first time in many fortnights.

I'll get over him. I know I will. *This too shall pass.* My brain is apparently swimming with cliché saying now that my heart is unbreaking.

I break the silence and say, "You're the best, you know that?"

"No, you're the best!" she counters and we both laugh and I notice the rain has stopped.

"Turn this song up! I want to jam out to Queen and let this emotional freedom wash over me!" I say.

Juniper gets what I'm saying and throws the volume dial up as loud as we can handle. We roll the window down and sing so loud our lungs hurt, finishing this last hour of our drive to Savannah with music in our ears and one hand out the window dancing with the air. Feelings are freedom. Mistakes are normal. Processing is healthy. I can't believe it took me this long to learn all of this.

Chapter 21

Present Day

February

Our stomachs are grumbling by the time we arrive, so we swipe the first parking spot we see in downtown Savannah, revealing all the excellent eateries nearby. I hop out, giving my legs and torso a good stretch before Juniper and I stake out the best spot to fill up our bellies until we're milk drunk like a couple of newborn babies. The smell of garlic and onions fill the air as the restaurants gear up for the lunch hour.

We pick a cute little Thai restaurant with the cutest awning and tree coverage. Mainly because the name sounded awesome, but also because their special is a delicious side order of mangoes and sticky rice if you purchase an entree. We walk inside and the waiter seats us at a table for two.

We order right away and stare out the big windows looking out to the sidewalk. Savannah has a nice vibe to it. Not actually a town you would think to be in the south. They're hip here. It feels more like a west coast town. I've seen more tattooed sleeves here in the past twenty minutes than I've seen in my five months in Georgia altogether.

"I like it here," I say to Juniper without making any eye contact. "It feels so free."

"I agree." She sounds mesmerized and I look over to see her gaze following a pair of friends walking in front of the restaurant. "I could see myself living here someday." She continues, "I don't feel like people are staring at me or my tattoos here. Back in California I go unnoticed, but here in the South I feel like half the people give me the stink eye after looking at my arms." She looks down and fiddles with a dandelion tattoo on her forearm.

"Why do you think people in the South do that?" I ask furrowing my brow.

"I can only assume it's because they just have a different way of life, like having two full tattoo sleeves isn't a 'clean' enough look or something." She looks up and gives me a half smile.

"Dang, I'm sorry you have to deal with that." I flatten my lips.

She shrugs it off. "Meh, It's not a huge deal. I'm just mildly aware of it."

"Well, that's good, because you are the cat's meow and I don't want you feeling stared at." I pat her arm across the table.

"Thanks friend!" She tilts her head then she asks, "So what did you order? I was so busy looking at all the people walking past the restaurant outside that I didn't catch it."

"Oh! I ordered fried rice to get their special," I say practically drooling. Mangoes and sticky rice is my favorite Thai dessert!

"Nice." Juniper folds her hands in front of her and leans on the table, "I'm hoping for you that this place doesn't disappoint with their fried rice recipe."

I perk up at her mention of my Thai restaurant traditions, "Thank you!"

Our food eventually makes it out to us and we dig in. The Thai fried rice was amazing, it really hit the spot. I love when a food is made so well you want to harness the power of a 4th century roman stuffing your belly, ready to visit the vomitorium later to only stuff yourself more afterwards. We however won't be vomiting this food up so the comparison ends there, at the 4th century romans full bellies. We got the check and left the restaurant full and ready to explore the city.

We'd told the waiter we were new in town and we asked him where a cool place to walk around would be. He told us how to find a place called Forsyth Park. *"It has a great fountain in the middle and it's lined with Spanish Moss trees. If you're looking for 'iconic Savannah' you won't go wrong with Forsyth Park."*

Walking the streets of Savannah feels like I went back in time. I look around for a magical time traveling portal we could have walked through, but I see nothing out of the ordinary. The magical portals in my *Thomas Taylor* books are definitely in my head, influencing my thoughts. I look back at the houses we are surrounded by, old Victorian architecture lining both sides of the street. They don't make buildings like this anymore.

All the buildings have pillars with front porches. The intricate, small designs on the top of the pillars have no reason for them but to be beautiful. I can't take my eyes off the architecture as we continue walking. I want to live in a house that has a porch wrapped around it with spherical roofs that come to a point. They look like modern day castles. I look in the upper windows for a princess, who should be daydreaming about a prince.

Above our heads is a canopy of tree branches that have hanging moss. It feels like we are wrapped in an earthy, spongy hug. If I reached up and jumped I could touch the moss. But I won't. *Yes I will...oooph...nope can't reach it.* These must be the Spanish Moss trees that the waiter was talking about.

We round another corner and see Forsyth Park ahead of us. It's a luscious haven of greenery. As we step into the park we are greeted by red pavers underfoot. Over our head is more canopy tree coverage. It's late February so there aren't any flowers blooming, but I can see flower beds that would add a nice pop of color to the scenery in the spring. That doesn't take away from its beauty though. The green moss that is hanging down off the trees gives us the right amount of whimsy. It's like walking through a fairy tale land. Ahead of us is a giant water fountain that, surely, a prince and princess would find themselves coming to after a night of getting to know each other at a masquerade ball.

The fountain is gorgeous with its many waterspouts spraying up as if to high five the sky. I'm mesmerized by it as we close the gap. "Can you believe how pretty this is?" I ask Juniper as she too hasn't said a word in this new fairy-tale land we have found.

"I'm awestruck, actually," she replies. "Do you want to sit and soak it in?"

There's bench after bench that line the red brick path we're walking on. I feel like Dorothy going to a different Wizard of Oz. Not the one in the emerald city, but maybe the one in the ruby city. We make our way over to a bench and sit down to soak in the beauty.

"Does this place remind you of anything?" Juniper asks.

"Yes! A fairy tale. I'm imagining a mashup of princesses and the Wizard of Oz," I say as I look in as many directions as I can, doing my best to take it all in. I'm realizing that's one thing I like about myself. I enjoy sitting and peacefully taking in my surroundings.

"Me too! It's like, where the maidens would sit to clean the washing together and the blokes would congregate to sharpen their swords. I just want to sit here for hours," she says eyes glazed over and awestruck.

"We can sit here for as long as you want. I'm captivated too," I say looking up at the sage green of the moss coming down, trying to reach as far as it can to tickle my nose. I smile at the thought.

"You know," she pauses and takes a deep breath before continuing, "I've been thinking about the next place I want to live. I want it to be somewhere that brings me life." I know she has been disappointed in the town we're currently in so her confession doesn't surprise me.

"I hear you. Our little town in Georgia is kinda boring and doesn't have a lot to offer. I don't think I want to live in a small town for the rest of my life either." I breathe in the air and I can smell the musty earth, it's so strong that it's probably rained here today.

"I'm starting to realize that I'm starving for a city that can offer a bigger way of living again," she says, looking lost in the forest of Spanish Moss even though we are in the middle of downtown.

"I can understand that. The only example I have of big city life is my three months in Thailand." I watch a few people walk by us who seem to be enjoying the scenery too.

"It's the best. It's culture. It's variety. It's acceptance of not just the typical, everyday person, but the unique, thriving, eclectic person. I want more variety. I love not being stared at because of what I look like. I feel so free here." She opens her arms as if to give the town a big hug.

"Ahh. That sounds lovely. I want that too. I can't wait to see where we move to and see us come alive as people more. You deserve that and I deserve that." I nudge her with my shoulder. "And just to give you more compliments because you've been there so much for me; you're such a beautiful soul, your sleeves are awesome, your whimsical clothes are captivating, and you are the best friend anyone could ever want." I reach over and give her a hug.

"Thank you, love, thank you. Sometimes I need to hear things like that too," she says and I realize that not only do I need her words of encouragement, but she also needs mine. We women need good friends that can lift us up in life and remind us that we are incredible.

"You're welcome. Your friendship has meant so much to me. I don't know how I could get through all this emotional sludge if I didn't have you. You're the best fairy godmother." I scrunch my nose and lift my shoulders with a smile.

"Your friendship has meant the world to me too," she replies with a returned nose scrunch.

I smile at our shared mutual appreciation and then my eyes look past her and land on the fountain in the middle of the park. "I bet a lot of people have pictures taken in front of that fountain."

"No doubt," she replies as she follows my gaze.

"Let's take a photo so we can remember it!" I put my hands on my knees and pop up.

"Yes! I'd love that," Juniper says and we walk to the fountain.

We get in our position then I pull my phone out and get our faces in the screen. CLICK. I examine it and see that my eyes were mid-blink. "Let's try again," I say and hold the phone out for another photo. CLICK. One look at the picture and it's great. I got the fountain in the background and our beaming faces in the front. That's perfect. We're both satisfied with the picture and I put my phone back in my pocket without looking to see if I've received any text messages from, you know who, best not to be disappointed again.

"What do you say we continue walking and figure out what we can find? I love a good bookstore. It would be great to find one," Juniper says with a gesture toward the opposite end of the park.

"I'm into that. Let's do it!" I say with enthusiasm.

We continue walking down the street lined with shadows from the tree branches above and whispers of sunlight poking through. After quite a few blocks of walking we stumble upon a boring little storefront displaying a sign that says, 'The Book Lady.' Quite the inviting name, even though the outside isn't screaming for attention.

"Oh my gosh, look! That's exactly what I wanted to find! Let's go in," Juniper says and we cross the street with a little skip in our step.

The bell on the door rings when we open it. As we get fully inside and the sun is gone from our eyes we are welcomed with the most amazing view. It looks like a book monster has vomited all over the walls with books upon books covering every inch of this place. There is not one spot of The Book Lady's store that does not have a bookshelf or stack of books on it. It's the purest definition of organized chaos.

We look at each other, and immense joy crosses our faces as we start to walk the aisles. Juniper looks like a fresh twenty-one year old in a liquor store ready to buy everything in sight. As we get further in we see a staircase that heads upstairs with a 'Private' sign on it. Not that you could go up there, because it too has been chosen as a spot for book vomit. There's a stack of books ten high on each step. The overflowing amount of books in this place feels like a secret haven for the spinsters that Juniper and I are sure to become.

Random Victorian era chairs and loveseats are sprinkled throughout the store. For those people who wish to fall into a book right there on the spot. Juniper pulls a book off the shelves and flips through it. I look at the shelf of books in front of me and see a book cover that catches my attention. The fourth book in my series of *Thomas Taylor, the Flask of Destiny*. We're both flipping through our respective books in hand and

WILL TEXT FOR LOVE

find ourselves to be the exact person these Victorian chairs were meant for. We fall prey to the setting The Book Lady has provided and sit down, engulfed in our reads.

After devouring quite a few chapters of my magical novel I say, "Do you want to explore some more?"

Juniper looks up from her book and reluctantly replies, "Yeah. Sure."

We get up like two cats not ready to leave their cozy haven and venture further into the bookstore to find a little coffee shop. After getting our drinks we discover a secret garden in the back that you have to climb out a window to get to. It was the perfect place for a photo op and to waste time in our very captivating books.

I look over at my phone to check the time. "Holy crap. It's been an hour, Per!" Shock written all over my face.

She leans in to look at the time, "Oh gosh! I want to check out other parts of Savannah. Let's get out of here. I really want to go to the waterfront." She closes her book and stands up.

"Oh yeah! That sounds good. Let's walk back to the car so that we can drive up to the waterfront. Otherwise the walk back is going to take foooorevvverrr," I say as I dramatically flop my body onto the table between us.

"Brilliant. Good plan." We leave the secret garden and buy our books, then head out to the streets.

We enjoy the canopy of trees and Victorian architecture for the second time as we walk back.

Once we're at Juniper's car we get in and follow the signs that lead us to the waterfront like good little tourists. It leads us to the Savannah River and there's a bunch of shops, restaurants, and boutiques lining River Street. There's only one parking spot left, right on the river.

The river is so cool I suggest another photo. CLICK. I take a photo of our feet with the river behind them. Then I flip the camera on the phone to the front one and try to get us in the frame. CLICK. I look at it and it's great, it kind of came out artistic with the photo being at an off-center angle. We look like we're starting down a road to living our best lives.

"This is so fun!" I say. "Thanks for entertaining my random whims or else today wouldn't have been possible."

"No problem! Happy to be of service." She curtseys and we cross the road to start walking down the street, window shopping. We went in and out of a couple boutiques, tried on clothes like we were in a fashion show, and bought a couple of outfits. A nice cap to the end of our time in Savannah. I feel only mildly aware that it's been thirty-six days since I've texted Dean.

Chapter 22

Past

September

I t's been two weeks since Dean flew back home. A strange feeling has slowly started to creep over me since he left, I'm now very uncomfortable. A shiver runs down my spine and my whole-body shakes. I can't turn off this feeling in the pit of my stomach, like vomit trying to spew out of me but without any nausea to move it along. I keep telling myself, *we had such a good time while he was here visiting, hold onto that memory. You don't have to start feeling weird about him,* but for some reason I can't stop feeling like I want to pull away and create a volcano of distance.

All of his attention is starting to make me feel like...it's just too much. I start pacing the living room floor and wiggle my relaxed hands in the air as if that will make the 'yuck' feeling go away. He's been texting and calling me just as much as we did before his visit, but something feels off on my side. I know we have feelings for each other and even though we kissed and had a wonderful time while he was here, I just don't want to have these feelings for each other anymore.

Is this what Forrest, Bethany, *and* Esther were talking about? Is this what I normally do with guys? They called it self-sabotaging, but I can't slow down the freight train of yuck I'm starting to feel from all his attention. Still wiggling my relaxed hands, I start to shake my head like a cartoon dog. Maybe I can make these unrequited love thoughts leave my head. I pause to test it and a second later the rush of yuck enters my stomach again.

I clasp my hands and rub the top of each fist. He didn't do anything wrong except like me a lot. I feel so bad. This feeling is coming after such a wonderful weekend, but I don't want to continue where we were going with this. My cheeks go red as I think about all the moments I flirted with him. I want him to slow down with this. I need to tell him that my feelings have changed.

I feel sweaty at the thought. I don't want to hurt his feelings. I also don't want to break our friendship. We've had such a fun time getting to know each other and if we could stay friends and keep up the texting and the talking on the phone, then I would love that. Like two platonic penguins agreeing to be celibate together.

I don't want to keep leading him on. Still pacing, I pull out my phone to check the time, ugh, he won't be off work for another six hours. I've been sitting with my thoughts for a few days now and they haven't gone away. It seems like the right time to tell him how I feel and I hate that I have to wait until the end of the day to do it. I need to make sure he knows that I still want to be friends and that this doesn't mean the end of everything. It just means, let's pull back on the pursuing.

He's pursued me so heavily and I liked it, but now it feels like an overwhelming tornado of attention and I need a breather. I hope he receives it okay. Actually, a wave of relief washes over me. He should receive it just fine because he's been so great with everything else I've talked to him about—my insecurities, my relationship with my family, my nerves about my move to Georgia.

I'm going to have a conversation with him tonight during our regular phone call. I head to my room and start packing my bags for Georgia. I run through the compliment-words-sandwich I want to use.

"You are such a fun person, but I need this to stay just friends."

"I love having you in my life, I just don't want it to be romantically."

"You're a funny guy and I still want to keep talking, but not every day anymore."

I rub my belly to try and settle the butterflies trying to crawl out of my stomach just thinking about this conversation with Dean. Not the good kind of butterflies though. Not the ones I started out having when we flirted the whole time at Fremily's wedding. No, this is the nervous kind of butterflies that sit in your stomach until the thing you have to get done is over. Doppelganger of the public speaking butterflies.

Regardless, I respect honesty. I want to show him that I'm not afraid to be honest and I know how to have deep conversations. Most people prefer to ignore these kinds of conversations like an ostrich sticking their head in the ground and they just hope that person goes away. That's the easier option. That's a D- for effort. I scrunch my nose at the thought, I'm not that person. That leaves the other person constantly questioning what happened. I'm all about closure and explanations. People deserve to know it's not their fault someone else is changing their feelings. *But gah!* I lower my head and close my eyes. I don't want to do this. I stop packing and look at the time on my phone again. Five hours to go.

I go through the motions of the morning like I'm being moved around by the imaginary puppeteer that controls me, waiting for Dean to get off work so we can talk. I packed most of my bags for Georgia and went to go get my final paycheck from work. I look at the time again when I get home. *Geez, still four hours to go.*

I'm gonna watch a movie, that'll help the time go by. I plop down on the living room couch and try to put the time of day out of my mind. *Runaway At The Alter* is one of my favorite movies. The poor girl doesn't know that she's the one that keeps running away and that all the guys she walked down the aisle with only wanted to love her for who she is. It's not until she realizes that she needs to love herself first before she can let someone else love her. Poor girl.

When the movie finishes I grab my phone for the first time since I hit PLAY. I missed a text from Dean an hour ago.

"I gave my notice today! I'm excited to be done with this place come December! Jake from State Farm OUT!"

I smirk. I'm happy for him. I decided to put on another movie and go with *You've Got Letters*, such a classic.

You've Got Letters feels like Dean and my situation. We got to know each other not in person but over messages. The characters in the movie end up together, though. Unlike Dean and I will, it would seem.

When the movie finishes I know this time he's off work. I look at my phone. He's going to call me soon. Butterflies hit again. I was able to hold them off with the movies.

A few minutes go by and my phone rings. I take a deep breath...here we go. I stand up for the first time in four hours and start pacing in the living room again.

I clear my throat. "Hello," I say, trying to sound normal.

"Long time, no see," he says with a laugh, and my heart feels crushed that he sounds so normal and he's about to be blindsided.

I laugh awkwardly. "Righhht. How was work today?" I ask, looking at the ground and kicking the carpet fibers. I don't want to start the conversation off on a low note. Having lost all of my ability to banter and make jokes, I go for the surface level questions while I make a deep trail in the carpet below me.

"Same old thing. Except…I gave my notice today and it felt so good. I don't want to keep working there. I'm excited to be done with that place in a couple months. My official last day is gonna be on the first of December." He sounds so insanely happy.

"Oh yeah, you texted me that earlier." Every word I say sounds slow and forced. "Sorry I didn't respond. I'm so excited for you! I bet that feels amazing." I exhale. "I know that I felt so good giving my notice to my job. And finishing my last shift yesterday was better than words can describe." I tuck one hand into the elbow of the other arm that's holding the phone.

"I bet. My last day is going to be a mix of happy and sad. I like my coworkers, but the job has lost its luster." He laughs.

I smile slowly at his joke. "So long, Jake from State Farm."

We keep talking about our day for a while and then there is a break in the conversation, probably because I'm feeling so weird. I decide now would be a good time to talk about my feelings so I grab a blanket and walk outside to find a spot in the yard. I didn't want any listening ears in the house to hear me essentially 'break up' with Dean, so I found an evergreen tree in the front yard and put the blanket on the grass to settle in.

"Can I talk to you about something?" I ask him and I feel like all the air left my lungs.

I hear him catch his breath and he says, "Go ahead. Shoot."

"I just wanted to start by saying, I've really enjoyed our friendship." I hear him let out a heavy sigh and I close my eyes as my stomach burns from the inside out. I take a deep breath and continue, "Talking to you these past few months has been the most fun I've ever had with a guy." I cringe and my shoulders go up to my ears at how cliché I sound. "I don't want to stop talking to you or anything." I wave my hand in the air as if to stop a fly from dive-bombing my face. "I just want to let you know that I'm realizing I don't actually have deep feelings for you." I pause to see if he wants to input anything but after ten seconds I figure he's just processing it all. If, on the off chance he's hurt, I want to address that, "I'm not trying to hurt your feelings at all. I just wanted to be honest with you." I lay stiff on the ground, finally able to breathe as I finished getting all my thoughts out to him. *Phew!* I roll over to my side and bring the blanket over my face. I got past the hardest conversation I've ever had with a guy.

I wait longer than I'd like for his response and he finally says, "Oh...umm...no worries...I've been thinking the same thing...I uhh...I don't have feelings for you either...I really like your friendship too. We can keep talking and being friends...That sounds good to me."

I squint my eyes and tilt my head under the blanket, *that was almost too easy.* I knew he would be cool about it but shouldn't he have protested a little? I thought there would be more of a fall out. Skepticism aside, I can feel the weight leaving my shoulders that has been there for the past few days. I'm relieved that he wants to still be friends and keep chatting without the heaviness of a relationship hanging over us.

"Phew! I'm relieved to hear you say that," I pull the blanket down off my face and stare at my dad's garden that's close to my grassy tree spot.

After a minute of silence I say, "My dad's garden is doing so good." Now that the worst part of the conversation is over I can lean into the rest of the conversation without any hesitation.

"It looked amazing when I was there! The corn was so high and the zucchini was growing everywhere. How many vegetables do you think he's growing?" he asks with a monotone voice, but I push past the question in my head asking if he really was feeling the same way I was, or if he's lying.

"Oh man, probably like thirty. Corn, tomatoes, onion, beets, broccoli, zucchini, pumpkin, cabbage, potatoes, green beans, peas, spaghetti squash, I could go on, but I won't." I let out a squawking laugh. "He loves his garden."

"I could tell, it was massive. And he is good at the upkeep," he says, still no pitch in his voice.

"For sure! He learned from his dad. My grandpa has great gardens too." I keep looking at the garden, "Someday I'll grow the Berger green thumb and be out in my own garden."

"I'd love to learn how to grow a garden. I won't be able to if I never live in a house, though. I'm not sure I'll stay in Bothell long enough to grow rich and buy a house with enough land to have a garden." He laughs dryly, finally some personality coming to his voice.

"Yeah, it's pretty expensive up there." I twirl a blade of grass in my hand.

"Tell me about it. I've been looking at apartments and there's no way I can spend $2000 a month on a one-bedroom, one-bathroom apartment. Who makes that kind of money by themselves??" He scoffs and is finally starting to sound normal again.

"People in tech. Bothell has a giant tech industry. Places by the water are always coveted. Even though the weather here is depressing. Buckle up buddy, you've got a lot of rain in your future," I say with a laugh as I flick the blade of grass back onto the ground.

"Right." He went back to monotone. "So hey, umm, I have to do something last minute, sorry. I've gotta cut this short."

I sit up quickly and crisscross my legs. "Oh, okay. Yeah, I should go too." I lean forward. I have a sinking suspicion that he's ending the convo early because of what I said. He had a lot of long pauses when he said he was on the same page as me.

"Okay. Talk to you later, Berger."

"Definitely. Talk soon."

He ends the call before I even take the phone away from my ear. I stare at the black screen on my smartphone, replaying his response in my head. He definitely was more hurt than accepting. He's never ended one of our conversations before. I've always been the one to end them.

Chapter 23

Past

October

My final week in Washington *and* the move across the country was a whirlwind. I thought it would be a breeze to uproot my life and move 2,700 miles away. Turns out, it's not. It's quite stressful, actually. However, Forrest and I made it and got through the sibling fights and the stress in one piece.

I got a job right away which was more than nice. The day before leaving town I saw a listing on everyjob.com for a coffee shop barista and I applied. The owners called me within the hour and we set up an interview for the day after I arrived in town. When I got to the interview there was no question that we clicked and I would be a good fit. They hired me on the spot.

It's been so much fun living in a new town and getting to know everyone in our giant house. Fred, Emily, Juniper, and Forrest are obviously people I know already. I've been getting to know Fred and Juniper's parents better, Sarah and Mitchell, plus we have two extra roommates, Kim and Josh. I'm no noob when it comes to a house full of people that needs their own personal traffic guard, so we don't have any collisions. We have family dinner nights once a week, so that's been fun. It's creating a sense of community, something I'm always craving.

I got Juniper a job a month after me at The Grand Coffee when my bosses were looking for another employee to hire, so now she owes me her firstborn. It's been a great fit and I've really enjoyed having someone I know to work with. The best part is that it's just a mile away from where we live so I can walk to work. Not having a car hasn't held me back from taking this town by the balls.

Lately, when I've tried calling Dean he hasn't been available. He tells me he's in the middle of something and that he'll call me back but, jokes on me, he never actually does. We've only talked on the phone twice this month. Our texting has slowed down too. It took me a month to realize it, but we only text every other day now. I'm starting to wonder what's going on. I wanted him to not pursue me so hard core, but I didn't mean pull back all together and only have crickets between us. I feel more stressed out now than before I told him I just wanted to be friends.

I pull my phone out and type, **"Hey man, how's it hanging?"**

I sit down on the couch in my new living room and play a movie that I rented yesterday, Drop Dead Gorgeous. Dean asked me to watch it over the summer, when we were closer, but I kept pushing it off...until now. Watching it makes me feel like we're still close. I bring my knees to my chest and hug them. I miss him and want to feel some kind of connection to him again. Like this cult classic from 1999 will somehow be the two-by-four's that will bridge the gap forming between us.

Just as Amber is fixing Mary's hair in the hospital on Drop Dead Gorgeous, my phone chimes, I grab it faster than lightning and read Dean's text even quicker.

"Good, just got back from a hike."

Nice, he responded quickly! *Maybe I was reading into his silence wrong.* I pause the movie. **"Can't help yourself, huh? Still need to**

risk hitting your head, if you fall, out there on the trail? Lol." I stare at my phone when I hit send. Hoping to get a response back just as quick as I sent one.

"I guess," was his dull reply back.

I hold the phone with both hands as I read and reread his text. That response feels so off. What's happening? Oh crap, I lift my head up and start at the paint on the living room wall. *This was me self-sabotaging again, wasn't it? Dammit.* I look back down at my phone and stare at it. *I need to fix this.* I start to type, **"Is everything..."** but don't finish the sentence. I hit the delete button to get it off my screen.

But wait, I need to know if I'm the one who caused this massive chasm between us. I'll ask him the elephant in the room question. I start typing again, **"Is everything ok, Dean?"**

It doesn't take long for me to get a response back.

"Yeah, why?"

I know something is up, but he's not telling me. I have the intuition of an eagle and this guy is being fishy. I play into his ploy though. **"Oh, I just feel like we talk less. I wanted to make sure there wasn't anything going on."**

"Nope. Everything is the same. I've been busy this month with some projects I need to get done before moving to Bothell. How has it been living in the big house with the whole fam?"

I decide to bait him further, hoping to smoke him out of this foxhole he's digging,

"Oh good. I'm glad it's not because of what I said a month ago!" I hit send and decide to wait a minute before starting my next text. Hopefully giving him enough time to read and respond without realizing that I'm gonna send another one on its heels. I don't have the text bubble feature on so he won't see me typing. I start slowly, **"It's been fun here! I love living with this whole group. We're all doing our part to keep the house clean and we all have our own cabinet with our food. Feels like we're living our own lives separate but together. I like it."** I hover my finger over the send button to give him just a few more seconds to respond to that first text. After another minute goes by I figure he won't be responding so I just hit *send*.

"That sounds fun. Fred's family is pretty chill. I can see it being an easy transition to live with them." He responds, completely avoiding my first text. I look up as Juniper walks into the room. I give her a blank smile as she sits on one of the couches.

I look back at my phone to respond, **"It has been."** I don't know what else to say. I feel sad that he won't talk about it. I lay my head down on the armrest of the couch and curl my knees up in the fetal position.

I pull my phone up to look at it. I don't want this conversation to end there. With this new version of Dean I've been getting lately, I know that a short three-word text like that means he's going to stop responding back to me soon. I purse my lips as I think about the Dean of two months ago who wouldn't dare let a short text stop him from responding and hearing back from me just for the chance of a good bantering thread. So I start moving my thumbs around the keyboard. **"And school's been great. Learning a lot of new things that are blowing my mind. Homework isn't hard either."**

"That's good. Sounds like you're thriving there."

His text makes me feel so empty.

"I feel like that too." I replied. I put the phone down at my side and think, *"wow, these texts feel sour and I don't like them."*

He doesn't send me another text back. I lock my phone, put it down, and stare blankly at the TV as I push play.

"Hey Per," I say over the noise of the beauty pageant mockumentary, "when this is over do you want to go grocery shopping together?" Juniper's the one with the car. I could ask to borrow it but I wanted to process with her about what's going on with Dean. Since Fred, Emily, Sarah, and Mitchell all know Dean so well I don't want them hearing that I'm starting to feel insecure with him.

"Sure," Juniper says while still looking down at her book. "I've been needing to get a few things too."

"Sweet," I say as I pull the blanket off the back of the couch and lay it over me to finish this movie. The movie I started in hopes to feel closer to Dean, but instead, is making my heart ache inside.

When the movie finishes we grab our bags and head out. As soon as the car door makes contact with the latch I turn to Juniper and say, "So I wanted to talk about Dean." I haven't yet told Juniper about me essentially 'ending feelings' with Dean.

Putting her seat belt on, Juniper slowly looks up at me and says, "Oh yeah, how's that guy doing?"

"He's doing fine. Though, things are starting to feel off with him. He doesn't text me as often as he used to and I'm getting really confused. We used to text all the time and now I only get a text every now and then. As opposed to hundreds a day. I used to not be able to count his texts on one hand in any given hour," I say holding out my hand with all the fingers spread apart and shaking it in the air.

"Oh, maybe he's busy?" Juniper suggests, steering the car onto the main road.

"I don't know...it's been like this for the past month. I would expect that to be the case if it was just a few days. Or if we didn't have a history of all-day-long texting, but now it's becoming his normal with me. You know him well, does this seem normal to you?" I whine, looking over at her with desperate eyes, searching her face for some kind of answer to my new problem.

"I wouldn't worry about it," she shakes her head. "Dean gets distracted easily."

Hmm. That's not how I've experienced him all summer. Her response doesn't settle the inner turmoil that is starting to bubble up inside of me. Even though I feel like I've landed on a foreign continent and don't know my way around this new world, it feels good to talk to someone about Dean.

"Okay. I hope you're right. I still like talking to him and don't want us to stop being in each other's lives," I look out the window at the building passing us. I'm starting to question why I ended things with him romantically. I absolutely thought I didn't want him as more than a friend, but now that I feel like I'm starting to lose him I feel confused. This distance is making me realize how much he meant to me.

"Why would you stop being friends? Did something happen?" she asks.

"Umm. Well...a week before I moved here, I told him that I just wanted to be friends and not be anything more. I felt really good about telling him that, but he's been really weird ever since." I put my feet up on the dashboard to hug my knees and look over at her.

"Elise! You didn't!" she says, with a little yell in her voice. "You probably broke that boy's heart."

My head is spinning as I stare at her with wide eyes. "But he told me that he wasn't interested in being something serious with me either. He didn't say that he was bothered."

"Oh hun, he's not going to say that he's really into you right after you tell him you don't want to be with him. That's just asking for more pain." She purses her lips.

"Oh my God, did I break his heart?! That has to be why he's been pulling away this past month. How could I be so naive that I didn't put this together?" I open my mouth in shock. "I mean, I thought for a minute he might be hurt during our phone call, but because he never said it with his words, I figured he was feeling the same way I was."

"Do you really feel that way? I thought you guys really had something." She turns the car into the grocery store parking lot.

"I'm actually starting to think that I do want to be more than friends with him. I don't know if it's the reality of him pulling away from me or if I always had deep feelings for him but just ended up self-sabotaging it. Ugh. I had a couple people this summer tell me not to self-sabotage things with him but...did I end up doing that without realizing it?" I put my face in my hands and sigh.

"Maybe it's not too late? Maybe you can let him know that you messed up and would love another chance if he's still interested. He might be willing to admit his feelings to you if you bare your soul?" she says, as she puts the car in park.

"Yeah, maybe I can do that. I'll try to have a conversation with him." I look down at my folded hands, "Damn. I think I really did like him and I was just scared so I ran. Just like the *Runaway At The Alter*," I say, trying to keep eye contact with her and feeling like it might actually be too late.

"Did I tell you I was watching the *Runaway At The Alter* the day I told him I didn't like him? That was a bit of foreshadowing if I ever saw one."

"No, you didn't tell me! How poetic," she says with wide eyes, now putting the car in park.

"Yeah, I wish I would have realized what was going on inside my head before I told him anything. Our story would be playing out much differently now." I open the car door and we start walking into the grocery store. Nothing feels more strange than my feet do in this moment, walking toward a normal activity while my brain is screaming at me to not let him get away. I need to fix this with him. *I hope he'll let me fix it.* I hope the story of us wasn't momentary.

Chapter 24

Past

November

B eing a barista makes me so damn delighted-I couldn't be more thrilled working at The Grand Coffee. I'm two months in, and I love it here. I'd pitch a tent in the meeting room if they'd let me. Coming into work at 5am and doing everything, from grinding the coffee to flipping the OPEN sign, fills me with bliss.

I could care less that Dean is, at this point, not texting me back but every couple of days. I have so much going on at work to distract me. The last thing I said to him was **"I've never thought about raisins being a fruit...but I guess you're right."** So far it's been crickets. It's fine though. It's fine.

When Juniper hands the final customer of our rush their drink through the window I say, "Today might be the funnest day here I've ever experienced!" I wipe off the steamer wand and smile, extremely proud of myself and not opposed to getting some sort of medal or gold star for not stressing out.

"I agree. I don't think we've ever made thirty drinks in twenty minutes before. The middle of that big rush was insane for us," she replies as she grabs her book off her chair to sit down for the first time since she arrived.

I finish wiping the coffee grounds off the countertop near the espresso machine and say, "Right! I'm proud of us for keeping calm and carrying on." I smile down at my hand.

"Switching subjects though," I clear my throat. "I know this topic might be getting annoying, but I just wanted to update you. It's been three days now since I've tried to call Dean. To, you know, let him know that I actually have feelings for him and want to see if he has them for me. He hasn't called me back though." I give her a pouty face. *Ok, maybe I care a little*, "I don't like that he isn't explaining anything! I mean, what started all this is when I shared my feelings. I wish he would just tell me what's going on inside his head so I'm not starting down the crazy path over here!" I grab my book off my chair and sit down.

"Ahh, Love. I'm sorry. That must feel awful to not have your call returned. It's good that you figured out your true feelings and you're trying to honestly communicate with him, though," She looks over at me with encouragement in her eyes.

"Ugh. I feel like I'm acting all obsessed with him, when he's actively avoiding me." I put my head on my book, feeling a ten-car pile-up of emotions. "I'm desperately pining for him. For the relationship we had two months ago. For the person I felt like I could always count on being there. For our long-ass nightly calls. Because talking on the phone for seven hours every other night and then having that all taken away in a matter of months just feels wrong."

"Okay. Okay. Don't get in your head too much about this. I'd wait one more day and call him again. Maybe he just forgot," she says while holding a hand out in the air.

"Yeah, maybe you're right. I could do that." I exhale a deep breath. "My heart is starting to ache..." I trail off.

"It doesn't need to ache yet. You don't know what he's thinking." I can tell she's trying to stop me from doing something that comes so natural to me, spiraling.

I look over at her, my head starting to get indents from leaning on my book. "But I'm a great spiraler. Always have been, always will be."

I turn my eyes to the ground and start thinking about all the 'if only's'. *If only I could go back into the past and keep my silly mouth shut. If only I could have played out both scenarios to see which one would break my heart the least.* I've thought about our future together. We'd travel the world. We'd go on hikes. We'd laugh and talk while we made dinner. We'd get a cat and buy a house. We both said once that cats were easier to take care of than dogs and we didn't want a dog to strap us down. Who needs those loyal little bastards anyway.

I've thought about the babies we would have with their dark hair and blue eyes. We'd take them on our hiking trips. We want a life that is fulfilled by adventure and love. The book I hold in my hand is no match to the photograph reel of memories that is playing all through the hopes and dreams we talked about. Now I'm wondering if any of it was necessary. Should we have even gone to those deep parts of our hearts if it was all going to end up like this? How could I not see that I was self-sabotaging AGAIN?! This is all my fault.

A customer walks in and we both stand to attention. I shake my head to try and focus on the order I'm making. I watch my hands do the work in front of me as my mind trails off. *I hope I still get to see him on New Years when he moves to Bothell. I hope that he's still planning on stopping by my parent's house up there, so we can hang out for a day and a half again.* I squeeze the paper cup when I try putting the lid on and half the latte spills onto the floor. *Damn.* I collapsed to the floor with a rag. *I desperately want to talk to him like we did over the summer. I need to try to call him again. Right now I feel like I'm still holding onto someone that's trying to walk away from me. I don't want to feel like a child wrapped around the leg of my person, trying to keep them from leaving.* I throw the rag away and grab another paper cup to start making a new latte. *It feels like the script has flipped and now I need closure from him. Without any closure I have no other way of knowing what his thoughts are. I'll just keep pursuing him the same way he pursued me during the summer. Maybe that will make him eventually start seeing that I care about him and he'll be interested in talking again? Or it'll embarrass the heck out of me and I'll feel like a loser.*

Once I hand the customer their finished drink I sit down and look over at Juniper, "I think it's the closure. I know he doesn't owe it to me, but I need an explanation of his feelings. Not getting closure and just being ignored makes me feel insane." I make a grabbing motion around my head. "I'm gonna try to get him to talk to me again, but if he just doesn't respond to me like he used to, well then, I won't know what to do with that," I say, as I slump down in my chair holding my book again.

"Not getting closure would suck," she says, putting a hand on my shoulder. "But if he can't give that to you or doesn't want to give that to you then you just have to accept that. I don't think you need to spiral just yet. Give it more time. You just moved and he's about to move. There's a lot going on in both of your lives right now. Wait and see how it plays out, before being led by your emotions."

"You're right." I look over at her and sit up straighter. "I'll try my best not to." I smile. "I'm glad I have you to process this stuff with. I don't know what I would do without you."

"I'm happy to help." She takes her hand off my shoulder, and we both open our books to read during this lull.

Chapter 25

Past

December

Thanksgiving goes by in a southern blur. I'm not used to having cold weather holidays in a warm place. But all of that is in the rear-view mirror, it's finally time to go to Washington for Christmas and New Years! I've been looking forward to this for months. Not just because I hope to see Dean at the end of it all, but also because I miss my family and want to see them at Christmas.

I've been stuck in limbo with Dean for a few months now. We only talked on the phone four times since the end of the summer. Every time I've tried to call him there's always something that he's doing and never enough time to call me back. I still only get a few texts back here and there but nothing more than a quick snippet of each other's lives.

I was actually shocked when, in the middle of December, I got a text from him that said, **"I can still come through Yelm, after New Years, on my way to Bothell, if you want."**

I felt a slew of emotions, a combination of giddy and hope and 'what if he bails', all at once when I replied, **"Yeah! Absolutely. I'd love to see you. We can finally have time to chat since our timing has been off all fall."**

He had texted me back, **"Cool. I'm looking forward to it. Tell Michael I'm winning Clue again, LOL."**

"Oh, I definitely will. He's gonna ramp up his competitive side though. You've been warned." I'd replied with a smile on my face that I wasn't been able to wipe off, even though that was our last text for the day. He was actually thinking of spending time with me. That's the first step to getting him back.

Christmas with my family is not for the faint of heart. Every Christmas we get together, we have a massive gathering. There's easily one hundred presents under our tree, so much so that it feels more like it's a home for the presents than for the family.

My family tries to make the most out of the Christmas holiday. It's all thanks to my mom, she never liked the kind of Christmases where everyone rips open their presents like a bunch of feral cats attacking all at once and it's all over after ten minutes.

My mom taught us how to slow down as if we were Laura Ingalls Wilder on the Midwest Prairie. She'd let us open up one present on Christmas Eve. Then on Christmas morning we would open up two presents before breakfast. After each milestone of the day we'd get another present. Ending finally with the last couple of presents before bed.

Now that my siblings and I have gotten older we've added even more activities so that our Christmas isn't just a day, it's almost a whole week! It helps us get into the Christmas spirit and wipe off any Scrooge that's left on us from the year.

Our Christmas tanks are full of joy by the end of a week filled with antique shopping, sledding, ice skating and last-minute Christmas Eve shopping. We end the week fully satisfied that we used up our time off to the fullest. It's rare to find a family that wants to do everything together, but we are that family. We don't get sick of the hustle and bustle around each other in our childhood home. We seemingly thrive off it.

During this tinsel-tastic week and a half that I'm in Washington with my family, I text Dean a few times. It was playful and banter-y. He's been quicker to respond than he has been for the past three and a half months, since my un-confession of feeling toward him. It almost feels like we could find our way back to each other again. My emotions won't waver this time. I like the guy and I've decided to tell him when I see him on New Year's Day.

The plan is for him to leave San Diego on New Years Eve, spend the night in Redding, then arrive in Yelm on New Years Day. I hope nothing derails it.

We finish our family-fun-Christmas-traditions and move onto thinking about the New Year and our resolutions that we're going to make. Maybe mine should be, "stop hiding from guys who like me," and "spiraling less."

On New Year's Eve I'm so excited I could poop out an ornament. I can't wait to get *the* text from Dean that says he is leaving town. I keep picking up my phone and putting it down all morning. I don't want to text him first in case he's in the middle of something, but I'm unable to settle myself enough to forget that today is the day he'll be eight hours closer to me.

I finally give in after cleaning the whole kitchen and living room when I see that it's 1pm. He should have at least said something by now, so I text him, **"How's it going?"** Casual, not antsy.

He texts back, **"Hey, sorry, I haven't left yet. I keep forgetting stuff that I need to do before I leave. I should be leaving soon though."**

I slump down onto the couch next to Forrest, and reply, **"Cool! Let me know when you leave."** All the energy has left my body and I give into the fried potato feeling that is consuming me. Forrest is watching *Logan's Heroes* as I'm regretting all my life choices from four months ago.

After 4 hours of *Logan's Heroes* I still haven't heard from Dean and I text him again. **"Sorry to bug you. Left yet?"** I scrunch my lips and place the phone down on the couch. I'm trying to be understanding with what his day looks like. Now that it's 5pm I can't imagine he'll want to get to Redding by 1am.

I feel my phone buzz on the couch sooner than I expect, I snatch it up quicker than a snake bite. **"Not quite. My sister needed to show me something at her house and that is taking up a lot of time."**

"Oh ok. Are you going to make it out of town today?" I ask him knowing that it takes ten hours, with stops, to drive from San Diego to Redding. He won't be able to make it there any faster, unless he was practicing going after his first Formula-1 race, but he's not.

He replies, **"I'm actually not sure. I've been thinking it's getting too late to head out and I still have to get a few things all buttoned up before I leave."** Then, after a minute, I got a second text. **"I think I'll leave early tomorrow morning."**

I read it and let out a breath that feels like fire.

I close my eyes and grab my shoulders to rub them back down to a normal level. If I was a fried potato four hours ago, I'm now a block of concrete, heavy and completely lifeless. The couch is my new home. *Be understanding Elise.* I should find a good lay-z-boy to buy, because I don't think I'll be able to move from this spot for the foreseeable future. *Be understanding Elise.*

"That's okay. Do what you need to do in order to leave. I don't want you to feel like something is left undone." I don't want to push him further away than he already is by letting out that I'm bummed.

"Thanks. I will."

I place my phone back on the couch, cross my arms and accept my couch life fate. I didn't hear from him for the rest of the day.

The next day I sleep in. I was able to ring in the New Year last night with my family, but I was half distracted. Thirty minutes after waking up I sluggishly roll over and grab my phone. I pop straight up when I see the text from Dean.

"I'm officially on the road this morning! Left bright and early, the sun wasn't even out! No birds were singing, no roosters were crowing. I'm gonna try to drive the whole way to Yelm today and just stop for an hour in Redding to see my pals there."

My eyes go wide and get a little watery. My lower lip starts to quiver as I realize he's actually going to try and make it here today. I thought he was going to push everything back a day, but I'm glad he's doing the unexpected. My chest lifts with joy at the time we'll still have together.

I start typing so fast the buttons can't keep up. **"Ok! That sounds good to me! I'm excited to see you today! Thanks for making it work."**

The left side of my brain tells me to wait patiently and not worry about where he is on the road; it'll only make me anxious. The right side of my brain wants to dance in a field of flowers, because I can't help being excited to see him, and only want to think about where he is and what kind of progress he's making.

I need something for my hands to do, so I get out of bed and go to the kitchen where everyone is finishing up their breakfast. Fred and Emily made potatoes, eggs, and sausage; it looks like. I smile at Emily standing by the kitchen counter when I go for my mom's recipe box, and start flipping through it for the Christmas cookie recipe. Once I find it in the Rolodex, I pull out the flour and sugar from the cabinets. I've mentioned to Dean before that I love having rolled out sugar cookies and my family has already eaten the ones we made on Christmas Eve.

"Oooo. Making more cookies. Noice!" Forrest says, as he walks thru the kitchen to get a glass of milk out of the fridge.

"I figured we needed more," I tell him without going into detail about the reason behind making them. I need to keep busy.

I finally get an update text from him, as I'm cutting out all the tree shaped cookies with a cookie cutter.

"I've made it to Redding! Going to stop here and I'll let you know when I leave town."

I scoop my tree, Santa, and jingle bell shaped cookies off the counter and onto my cookie sheet. I pull out the first batch of cookies from the oven and pop the next tray in the oven. Before I can pick up my phone I go to the sink and wash the cookie dough from my hands under the running water.

I reply, **"Great! Don't have too much fun! lol."** Then put my phone back down, and continue to cut out more cookies with a smile on my face.

A couple hours later I get a book report of a text from him.

"I think I'm going to stay here for the night. It's raining really bad and I don't want to drive in this kind of weather because I'm not used to it."

After reading the first two sentences, I sink onto a bench stool tucked under the countertop.

"**Plus, I haven't seen my friends here in eight months and it'll be nice to catch up with them. Don't be too disappointed in me.**"

My eyes start to tear up as I continue reading.

"**I'm going to leave early again tomorrow so I can make it to your place by the afternoon and we can have a few hours to hang out before you have to fly away. I know it's not a lot of time but it's something?**"

Be understanding Elise, you owe him that, "**No, I get it. Thanks for the update. Have fun with your friends. I look forward to tomorrow. We can still make the most of it.**" I hit send, and drop my hands to my lap. I let the tears fall on my phone.

"**Thanks! Talk to you tomorrow!**"

I grab for a warm cookie next to me and take a bite of Santa's leg. I finish the whole thing, wipe my eyes, and decide to go to my room for a nap. I'm getting dizzy from all my emotions and it's drained me.

The next day I sleep in again. When I wake up at 10am there's a text on my phone from him, "**I left Redding at 6am and should be to Yelm by 2pm!**" An involuntary smile crosses my face. I still find myself excited that we're going to get some kind of hang out in, before I have to fly back. I can't help it. The heart wants what the heart wants.

I reply quickly, scrunching my forehead, "**That sounds great! How's the driving going?**"

He responds back, "**Not good I'm afraid.**"

My heart sinks, not again, he's grossly unaware that he's emotionally beaten me to a pulp and left me out to dry into a piece of leather fruit, and now these words are the blow torch to finish me off. *Stop being dramatic.*

"The rain is so bad I'm only going 40MPH. So it's taking me twice as long to get there."

With sad limbs I get out of bed and start packing up my clothes and Christmas gifts from the week. I'm gently placing each item into my suitcase as I consider where my headspace was at these last couple days. I was daydreaming about what kind of convos we were going to have. I realized a couple days ago that I hadn't taken him to a few spots in town, so I was going to show him those while he was here. Now he won't be here and my emotional left brain has fully taken over my conscience now. My arms feel robotic as I continue getting ready for my flight back to Georgia.

I text Esther, **"I might need a ride to the airport today, do you think you could take me?"**

"Yeah, no problem. Is Dean not coming?"

"I'm not sure. The rain has thwarted my plans with him today." I slump down on the bed at the thought. The only thing the weather does in the winter is rain, I should have expected this, I'm a Washingtonian after all.

"Oh dang, that's a bummer. We'll be there at lunch today. Then maybe we can play a boardgame?"

"I'd love that for the distraction. See you soon."

When I'm an hour from needing to leave the house, and in the middle of a game of Monopoly with Esther and Forrest, my phone buzzes. I almost don't want to look at it, because if it's him, and he's not coming, then I'd rather not read that.

Ugh. I can't help it, my mind goes on autopilot, and I reach for my phone to read his text, **"Hey! Just entered Yelm. I should be at your house in five minutes."**

Wow, he actually made it in time to say a quick hello.

"That's great! Thank you for doing all you could to come visit."

"I know this has been disappointing, but do you still want me to come over and drive you to the airport?"

I play with the corner of my phone, as a swarm of moths twist my stomach in seven different directions.

"Elise, it's your turn, do you want to pass GO or collect $200?"

"Hmm?" I look up and then back down, half registering what Esther just asked me.

Of course I will want to see you, I like you mister, "Umm, I'll collect $200," I tell her. As she counts out the money for me I reply to Dean, **"Yes, I would still like that."**

I look up at Esther and say, "I guess I won't need you to take me to the airport after all."

She gives a quick clap like two symbols being banged together and says, "Yay! He's coming! That's great!"

Dean arrived at my parents house, just as I was about to collect my Park Lane real estate. We stopped the game to welcome him in. My cheeks go red when I see him, and I hide in the back of my family group. Everyone in my family likes Dean, so they've all been looking forward to him coming to visit as much as I have. I didn't tell anyone that my heart has been sad these past two days, because it wasn't actually Dean's fault that things held him up.

He's so cute, I can't believe there was ever a time I doubted it. I tilt my chin down so he doesn't see how insecure I feel being near him.

"Hey Forrest, see any good movies lately?" He pats my younger brother on the back.

"Yes actually, we saw an action movie last week." Forrest returns the pat.

"Excellent." Then Dean looks at Michael. "How's that move to Spokane going?"

"Great. We settled into a nice little downstairs apartment and got a new cat," Michael responds from the couch.

"Awesome. I'm happy for you." Dean gives him a thumbs up.

"It's good to see you, Elise," Dean finally makes eye contact with me and gives me a hug that I wish lasted longer than a few seconds. Just being in his presence makes me want to melt into his arms like butter in a pan. Was I reading into his texts too much? Maybe he was just busy and needed to finish his move before we could go back to normal?

When Forrest asks Dean about his move to Bothell he says, "I'm really excited about it. I love new adventures and this is definitely going to be my biggest one yet." When Michael asks where he's going to be living he says, "With an old friend. He's the one that convinced me to move to Bothell in the first place. It better be as great as he says it is or our friendship is over."

I chuckle.

The hour zooms by and it's already time for me to say my goodbyes and head out. My family wishes me a safe flight, and wishes Dean a good time in Bothell. When Esther gives me a hug she whispers, "I want to hear everything about this car ride when you get a chance."

I let out an airy laugh and said, "Oh, you most definitely will."

When we start driving, Dean asks, "How's everything going?"

281

I snap my head to look over at him, then push down my insecure thoughts of being too much, too clingy or too desperate. This might be my only opportunity to talk to him about how I feel. I'm not exactly in the best state of mind to pour my heart out, but with his unavailability lately to answer my phone calls I'm not sure I'll have another chance. We have an hour after all. We should have time to hash it out and get to some sort of conclusion.

I clear my throat, and without any banter I say, "I'll get right to the point. I've been really struggling these past few months. I don't like how little we've talked." I look down and start fiddling with my hands. "We used to talk all the time but now it's dwindled down to nothing. I can't help but feel like it's because of the last time I talked to you about my feelings. I thought I just wanted to be friends because I was feeling so uncomfortable with all the attention. But it turns out..." I trail off and pause for a second to decide if I'm really going to say this. My brain screams, YES, at me so I continue, "I do like you. A lot. I would like to see if we could continue our relationship in the same way we had been doing over the summer. And maybe see where this can go more romantically?" I phrase the end as a question. I genuinely want to hear from his mouth if he wants to continue things from where we left off.

We sit in awkward silence for far too long, when he finally says, "Thank you for telling me and I'm sorry it's been hard for you." He lets out a heavy sigh. "Unfortunately, right now isn't a good time for me. Freshly moving to Bothell and trying to start a life here will take up a lot of my time and I don't want that to take away from you and I, if we did try to start something. Maybe we can be together someday. Just not now," he says as he slams the door on us, but leaves a crack open for the future. I can almost hear the squeak of the metaphorical door being left ajar just a tiny bit.

"Oh," I say, not expecting to hear this kind of response. Slowly, as if the words don't want to leave my throat I say, "I understand." I'm losing my confidence and myself now. "Thank you for being honest with me." I flatten my lips into a half smile.

If he was trying to end things, he did a very confusing job of it. He left the door cracked a little as he tried to walk out of it. I look out the window as we go North on I-5, and sift through my mixed emotions. My eyes start to sting as I hold back the tears. His words are saying he's breaking things off, but only until things settle down. My eyes start darting from side to side, as if I'm working out a complex geometry problem, but maybe we will be an official couple someday.

"No problem. I hope you can understand, or at the very least, thank you for trying to understand," he says, sounding solemn beside me.

"Yeah...yeah...I do...I do," I say, trying to sound like everything is normal when on the inside my world is crashing. "Does this mean you don't want to talk anymore?" I ask, as an ache starts to settle into my heart.

"NO—no. We can still talk. We're still friends, Berger," he says as he elbows me across the car.

"Oh, cool. Okay. I like that. Because I do still want to be friends." I playfully nudged him back.

I don't want to continue to make it awkward, so the rest of the car ride is spent in comfortable conversations about what we've been up to lately, and what we hope to do with our lives in the next few months. When we get to the airport he helps me get my bags out of the trunk, and then he gives me a hug. This goodbye feels different than the last time we were at the airport. The last one was filled with hope, joy, and adoration. This one is filled with questions, pain, and no future.

Chapter 26

Past

January

I feel like an empty pistachio shell after seeing Dean.

It's two weeks into January now and he's only texted me twice. It was in response to texts I sent him though, so he wasn't the one initiating. I put my head in my hands as I sit at the kitchen table. I hate these long stretches of time between talking. I want to hear him say that he doesn't like me, and we need to move on, instead of staying in this limbo together. I feel like I'm stuck in a labyrinth with him and I can't get out. He didn't shut the door, he left the door hanging on its hinge. I'm over here waiting for one gust of wind to blow it wide open.

I let out a breath as I push my arms flat on the table and lay my head down. I've been thinking about him constantly. My ears perk up anytime someone in the house talks about him. I've talked to Emily about it since being home and she just lets me talk and sympathizes. Wishing that things were going to turn out differently but not quite sure what else to say, I want to ask Fred if he's talked to Dean at all but that feels intrusive. I don't want to put him in the middle of this drama. I also don't want to come off as desperate and insecure in case that gets back to Dean. But, I'm flipping desperate and insecure!

The day after I fly back I tell Juniper the whole story, all the annoying details. Before I can tell her the part of me telling Dean that I still like him, I veer off topic and start talking about kissing him.

"The worst part is that I just wanted to kiss him again, ya know??" I say, as I jump and do a belly flop right on top of my covers, face in the pillow. If she wasn't here I would probably let out a muffled scream. I continued, "And we didn't have any alone time at my house before driving to the airport to fulfill a makeout daydream I was thinking about." I turn back to Juniper as she sits on her bed looking at me patiently with her legs crossed. "I tried to get him to go back into the back of the house with me to 'get something,' but he was so tied up talking to my siblings that he asked me if I could just get it without him." I threw my head back into the pillow and decided to let out a little scream that sounded like a baby kitten. I'm feeling all riled up from reliving the day again.

"Maybe you can make it up by telling him that you like him? Maybe it's not too late and he'll open his heart up to you again? I know he likes you. I just know it," she says like an optimistic yoga instructor, telling you to breathe through the pain of the handstand scorpion pose that you've tried once before, without success.

"Oh! I didn't get to that part. I rabbit-trailed hard with my hopes-of-kissing-him, sorry. I actually tried that in the car on the drive to the airport. He turned me down. He said, 'Maybe we can be together someday. Just not now.' I'm feeling so desperate, though, I'll try anything. I could ask him again. I'd try haggis if it meant he'd pay attention to me like he used to. He's just still giving me few responses and little communication. Not hearing from him is making me feel crazy."

"Well, crap. That sucks! I hate this for you!" she says, as she slaps the top of her leg.

"It's so dumb that I'm sending him text messages he's taking days to respond to. It's making me feel, and come across, even more desperate than I actually am. Because if he would just RESPOND back to me then I wouldn't have to seem like the psycho girl who won't leave him alone." I kick my feet on the bed. "Man, just when I thought I was the confident girl, this happens, and now I'm tipped over the edge to the far end of 'crazy.' Ugh."

"Yes! That's rough. It's unfortunate he's left you in limbo like this," she says, as she lays down.

I nod my face vigorously into my pillow. I tilt my head to the side so she can hear me say, "Then, when he finally texts me back I devour his words, like a hungry lion eating an antelope, and I return a text back right away, like we both used to, and then I'm left waiting another two days for a response back. I don't get it. I don't get it!" I say with another baby cat scream into the pillow. "I'm going crazy. Am I going crazy? Am I not seeing this correctly? Were we not close at all last summer, and now I've just created something in my head that was never there?"

"No dude, you're not crazy. You did have something with Dean, and he felt it too. He came to your house for Christ sakes and you guys made out in the parking lot of the movie theater. Of course you guys had something. He's just being a dude that decided ignoring a girl is better than communicating with her. I'm so sorry. I wish I could fix this for you," she says. "You're just going to have to ride the wave and get through it with time. Keep texting and calling if you need to, but just be okay with it if he keeps not responding back. Don't let it get to the point that it feels like he's stringing you along," she says.

"Thank you. I appreciate the advice," I say. "I think I need to be alone now. I'm going to stay on my bed and think about my life choices," I say dramatically as I turn around and face the wall.

"Okay, love, I'll let you have some time alone," she says, and I hear the door click a few seconds later.

I lay in bed for an hour, thinking about how to make my desperation go away. Maybe I should breach the topic with Fred. He knows him well enough, maybe he'll know what to do. Maybe Dean has even talked to Fred about this over the phone, and Fred can tell me what Dean is thinking, since Dean is clearly not saying anything to me. I squeeze my temples with my hands to release all the running my brain is doing. I decide to take a nap, so the stress I'm feeling will melt away into the floral sheets below me.

When I wake up I go find Fred to talk to him about this something-ship with Dean. When I find him he's making a sandwich in the kitchen with Emily.

"Hey guys, how's it going?" I ask, looking at the sandwich meat they have out on the counter for their soon to be lunch.

"Good El, how are you doing?" Emily asks as she spreads mayo across her bread.

"Well, since you asked..." I put both my hands on the countertop. "I'm feeling sad." I give a quick head nod, then continue, "Because Dean hasn't been texting or calling me back and I just don't know why he would do that when he said he still wants to be friends." I look over at

Fred who is staring intensely at the Havarti cheese in his hand. "It feels like Dean's ignoring me." I search Fred's face for a reaction.

"Oh man, sorry to hear that, El. That's not what I want for you guys," Emily says, as she puts her knife down to give me her undivided attention. She's always been good at that. She never wants someone to feel unimportant. I've always appreciated that about her.

"What's going on with him?" I ask, turning to Fred, and Emily follows my gaze.

Fred looks up to see that I'm looking at him and says, "Umm. I don't know. I haven't really talked to him much about it."

"You're no help then," I deadpan.

"Babe, should we just try calling Dean and see what's going on? Elise needs some answers, and maybe we can help her out a little bit by nudging Dean to communicate with her." Emily grabs Fred's arm and gives him a sweet smile.

"Yeah...maybe we can do that. I'll text him and set up a time to talk," Fred says, looking unsure. I have a feeling he doesn't want to be doing this, but he loves his wife and he'll do anything she asks him.

I stand up straighter as the sad little gnome inside my heart does a backflip. Maybe this will actually give me some answers. I'm holding out hope that this conversation will somehow make Dean see the light, and come back to me. I cringe as I wonder what Fred and Emily are thinking of me. We've all been in that relationship, or something-ship, where we've looked like the desperate 'clinger 5000' because the person we are essentially 'clinging to' isn't giving us enough closure to end things properly. Right? Or is it just me?

A couple of days later Emily and Fred tell me that they've talked to Dean. They let me know that it isn't their place to tell me what Dean has told them, but that Dean will be calling me sometime tonight to talk things over. "We told him to stop making it a grey area and give it to you in black and white," Emily informs me.

I'm so happy that I'm going to FINALLY hear back from him that I don't even think the outcome of the call could be a bad one. All I'm thinking about is that he's CALLING ME! Like he used to.

A couple of hours later I'm in my room, and my phone rings. Cue the flying ants in my stomach. I pull the phone out of my pocket and say, "Hello?" with a pep in my voice. I start to pace back-and-forth in-between the two beds.

"Hey Berger, how's it going over there in Hot-Lanta?" he asks, with a calm tone.

"Pretty good. Except it isn't hot right now. Just mildly cold. It's January, which means 60 degrees in the south. Nothing to write home about," I say. "How are you doing?" I'm trying to keep my side of the conversation airy and free, no heavy feelings. I'm feeling a mix of wanting to talk about "us" and just wanting to talk like we did in the summer. I naively just want our normal back.

"I'm doing good as well. Settling into life here in Bothell. My friend and his roommates are a great bunch to be hanging out with most of the days, so I don't have any complaints. Work is boring but that's to be expected with an office job." He chuckles.

"That's great to hear! Not the part about the boring office job but the settling in part," I say trying to sound supportive, hoping he doesn't feel any desperate vibes off me.

"Yes. I agree," he says, then he pauses and I can tell I'm about to finally hear from him on the topic of us. "So umm listen, I've had a good time getting to know you these past eight months. I really don't want you to keep holding out for me," he says, completely closing the window he left open.

"Oh," I pause, "Okay." I'm shocked he said it that way. I need to let him know that my feelings still haven't changed since New Years, so I say, "Umm I've been trying to call you and talk to you again. I know you said you didn't want to start anything right now, but I really do like you and I don't want to see this end."

"All relationships end though," he says and his words punch me in the gut.

"Ouch..." I whisper as I stop pacing in my room. "That's not what I expected to hear," I say, being honest with him. "Can we talk again in the future? Like the good ole days? I miss our hours of talking and texting." I try another angle, I know I'm sounding desperate.

"No. I don't think that's a good idea. We aren't going to be together in the future," he replies with another gut punching phrase, and I drop to my knees on the carpet. That one knocked the wind out of me.

"Oh," I say, breathing in shakily, trying to catch my breath.

"I'm sorry if that makes you sad," he pauses. "I'm just being realistic," he says and I can hear the sound of a pen or pencil tapping against a desk. I wonder if he can't wait for this conversation to be over.

"N-n-no problem," I stutter, trying to get words out. "Those are your honest thoughts. I needed to hear them," I say as my brain feels like it's short circuiting. I don't know what to say or how to feel anymore.

"Yeah, well I hope the best for you," he says, pushing the conversation to an end.

"Oh. Umm. Thanks," I say, still on the ground, still catching my breath, still short circuiting.

"Have a good night," he replies.

"Thanks," I say. And that's it. We get off the phone and I fall all the way down to the ground. That was the blandest goodbye. For all the time we gave to each other, phone calls and text messages, that last conversation didn't honor what we built. He zoomed through that conversation so fast I felt like a ghost just passed through my body. Now I'm left feeling icy cold chills.

I don't feel like this is real. I close my eyes and breathe in the carpet underneath my nose. I don't know if I'll be able to stop myself from texting him anymore. Cold turkey has never been my strong suit.

After twenty minutes I leave my room, dragging my feet as only lifeless zombies can. When I get to the end of the hallway, I pass Fred, and say, "He ended it." I can barely make eye contact with him.

He gives me a sad smile and says, "I'm sorry to hear that. This must be hard." He gives me a pat on the shoulder. "But hey, I know this won't fix the pain, but you should read the *Thomas Taylor* books. They're a good time and might help you keep your spirits up while you go through this."

"Okay. I don't have the books though," I reply, sounding like Garfield after someone ate his lasagna.

"I have the first one. Let me get it for you," he says and he leaves to return a minute later with the book.

"Thank you." I grab it from him and walk to the kitchen to get myself a glass of milk.

Chapter 27

Present Day

April

I dog ear the corner of my book to keep my place in *The Gnomes Tale* marked so I can join the conversation with everyone in the house.

"We should have a fun dinner where we all talk in British accents without breaking character," Sarah suggests to the group.

We haven't seen everyone as a whole in months and we've been talking about having a house family dinner where we all take time off work and time away from girlfriends/boyfriends to reconnect with our magnificent nine.

I scrunch my nose and cringe, then slowly soften to the suggestion, "As embarrassing as that may be, I actually kinda like that idea." I've been trying to say yes to more things that make me happy, lately. It started with going to a volleyball open gym night to be a sub for a team that needed a sixth player. And it's not going to end anytime soon because I'm learning to love myself.

"I'm in," Kim says.

"Oh my gosh, you guys, this sounds like so much fun! Let's do it!" Emily says like a cheerleader trying to hype up a crowd.

"Okay," Josh says reluctantly. Out of everyone in the house he is the most reserved. I've tried to have conversations with him, but they don't flow and it feels like pulling teeth to get a conversation going. I'm not a dentist. He's a nice guy, though, so I just give him his space to decide when he wants to join our Brady Bunch shenanigans.

Everyone else agrees that we should do this 'British accent family dinner' in one week. Juniper makes a sign-up sheet where everyone can put their name on a dish to make for the evening, so the food doesn't land all on one person. It almost feels like we're having Thanksgiving in April.

When I went to put my name down on the sign up sheet I was happy to see that 'desserts' hadn't been taken. Baking is another thing that makes me happy. I looked up a bunch of fun recipes that only Buddy the Elf would enjoy. I decided that since it's a special occasion this is the best time to whip together recipes that everyone has never had before.

On the day of our Thanksgiving-esque-family-dinner-British-accent-party, I made a Black Bottom Pie and an Avocado Pie, which might be the only green veggie we eat tonight. I also decided to make my mom's homemade Pumpkin Pie. This one gives you all the basic girl, sweater-wearing, warm and fuzzy feelings inside. With pumpkin and all the earth warming spices it is sure to be a crowd favorite. I had to throw them a bone and give the group at least one pie they'd recognize.

When we all finally finish making our dishes for dinner, we place them on the center of the table and each take a seat in one of the dining table chairs around it.

"Waaaill, goood evening all," Sarah starts out, trying to sound British but it accidentally comes out sounding southern. "It's lovely weather we're having, uh, spit spot. How have you all been?" She clasps her hand and leans on the table as she looks us all in the eyes, one by one.

Everyone stays silent. All eyeballs looking left and right as we try to figure out how to put aside the embarrassment and join in the fun.

"I had a right fine day out in the warm rays of the sun earlier this afternoon." I attempt to sound British but my vocal chords could only conjure up an accent from early 1800's America. I clear my throat and touch my cheeks.

"That sounds swail," Fred continues with the theme of botching the British accent.

We all laugh at what we're even doing with our lives, but still forge on because we're not a bunch of quitters.

"I for one am very pleased with the spread of food we have before us today," Forrest says, joining me in the early 1800's.

"What kind-uh pies you make, El?" Emily asks me, not able to switch out of a southern accent just like Sarah.

"Well, I've made a mighty fine one called Black Bottom Pie..." It comes out too southern, so I adjust, "and an Avocado Pie." I switched to sounding like George Bailey from It's a Wonderful Life with a low deep tone, so I adjust again, "then I made a pumpkin pie for all of yous to enjoy." Back to southern. Damn this is hard, but I can't wipe the smile off my face. Or the warm feeling growing in my belly. I have a tribe, a community that has seen my most embarrassing moments and still loves me for it. I have learned to love my insecure parts and share my deepest pain without hiding away. I'm a strong woman who knows how to not stay a wallflower but show people that I'm fun and free.

"Oh, how lovely. I can't wait to try these tasty morsels," Kim chimes in with her attempt at a British accent.

"Does someone want to pass the mash please?" Juniper asks, reaching out her hands to take it from the right side of the table. She came up with the closest attempt at a British accent we've heard so far.

"Absolutely," I reply, back to the 1800s. It's harder than it sounds to try to find the right accent to get out. With so much access to all sorts of accents it's hard to figure out how to make your tongue move around your mouth in a way to mimic the old mother land.

Josh and Mitchell stay the quietest. Saying quiet requests for food to only the person sitting next to them. I don't point it out. These games aren't for everyone. I would've joined them in their silence a month ago but the more I've found internal love for myself, the more I feel comfortable in my own skin.

"Does anybody want a cuppa tea?" Josh pushes out his chair to get up and surprises us all with a spot-on British accent. We all erupt with cheers and claps.

With a final whoop a few people accept his offer for tea, and we go back to trying to talk to each other without breaking character. This tribe has the best time together. I almost let my insecurities blind me from being present with them. The cracks in my heart are feeling more healed with each splendid time I laugh at someone across from me. I've realized that I don't need a call or text back from Dean when I finally know that I'm worthy of love, and I won't let myself self-sabotage again. I've lost track of how many days it's been since I've texted him. He's slowly fading into the background of a life I once had but don't hold space for anymore.

Chapter 28

Present Day

July

A few months later and I'm swinging my arms big, as I'm walking across the parking lot of a small theater in Georgia with my favorite people. Fremily, Sarah, Mitchell, Juniper and I are all going to see the sixth *Thomas Taylor* movie on the big screen. My skin is itching with excitement and I can't wipe the smile off my face. I feel like this is the peak of my growth. Doing something I love with people that have loved me through my growing pains. Being shown acceptance from this group of five people has made me learn how to accept myself. Even at my worst, I'm freaking incredible.

I finished the final book of the *Thomas Taylor* series, *The Last Wand*, a month ago. If Thomas has taught me anything, it's that the community you have around you, supporting you, is the most important thing in life. I'm not sure Fred realized that this was the message I would get when he suggested the book series to me, but if he did, he's one smart guy. I look over at Juniper talking to Fred and Emily, and wonder if I would've been able to make such big growth if I didn't have them around.

As we come within view of the theater entrance I say to Juniper, "Hey look! We're not the only ones!" I point at the line waiting to get their tickets. About ninety percent of the people in line here are also dressed like they've just received an acceptance letter to Stiltsen School of Witchcraft and Wizardry.

"I was going to wear my Nimblefoot scarf but couldn't find it. I feel so naked," Juniper says as she grabs at her neck as if she's searching for the red and yellow ensemble to complete her outfit.

I snap my head over to her. "You still look great! You have the Nimblefoot colored ribbons tied into your hair and the right colored shirt." I push one of the ribbons off her shoulder. "Nobody will notice that the dryer ate your scarf and won't give it back," I say, trying to help lift up her spirits.

"It's always the dryer." She shakes her head and bows it in grief.

As we all walk through the doors, skipping the ticket line because we're the winners that purchased ours online, I think about the big growth I've made. I've made massive strides in healing my self-worth and changing my self-talk.

We walk up to the concession stand and pick one of the long lines. "Wow. I love that we arrived early because this crowd is insane," Sarah says, looking around at all the people as we wait to order popcorn.

"Kudos to us for being proactive," Emily says, "We should all give ourselves a giant pat on the back," and she reaches her arm around to give herself a pat. Then Fred gives her a loud pat on her back too. "No babe, not to each other, do it to yourself." Emily laughs and turns to the rest of us, beaming at her husband's silly joke.

I let out a full belly laugh and smile at their interaction. Watching them be adorable doesn't hurt anymore. I might've accidentally been the *Runaway At The Alter*, leading lady, of my own life, but I know now that I don't have to be scared of someone showing me attention and being captivated by me. I've learned that I'm so damn loyal, the toxic flaw of that is not letting someone go even though they're trying to leave. I won't fall back into that toxicity again because I'll see it coming.

Everyone is reading the concession board, and deciding what they want to order, while I am looking at all of their faces and writing them in my memory. My community didn't let me fall down the mudslide of life and I'm so grateful for them. As I'm standing in line with my people, listening to them chatter back and forth with each other about the movie, and what they hope the filmmakers put in it from the book, a clown sized smile crosses my face and I realize I'm the happiest I've ever been. I'm almost sad to be leaving them.

A tear leaves the corner of my eye as I see them fold over laughing, and grabbing each other's arms to hold themselves steady. I decided at the end of the summer, I would be going to Thailand and continuing my humanitarian work there. Living in a house full of nine people really cut down on rent, and allowed me to save up so much money that I'm able to support myself for a whole year out there. I leave next week for Bangkok. This movie is my bittersweet going away party.

Who knew that when I talked about loving who I was when I was in Thailand, on that day we went to Cafe Intermezzo, that I would actually be going back to that country. I wipe the sliding tear away when we get to the front of the concessions line, and we each order our own bucket of popcorn and our own box of candy.

The energy in this place is pulsing. The Thomas-head's are a bunch of polite people, who wish they all could actually send out magic from their fake wands. As we head to the theater hallway to find theater number-one, I pass people that are pointing their wands at the ceiling lights and at the doorways, to try and magically move everything around them. It feels like we are actually walking the hallways of the old Stiltsen castle.

This movie, with these people, fills all the cracks left in my heart. I am known. I have a place. These are my people. *Thomas Taylor* gets it. It's all about who you surround yourself with. I shovel popcorn in my mouth and wiggle in my seat, as the lights dim, to settle in for the next two and a half hours.

When the movie ends I am in awe. I wouldn't be able to talk even if I was captured and found myself forced to be in a spelling bee, I'm so speechless. I loved every minute of it. Walking behind Fred and Juniper, I overhear them talk about how they wished it had more of Angelore's back story, or that it brought you along the storyline of Thomas and Wren better. I quietly think to myself that I didn't even notice that those moments fell short in the movie. I was more focused on the atmosphere of the movie, and how it brought Stiltsen to the big screen. I will sleep well tonight knowing that I've officially been adopted into the *Thomas Taylor* family, now that I've seen one of the movies at the theater.

Chapter 29

Present Day

July

I'm packing up some last-minute items before I leave for Bangkok tomorrow. It's been an emotional year, and looking back I feel like I've grown so much. I realize now that I had been stuck in the same pattern of behavior for so long, and having snapped out of it I really do feel like a new person. Ever since my first real heartbreak, back in high school, I had been stuck in this loop, letting my need to be loved and fear of rejection influence every part of my life. I would always dissect all of my interactions with others to check if I was funny enough, smart enough, attractive enough...It was exhausting having such a large part of my energy constantly being drained by my insecurities.

I used to think I had such bad luck with guys, never really realizing I was stuck in a loop of my own making. During my work with the humanitarian group, for instance, I met a guy named Richard. We spent every day getting to know each other for the three months we were in Hawaii. Then we each went on an outreach trip to Southeast Asia, where he went to Bangladesh and I went to Thailand, and were apart for three months. Before taking our flights he told me he liked me, but I turned him down saying I wasn't interested.

During the three months away from him I daydreamed, like a teenage girl, about being with him and started to develop feelings, or maybe just realizing they had already been there. I was excited to tell him that I was wrong and I actually did have feelings for him when we met back up in Hawaii. I wasn't nervous, I was confident. I asked him to go for a walk and let him know my new realization about my feelings. My happy bubble burst when he told me he actually didn't have feelings for me anymore and just wanted to stay friends. He spent the next two weeks ignoring me and not talking more than a few sentences to me.

Looking back at the whole Dean situation, I see how I did pretty much the exact same thing with him. It's like I can only admit to myself that I like a guy once he tells me he doesn't like me. It seems so obvious in hindsight.

I know now, that I am so scared of being rejected that I reject them first so they don't have the chance to hurt me, but then my subconscious catches on that I made a mistake and actually do want to be with them, but like a true masochist, I wait long enough to take action so that they don't like me anymore and end up rejecting me anyway. It's like that mean and insecure little gremlin that lives in the deepest part of my subconscious wanted me to get rejected so it could use it as proof to say, "See, you're not good enough." No matter how sweet the men were, I always ended up creating a scenario where I got rejected and was left feeling heartbroken. Even when it was pointed out to me by others that I was self-sabotaging, I still couldn't see my way out of it, too entangled in the mess of my own feelings to break free.

But I see it now, clear as day. With the help of my family and friends, especially my fairy godmother, I now know deep in my heart that I deserve to be loved. By others *and* by myself. Changing my self-talk hasn't been easy, but it has been so rewarding to see myself in a better light. In turn, being in a better place has also made me better at taking accountability for my own mess-ups. I understand now that I can make mistakes and still be a good person, but that I simply need to take accountability and make things right whenever I make a mistake. No more punishing myself endlessly only to end up projecting that onto others.

I'm excited to close this chapter and start a new one. My plane leaves tomorrow morning and I truly feel like this is the right move for me. Doing work that brings me joy and purpose, while giving myself the time and space to continue learning and growing as a person. There is only one thing left that I need to do before I can really close this chapter, and that's to truly give Dean the apology he deserved from me all along.

When I broke things off I wasn't being honest with myself, and so, I wasn't honest with him either. I did tell him I was mistaken and that I did have feelings for him when he came over after New Years, but I shouldn't have asked him for a second chance without properly apologizing first. True accountability means apologizing to those you've wronged without expecting something in return, so in hindsight, I might not have handled that conversation that well.

It's been a long time since I have texted him, and even longer since he texted me, so I don't know if he even wants to hear from me, but I think it's the right thing to do. I consulted Fred about my epiphany and asked him if he thought it would be a good idea, not wanting to do more harm than good. But Fred said he thought it would be a good idea. He didn't know if Dean would respond, but he said that he imagined Dean would appreciate getting the real reason for the way I suddenly broke things off at the end of the summer. So...here we go.

"Hi, Dean. I know it's been a while since we've talked, and you might not want to hear from me at all, but I wanted to send you one last text message to fully close this chapter. I don't

expect anything in return from you, so you really don't have to respond...I just feel like it's the right thing to do. When I broke things off between us, I was very much in denial about my own feelings, so I didn't really give you the true reason for it...

I truly did like you. So much so, that it scared me. I've come to the realization that I have a tendency to run away from good things because I'm scared of losing them and being left heartbroken. I think deep down I knew how much I felt for you, and losing you would've been too painful to handle. So instead of waiting to see if you would reject me, I beat you to the punch.

You were nothing but amazing to me and you deserved so much better than to suddenly have the rug pulled out from under you like that. I've done a lot of self-reflection, and I understand why I acted the way that I did, I only wish I had seen it sooner so I wouldn't have put you through that. I don't expect anything from you, but I just needed it to be said: I'm sorry!

You're an incredible person and I wish nothing but the best for you in your future!! I know you will find the perfect girl for you who will love you unapologetically, like you deserve.

Much love, Elise xx."

I read over the text to check if I said the right things, but as I feel the insecurities trying to creep back in I decide to just hit send. I spoke from the heart and now it's over. No more spiraling and overthinking, I am closing this chapter for good. I check one last time to see if my alarms are set for the morning and then I plug my phone into the charger, putting it down on my nightstand. Zipping up my bag and putting it in the corner with the rest of my travel baggage, I look around my room and truly take it in one last time. I am so grateful for my time here in Georgia, getting to live with the most incredible people you could ask for. It's bitter-sweet knowing it's coming to an end, but I am ready for my next adventure. Thailand, here I come!

Chapter 30

Present Day

December

I joined the same humanitarian group in Bangkok that I went with a year and a half ago. The base operation is in a four-story building with roof access. The bottom floor is our living room, kitchen and laundry room. The next three floors are all bedrooms. The roof is where we spend our nights confessing our deepest secrets while being wrapped in a blanket of warm night air.

The people that came here long term, or permanently, all get their own room and don't have to share. The short-term people that come for a month at a time get to stay in a room full of bunk beds. Fun little suckers. I'm thankful for this arrangement because I'm done being a poor college student trying to pay for my bills. In Thailand I feel like a queen with my private room.

Working with the women in the red-light district was the last time I felt like I was truly where I needed to be in life. I've found out, as I opened up and surgically dissected my own heart, that working with other women and helping them find out their own self worth is something that drives me. Thanks to my fairy godmother for further showing me the way.

I've made a couple friends these past six months here. My main friend's name is Moo. She has a long Thai name, but all the Thai girls shorten their names for the white people to be able to pronounce them.

I'm not going to lie, I feel seen and appreciate this more than they know. She and I have the same shift at the L.I.F.E. Foundation near the red-light district. The L.I.F.E Foundation is why I'm spending a year of my life over here with these amazing people.

The foundation is helping the women of the night learn a trade so they can make money that doesn't require them to sell their bodies. Moo is in her twenties and loves helping the women get out of the 'bar girl' life. She's always lived in Bangkok and has a young and bubbly personality. Every time she greets me in the mornings it's always with her hands in the air and each word is followed by an exclamation mark. "Hi! Good morning, Elise! I hope you slept well! Want some breakfast?!"

"Good! Thank you! And yes!" I reply with my arms in the air, returning the greeting.

Today is a normal day. We sit down at our table of four and have a breakfast of rice, eggs and bananas. I added a handful of muesli, what we call granola, to bring a little familiar American crunch to my breakfast.

After breakfast I tell Moo, "I've got to grab my camera upstairs, and I'll meet you back down here to share a ride to work."

"Sounds good, Elise!" She gives me two thumbs up and I race upstairs to get the item that got me this job.

The sounds of the city are all around us as the driver of our tuk-tuk weaves in and out of traffic. Honking their little horn for people and cars to get out of their way, these little three-wheel vehicles run the streets of Bangkok. They see the lines on the road as a suggestion, not a demand. I only travel by tuk-tuk because it gets places cheetah fast.

The section of the L.I.F.E Foundation Moo and I help with is called Hope Cards. They make all kinds of gift cards for people to buy their loved ones for any occasion; birthday cards, wedding cards, anniversary cards, etc. My job is to chat with the women and to use my photography skills to capture moments with them for our website and newsletter.

Hope Cards is bursting with activity when we get there. "Hi, Na," I say, waving to the receptionist. "I love your shirt. Blue might be your color," I say with a thumbs up and she laughs at me and tucks her head down to her shoulder. Thai people don't like to appear boastful, so when giving any compliments to them they quietly turn their head away and say nothing. It doesn't stop me though, these women need to know they are beautiful and that they matter.

Moo and I walk into the big meeting room that has over twenty tables with chairs all around them. The tables are covered in paper and craft decorations to help create gift cards. About forty women are seated around the room. "We're here again," I say to Moo with my hands high up in the air.

Moo laughs and says, "Best day ever!" as we split up and each go to find a Thai woman to sit with while they work.

We want these women to start building a community around them of people that are safe and supportive. I pull out my camera and take a couple shots of the overview of people today.

"Hey guys, can I take your photo?" I ask as I move toward them.

"Yes. Of course," Amanda, one of the other American workers, says to me as she leans in close to La-La.

"Say cheese," I say as I put the camera up to my eye and take a more close-up photo of them finishing a birthday card and putting it in a plastic sleeve.

I look down at the digital photo on my camera and feel a sense of peace. "Thank you. It looks great. You gals are so photogenic," I say, bringing my chin to my shoulder. The women make their cards and seal the clear covering with their signature stamp that will lead the money back to them. All the money they make from their designs they get to take home to their families. Half of them have children and husbands. And the other half are single, retired, bar girls.

I walk over to a woman I have sat with before and pull a chair out from the table. "Hi, Haa, how's your daughter?" I ask and I watch her hands finish gluing a heart on her card creation. I've seen Haa before, she likes to work alone but I know the value of community, and I don't want her to get away with being a wallflower.

"She good. Her broken arm is very better," Haa says without making any eye contact. I smile at her broken English. She has come a long way from when I got here six months ago.

"That's great! I'm happy to hear that." I close my hands in front of me and put them on the table. "How is she doing with her writing?"

"She doing well. Her penmanship better than mine," she says with a smile as she cuts out another heart from the red construction paper on the table.

I look down at her hands working on her livelihood and appreciate that she was able to get away from her abusive husband and find happiness with Hope Cards. Healing the cracks of her own broken heart with each healthy interaction she has here in our little family.

"You are a very good mother," I tell her and rest my hand on her arm. "You know what's best for her and you are finding every way possible to make her life better. I'm so excited for your future." I compliment her and I'm met with the same response that Na had.

Chin tucked to her shoulder, she smiles at me and says, "Thank you."

"Can I take your picture today?" I ask her, holding up my camera to show her. She's been turning me down every day that I've seen her, but I won't stop asking.

To my surprise she says, "Yes," and straightens her back to sit up taller.

I stand up and point my camera at her. I snap a couple of shots of her looking up at the camera and then her looking down at her hands. Perfectly photogenic. I pull my camera down from my eye and I look around at the other women making cards and the other workers like Moo and myself talking to them and making them feel seen.

This is the place I want to be. I want to be lifting other women up in the pursuit of a better life, a healthier life, a seen life. Coming here five days a week for the next six months is going to be so fulfilling. More fulfilling than a briefcase full of cash left on your doorstep. It doesn't hurt that Thai food is delicious too. I don't have to search for good restaurants like Juniper and I did when I lived in Georgia. Every street cart and restaurant is top shelf.

At the end of today's shift I'm the last one to leave. I start packing up my stuff after I say goodbye to the final worker. Just as I'm putting my camera back in my camera bag, I see movement out of the corner of my eye. I look up and I see Dean walking toward me with the golden sun that's coming through the window shining off his skin. I squint as my head registers what I am seeing. My heart doesn't take as long to understand, because it starts beating so fast I have to put my hand to my chest to settle it down.

I'm not sure if I've died or if I'm dreaming. Those are my only two options because this doesn't feel like real life.

How did he find me? Why did he come? I haven't seen or heard from him in almost a year, and now he's *here*? I feel this confidence rise up in me. I know who I am now. I know my self-worth.

"Hello," Dean says as he walks toward me, slowly. The smile on his face indicates that he knows he's surprised me.

"Hiiiii," I furrow my brows and say the word like it has six letters instead of two. I look around to see if I can spy any hidden cameramen ready to jump out and yell "GOTCHA," but nothing seems out of the ordinary. "How are you here?" I ask as I tilt my head to the side.

"A best friend's sister, a plane and a tuk-tuk." He holds up a new finger every time he says a new element.

I shake my head and rest on my back leg. "I should have known Juniper would be involved. She was always secretly rooting for this."

"She told me it was her duty as your fairy godmother, I think she might be my fairy godmother too." A smile spreads across his face as he uses the endearing term I've had for Juniper during my heartbreak era.

I laugh, then look down at my hands as I ask, "So then, *what* are you doing here?" Reality keeps my feet stuck on the floor like they've been superglued.

"I, umm...I realized I messed up," he says as he reaches the table I'm standing at.

Still looking down I say, "Yeah?"

When I look back up at him he starts talking. "Yeah. I've been thinking about that conversation we had at the end of last summer. The one where you told me you didn't have feelings for me anymore. I felt blindsided by the change of heart, and I felt like the rug had been pulled out from under me again. I guess I got triggered from the last time that had happened to me. And in an attempt to protect my heart, I couldn't see past my fear when you told me you were wrong and you did have feelings for me. I was scared to let myself fall for you all over again, only for you to potentially break up with me, but I knew deep down that you are my dream girl, and I just couldn't close that door completely. That was really shitty of me. I had no right to string you along like that, giving you mixed signals and playing with your feelings. I needed that wake-up call from Fred and Emily to realize what I had been doing to you was hurting you…I messed up," he says, then he starts to walk around the table to stand on my side of it.

He continues, "I should have told you that I did have feelings for you. Big ones. I should have told you that I felt like we had built something really special, and I didn't want to let you go. I was trying to protect my own heart, by not telling you how I really felt. I should have told you that it really hurt to hear you say all that, during our September phone call. I didn't want to get hurt, so I just lied and told you I wasn't feeling anything either. It wasn't until you sent me the text message, where you explained that you had let your fear of rejection get the best of you, that I realized I was doing the exact same thing. I figured, if after everything we went through, you still managed to find the bravery to take accountability for that, I should toughen up and do the same. So here I am, hoping you'll see my showing up unannounced as the first piece of proof that from now on, I will fight for you, for us. I will not let fear get the better of me again, because you are worth everything to me, Elise Berger."

I stare at his gorgeous blue eyes that are so genuine a baby kangaroo would trust him. He came all this way to make the nicest apology. I start to laugh and my eyes fill up with tears.

"What?" he asks, taking another step toward me.

"You never know what life is going to throw at you. Even the good stuff," I admit as I dab the corner of my eye with the collar of my shirt.

He shares my laugh and starts to reach out a hand, but changes his mind and puts it in his pocket instead, then says, "Elise, you are my dream girl. I'm sorry it took me this long to come find you. I want to fight for us. This is my grand gesture. I've been wanting you ever since I tried to cut it off at the beginning of this year. I want you back, if you'll have me. If you won't have me now then I will wait until you can see that we will be something special someday."

No longer happy with the foot of distance between us, I say, "Shut up and kiss me," and he closes the gap between us, sweeps me up into his arms and covers my mouth with his. Passionately finding each other again. My heart is lifted up into the heavens as he squeezes his arms around my back, and pulls me as tight to him as he can. Our mouths open and close around each other's lips as our kiss starts to speak louder than words. A crowbar couldn't break us apart. The butterflies are back. The ones I said goodbye to a year ago and haven't felt since. His arms rub up and down my back, like they're tracing the topography of it and searing the memory of me into his brain.

We pull away and I run my hands through his hair. "I love that you're not wearing a baseball cap," I say, smiling up at him.

"I felt like I needed a fresh look. I'm glad you like it," he says, still holding me tight and not letting go.

"I've always liked what you looked like without that hat. You're so freaking handsome!" I say, as I throw my hair back.

"Thank you! And look at you, hair down and flowing freely, like a new person. I've always wanted to see your hair down on your shoulders, and now I don't ever want to stop."

I blush and slowly pull his head down for another kiss, and this time, we go slow. He rests his hands on my lower back, and my fingers are running through his hair. He teases me with his tongue and I bite his lower lip. Our lips part for a couple seconds as we breath in the warm breath of each other and then he goes for my lower lip. Sucking on it like a lollipop and I feel warm all over.

When we finally part again I say, "Thank you. You are the sweetest man. Having you show up and declare your undying love for me was not on my bingo card for today. But I'm here for it," I freely run my hands through his hair.

"I'm not gonna let you get away this time," he smiles down at me.

I beam up at him and say, "Hey look! You just traveled to your first country! And it ended up being Thailand, which was on your list! How great is that!?" I can't hide my enthusiasm for him and this big moment.

"I know. It's pretty special. Taking the flight and navigating here has made made my little boyish heart happy, to finally be experiencing a real country for the first time." He reaches down to grab my hand, "And it looks like I'm going to be here for the next six months and do some humanitarian work with you. I'll just have to see where they want a guy to be helping out," he says, smiling down at me.

"I'm sure they'll find something for you. Even if it's mopping the floors of the base." I throw my head back and laugh.

He waits for me to finish laughing. Then he looks down and says, "I could also just hold up this camera bag right here." He points to the one I left on the table, right before being swept up into this moment with him.

A squawk laugh leaves my lips and I say, "That is a hobby of yours, if I remember correctly."

"I told you this hobby brings me to a lot of places. Now Thailand can be crossed off the list." He squeezes his hand around mine.

"It's true. You can." I step forward and rest my head on his chest. "What a crazy life."

"It truly is," he says and grabs my chin so I'm looking him in the eyes. He brushes a strand of hair off my face and says, "I have one question for you." His soft smile reaches his eyes. "Elise Berger, do you want to be my girlfriend?"

I let out a gasp and wrap my arms around his neck in a hug. "I would love to!" I say, and I never want to let go. I start to feel hot and cold, a rapid heart rate, and all of a sudden I'm tired. My symptoms sound like the onset of malaria. But actually, I think I'm in love.

After a final kiss that seals the deal I say, "Come on, bag boy. You have some people to meet." I grab his hand, then my camera bag, and lead him outside to take a trip back to the base where we get to stay while we learn about each other all over again. Plot twist! I finally got my very first boyfriend, and it happened in Thailand.